# 2084

UNSUNG
STORIES

Published by Unsung Stories, an imprint of Red Squirrel Publishing
"Red Squirrel" is a registered trademark of Shoreditch Media Limited

Red Squirrel Publishing Suite 235, 15 Ingestre Place, London W1F 0DU, United Kingdom

www.unsungstories.co.uk

First edition published in 2017

Hardback ISBN: 978-1-907389-58-0
Paperback ISBN: 978-1-907389-50-4
ePub ISBN: 978-1-907389-53-5

Editor: George Sandison
Copy Editor: Robert Clark
Proofreader: Katherine Stephen
Designer: www.coxdesign.co.uk
Publisher: Henry Dillon

Printed in the UK by TJ International

# INTRODUCTION

*How could you communicate with the future? It was of nature impossible. Either the future would resemble the present, in which case it would not listen to him: or it would be different from it, and his predicament would be meaningless.*
George Orwell, *Nineteen Eighty-Four*

This isn't a book about the future.

For all their trappings of science fiction, dystopias are about today. By creating them we explore our fears. In telling these stories we cast light on the world we see around us, explore aspects of the overwhelming complexity we live within. A nudge here, a trait amplified there, a concern extrapolated to its logical conclusion. They contain nothing that isn't already here.

They are most effective when they speak to a universal truth, when they tap into a nerve that's still raw. That's why George Orwell's *Nineteen Eighty-Four* still resonates today, decades after the year it predicted. It's built on shifting sand, where propaganda has defeated the truth. In the Party's rigidly controlled world, we recognise aspects of our own – fake news toxifying discourse, paranoia about outsiders, a mistrust in experts. What was once fixed becomes malleable, subjective.

This hits on one of the essential parts of our societal compacts – that we collate information that is true and reliable, for the common wealth. The age of the Internet has broken down countless barriers between communities and allowed for incredibly powerful connections to be made. But it can also be distorted. Orwell didn't predict the Internet, but he understood how we would learn to use the media – and how it could be used against us.

But this isn't a book about the media.

Or not exclusively.

The media exists between us by definition, the epistemological gravity well that we all orbit. It's the quintessential doublethought, an inescapable aspect of modern life, both connecting us and keeping us apart. You'll find stories here about how we interact with each other in and across societies and about the effect of technology on our relationships. But you'll also find stories about education, growing old, climate change and borders.

Our world is drastically more complex than the one Orwell created. His was a thought experiment, a medium – there's that idea again – to convey his discussion of totalitarianism. His world was born of 1948, when the planet was the same size, but didn't seem that way, missing the cornucopia of interconnections that is our new norm.

The media is ubiquitous, not omnipotent. And when you

ask fifteen writers to do something, expect fifteen different responses.

This isn't a book of predictions.

Orwell proposed a state of constant war across the globe divided into three super powers and the leftover territories. Yet democratic governments still existed in 1984, prevailing even today. Global political unity, of any form, is still a distant dream. So many of Orwell's predictions were proven wrong, but it doesn't matter. It's the truths about human nature that make up that vision.

Some of it raises a smile now, like the fears that Chaucer, Shakespeare, Milton and Byron will only exist in Newspeak versions by 2050. Instead we have carried great art on with us. We are creating new work and updating old in digital forms. We are starting to challenge the colonial-era cultural hegemony, slowly moving towards diverse representation.

Some of it is close to the mark, even in failure. Today there are only ten countries in the world not involved a conflict. The United Kingdom isn't a totalitarian state where all media is strictly controlled, but trust in a media owned by a few incredibly wealthy individuals is plummeting.

When we get to 2084, this will probably all be proven wrong. Or at least the settings will. The question becomes, what truths do we find in these stories? You will find they speak to us of fear and loneliness, of vanity and grief, of anger and guilt. Will we recognise ourselves?

This isn't a book of Orwellian stories.

What do we mean by Orwellian, after all? We use it to describe a dystopia where facts are taboo and objective truth impossible. Where language is turned against us, just like our cities, our families and our governments. Big

Brother is watching you, pleased at how you have adopted the language. Doublethink. Thought Police. What use do we have for Oldspeak?

Orwellian. The word that fails to encapsulate the tenderness and hope we find in the love between Winston and Julia, or the inability of Oceania to destroy the washerwoman's spirit. The Party can only force her into penury. It says nothing of the peace and beauty found in the forest, the susurration of wind in the trees beyond the cameras. Not Doublespeak, but Singlespeak, where it should be polyphonous.

What was a warning to us about the power of language has been diminished. *Nineteen Eighty-Four* tells us, 'The larger evils invariably escaped their notice'. The worm eats its own tail. So no, these stories won't dwell in Orwell's Oceania, or emulate his neologisms. They will embrace the complexity of the world. They will link today with tomorrow, and ask us to share in the responsibility.

This isn't the way we planned it.

The idea for this anthology first came to me in 2015, long before the EU referendum in the UK, or the 2016 US presidential election. The seventieth anniversary of *Nineteen Eighty-Four* was approaching, and propaganda was on our mind. Politics was lurching to the right. The tone of discourse was changing.

So we set to work commissioning the stories and, as is the way with near-future fiction, time had its way with us. It is perhaps appropriate that this project was conceived in a different world. Predictions of the future have a shelf life, with deviation only increasing over time. And some years we all have to recalibrate our expectations.

This book was supported by a Kickstarter campaign, which was launched the same day that the UK government activated Article 50, beginning the process of leaving the EU. Many people in the UK believe this took us one step towards a dystopian future and across the country there was an unclassifiable outpouring of rage, angst, jubilation, fear, vindication and frustration. Our community was seeking a focal point for all of that emotion. And there was our little book, in the middle of it all.

We couldn't have planned it better if we'd tried. We feel more kinship in our communities across the globe than ever before, and we play with forces larger than us every day. We act to create our future with such conviction, but the full consequences are impossible to predict. We are creative in times of adversity. We resist the coming darkness.

There are warnings in this book – we would do well to heed them.

*George Sandison*
*June 2017*

# BABYLON

## DAVE HUTCHINSON

They were three days out when they encountered a Coast Guard cutter. The pilot, his face almost entirely hidden by a VR set, spotted the vessel on passive radar and turned off the motor. 'Easy now,' he whispered.

'Who is it?' Da'uud murmured.

'Does it matter?'

Da'uud supposed not. He raised his head and looked out beyond the prow of the boat, but all he could see was a profound darkness. It was a moonless night, and high cloud hid the stars. The patrol boat was probably running dark; there was no way to tell how far away it was.

He lay down again on the deckboards and stared up into the night, feeling the long, powerful swell rising and falling against his back. He said, 'What will we do?'

'We will wait,' the pilot said quietly. 'And we will not make any noise.'

Da'uud closed his eyes and clasped his hands across his chest. The boat was stubby and low in the water, and it was constructed from materials which gave it the radar signature of a floating beer keg. He and the pilot lay side by side in the bottom, covered in waxy tarpaulins that smelled of camphor and dissipated their body heat into the sea via a network of hollow threads trailing in their wake. A stealth boat, Latsis had called it. One of a kind. Please do not break it.

He wondered where Latsis was now. He thought of the old man standing on the beach along the coast from Phocaea, watching as Da'uud and the pilot made their way out to sea, then slowly turning and plodding back towards the line of trees where they had hidden the truck the boat had been transported in.

'There are a couple of ways we could do this,' Latsis had

mused at their first meeting. 'We could put you in a stealthed hydrofoil and just run you across the Aegean at high speed at night, get you where you need to be in a few hours, but that's risky. So we're going to take our time.' He had seemed quite taken with the idea, scarred hands clasped on the table in front of him, the sleeves of his washed-out old blue work shirt rolled up to reveal forearms knotted with muscle. 'We are going to creep into Europe.'

Latsis, of course, did not know the purpose of the mission, and he was being well paid not to form any opinions which he might later feel obliged to share with the Turkish authorities. Da'uud's Uncle had told him that the old man had started out in the people-smuggling business back in the heady days of the first quarter of the century, before various crises had rolled together into The Crisis. The two of them had had some dealings in the old days, and Da'uud's Uncle had pronounced Latsis trustworthy, to the extent that anyone could be.

They were having this conversation in the family compound outside Berbera, overlooking the Gulf of Aden. Rebel forces had come through the area the week before, skirmished with government troops for a while, looted and burned a village, and departed. The family had been on high alert the whole time, manning the railguns mounted on the compound walls – they were just as likely to come under attack by the government as by the rebels – and Da'uud was still exhausted when his Father and Uncle had come to him with their proposal.

'You may decline, of course,' his Uncle had told him when the plan had been outlined. 'But someone else will go in your place. One of my sons, possibly.'

Da'uud remembered sitting back and staring at the map projection on the tabletop, almost overwhelmed merely by the distances involved. 'We have friends in Riyadh with an aircraft,' his Uncle had said, and he'd gone on to describe a crossing of the Gulf and an overland route across Yemen and Saudi Arabia as if it was a mellow school outing rather than a journey across some of the most dangerous territory on Earth.

'Do you not have friends in Nairobi who have an aircraft?' Da'uud enquired mildly.

'We are warriors,' his Father admonished. 'Descendants of warriors. Don't embarrass me in my own house.'

'And Nairobi,' his Uncle added with a smile, 'is in the wrong direction.'

'A great gift is about to come into our hands,' his Father said. 'We must be in the right place at the right time, and we must use it. We will change the world.'

The world is run by old men, Da'uud thought, bobbing on the midnight Aegean and wondering if he would live to one day join their number.

'Moving off,' the pilot murmured.

Da'uud listened, thought he heard, very faintly and far away, the sound of engines.

'We'll give it an hour to get clear,' the pilot said. 'Then we'll be on our way again.'

>•<

It took Da'uud almost a week to reach his destination. Driven by its whispery catalytic motor, the little boat drifted as much as made way, but that was deliberate. As Latsis had said, a direct approach at high speed would have taken a few hours at most. It would also have attracted the attention of every early-warning system the Europeans had sown in the Aegean. At night, tethered to the boat, Da'uud and the pilot took turns to swim for exercise. During the day, they stayed under a blanket of mimetic material which adopted the colour of the sea and hid them from satellite and drone surveillance. The boat distilled fresh water from the sea, and almost a month's worth of dehydrated combat rations, nourishing but tedious almost beyond belief, were packed under the deck. They were not, at least, going to starve. In fact, the importance of keeping his weight up had been drummed into Da'uud at virtually every planning meeting. 'I do not pretend to understand these things,' his Uncle had said, 'but I am told that body mass is important.'

One morning, the light just beginning to strengthen in the eastern sky, the pilot nudged Da'uud's leg and said, 'Dewline.'

Da'uud sat up, lifted the edge of the mimetic blanket, and looked out across the waves. For almost half a century, Europe had encysted itself behind concentric borders and buffer zones, the better to protect itself and its citizens from the likes of him. Wracked by financial collapses and never-ending arguments about whose shoulders the responsibility for security fell upon, the EU had eventually bullied the states of southern Europe into co-funding a line of distant early-warning sensor buoys stretching down the centre of the Aegean to the Egyptian coast, and across the Mediterranean to Spain. They monitored the passage of all surface traffic passing between Asia Minor and the Middle East and Africa and Europe. Mass-produced by American contractors, the buoys were small and cheap, and in the way of small cheap things they were prone to failure. No one would be especially alarmed when the ECM pod built into the boat's shallow keel disabled the nearest buoy and they slipped through the dewline, although a crew would be despatched to replace it, in time.

'I don't see it,' he said.

'At two o'clock,' said the pilot. 'We're almost on top of it.'

Da'uud squinted and finally located a small cylindrical object bobbing upright in the waves. It was no larger than a coffeepot. 'Are you sure it can't see us?'

'No way to tell,' the pilot replied. 'We'll find out soon enough.'

They passed the buoy, and there followed a tense few hours as they pulled away from the dewline, but apart from a handful of distant fishing boats and a couple of airliners stitching through the clouds they saw nothing at all.

The following day, the pilot said, 'We're here.'

><

They approached the island cautiously, under cover of darkness. Several huge ships were anchored offshore, lit up brightly enough to be visible from orbit. Da'uud could hear, faint but clear, the sound of music coming from them across the water. Beyond them, a string of lights outlined the edge of the island, thickening into a vaguely spade-shaped mass where the town clustered around the harbour and climbed into the hills.

Keeping well away from other shipping, the pilot circled the island. The far side seemed more or less unpopulated.

Da'uud knew the island from maps and photographs, but this was the first time he had seen it at night. He could make out the lights of two or three buildings against the great dark mass of the mountain rising out of the sea, but that seemed to be it as far as habitation was concerned.

'Shore patrol,' the pilot murmured.

Da'uud looked, saw the headlights of several vehicles moving slowly along the coast road, heard the sound of their engines. They passed out of sight, and a few moments later there was only darkness and the sound of the sea sucking at the island again.

'Gone,' said the pilot. 'Good luck.'

Da'uud grabbed his bag, said, 'You too,' and rolled out of the boat. The water was shockingly cold after the warmth under the mimetic tarpaulin, but he oriented himself and stroked strongly away towards the shore. Behind him, he heard the quiet mumble of the engine as the boat turned away from the island. He had no idea whether the pilot was returning to Turkey or had another landfall in mind; they had barely exchanged a couple of hundred words during the whole crossing.

Da'uud swam unhurriedly the kilometre or so to the island, his bag bobbing just below the surface behind him on a tether. Finally, his knee scraped sand and pebbles and he crawled up onto the beach. Despite regular exercise, his legs were still unsteady after a week at sea. He crawled along the beach until he came to a rocky outcropping which hid him from the road.

He stripped off his wetsuit and bundled it into a crevice in the rocks. There was a tab under the armpit; he tugged it hard and felt something pop, and within moments there was a fierce chemical smell as the suit dissolved. From his bag, he took a change of clothes. Western clothes: jeans, a T-shirt, a hoodie, trainers, all of them expensive brands but not new. In a separate pouch were paper identification documents – a Somali passport, travel permits, and so on – but they were meant only for the direst of emergencies. The first thing any encounter with the authorities would involve would be a scan for the microchip implanted in all refugees at their point of contact with the edge of Europe. Lacking such a chip, the most optimistic thing he could look forward to was a long and poorly organised repatriation, followed by many years suffering his Father and Uncle's sardonically expressed disapproval. Best not to risk that.

For the past 50 years, EU immigration policy towards the tide of refugees fleeing the chaos in Africa and the Middle East had been to hold the problem as far as possible from its northern states, stringing border wire along its southern frontier and sealing off the juicy heart of the continent.

Greece and Turkey found themselves on the wrong side of the fence – the former too exhausted by financial and political ruin to complain, and the latter still so cockteased by the unfulfilled prospect of EU membership that it would do anything at all to please Brussels. They were useful firebreaks where the endless flow of humanity could be halted, corralled, processed and repatriated. It was a labour-intensive task – probably the only growth industry remaining in Greece. Meanwhile, the Italians, a little better-off, but really not by much, were buying surplus US military drones and flying 24-hour patrols along the edge of their territorial waters, rocketing anything that displeased them. The Europeans had turned their continent into a fortress, but every fortress has nooks and crannies where a carefully prepared individual can slip through.

Da'uud took from his bag a small rucksack packed with a change of clothes, a battered paperback, a survival kit and a couple of other items. He rolled up the waterproof bag, stuffed it into the rucksack, slung it over his shoulder, and began to pick his way carefully up the beach. Reaching the road, he crouched in some bushes until he was certain no vehicles were approaching, then he crossed quickly and began to make his way up the hillside beyond.

'You know, I can't think of a single reason why I shouldn't just fly there directly,' Da'uud told his Uncle.

His Uncle sighed. 'Because you will be microchipped when you pass through Immigration and they will know where you are. The whole *point* of this exercise is that they do not know you are there.'

Da'uud looked at his Uncle and Father. These two old men had once wielded considerable power. Not in public, but in the shadows. In their pomp, they had created an intelligence network which encompassed most of Africa and extended tendrils into southern Europe. His Uncle was fond of saying that intelligence work existed independently of all temporal considerations, and the fall of the previous government, the appointment of a new security service, and their current state of house arrest, had barely slowed them down. They were not allowed to leave the compound, but they were still cheerfully destabilising small states and enabling dictators on the other side of the continent, and no one could stop them.

'You will have to be strong,' his Father intoned. 'The journey will be the least part of this business.'

'I'm not afraid,' Da'uud told him.

'Then you're an idiot,' said his Uncle. 'Or you're a liar. And we have no use for either.'

Da'uud got up and went over to the window, looked down into the compound. He had a very large extended family, many of whom had worked in intelligence with his Father and Uncle and had subsequently chosen to go into internal exile with them. His country had been in conflict for so long, it was said, that many in the West thought that *war-torn* was part of its name. War-torn Somalia, where even the populace could not be certain, from year to year, who was running things, or if things were even being run at all. His Father and his Uncles had raised the family to stand aside from such things. They hewed to no god, no tribe, no allegiance. They were schooled in infiltration, subversion, sabotage. The elders of the family looked upon their work and saw that it was good, and then they turned their eyes north, beyond the seething chaos of Yemen and the many tiny squabbling sheikdoms the House of Saud had left behind when it fled to Paris during the coup. It was the work of a moment for the wealthy to enter Europe – a fast jet, some petty bureaucrat waiting on the tarmac at the other end bearing residence visas and possibly a welcoming bottle of Krug. It was not, it went without saying, so straightforward for the majority.

Da'uud turned from the window, sixteen years old and a fraction under two metres tall. He could hack a government communications network, speak four languages, field-strip a dozen different types of assault rifle under combat conditions, cook a restaurant-standard meal, quote Coleridge, and kill a man with a rolled-up newspaper. Admitting to fear was not something which came easily to him. He had been schooled, from almost as soon as he could walk, to be *capable*. Fearing something meant doubting his own *capability*. Fear was the first step towards failure.

He said, 'If you can get me there, I will do this thing. You need not doubt me.'

The two old men exchanged glances and then looked at him. 'Go and say goodbye to your brothers and sisters,' his Father told him. 'You will leave after lunch.'

After so many dawns bobbing on the surface of the Aegean, this morning was an almost religious experience. Or it would have been, had Da'uud been remotely religious. Halfway up the slope of the mountain which rose at the heart of the island, he sat and watched the light grow in the eastern sky, revealing a fantastical vista of sea and scattered islands and, far far away on the horizon, a vague darkening which he thought might be the Turkish mainland. The sun, rising above the edge of the world, seemed to set the sea alight for a moment, flooding everything with colour.

From his vantage point, he could see for many miles along the coast road. This side of the island seemed sparsely visited, probably because the soil was so poor and rocky and there were no natural harbours. History and geography had settled everything ten or fifteen kilometres away on the other side, and it had not seen fit to spread very far. So far, he had only seen a handful of vehicles, apart from the shore patrol doing its hourly circuit.

There was a stand of stunted, weather-bent trees a little further up the slope. Da'uud moved among them, found a spot and began moving rocks and little stones aside until he had exposed the almost worthless soil underneath. Then he carefully scooped a hole several centimetres deep. When he was satisfied that it was deep enough, he sat back on his heels, reached into his backpack and took out a small transparent flask. Rattling in the bottom of the flask was a dull metallic object about the same size and shape as a sunflower seed.

He remembered his Uncle giving him the flask. His Uncle had been wearing insulated gloves. 'Many Bothans,' his Uncle had told him gravely, 'died to bring us this information.'

It was a family joke, but not one without a lesson: intelligence always has a cost. Da'uud and his siblings had been taught not to treat intelligence lightly, to remember that it was not simply words and numbers and photographs and video.

It was also true, in this case. People had died in order for his Uncle to offer the flask to him; it was well to remember that.

He had been warned not to touch the seed – the interior of the flask had some kind of protective coating – so he simply removed the cap and upended it over the hole. The seed dropped to the ground, missing the hole by a fraction, balanced on the edge. A faint wisp of smoke began to curl up from beneath it. Da'uud sighed, looked about him, found a twig and poked at the seed until it toppled into the hole.

He scraped dirt over it and sat back on his heels. Holding the twig up in front of his face and squinting at it, he saw that the end seemed to have been eaten away. Was *still* being eaten away; as he watched, it appeared to be disappearing in a tiny vague cloud of mist. He stuck it in the soil over the hole, scrambled away a few metres and made himself comfortable against the wizened trunk of one of the trees. He looked at his watch. Twelve hours, his Uncle had said. That, at least, was the intelligence they had. They were dealing with a Mystery here, and there would be variables. Da'uud settled back against the tree, set the alarm of his watch, and closed his eyes.

'It is a weapon of great power,' his Uncle told him. 'Our information is that it was developed by the North Koreans, who have become interested in technologies proscribed in the West.'

Da'uud, who was sitting on the couch in the living room of the main house with a tablet in his hands, reading the technical specs of the thing which had been delivered under cover of darkness last night, glanced up at his Uncle and Father. 'North Korea,' he said.

'Yes, we know,' said his Father. 'The last famine killed over a million people, and still they work on devices such as this.' He nodded at the tablet.

To Da'uud's mind, as well as the minds of most people in the rest of the world, North Korea had become a pressure cooker, an out-of-control social experiment presided over by a line of increasingly dangerous Kims. No Westerner had been allowed into the country for almost 30 years, and what intelligence did emerge came in the form of wild rumours about genetic experimentation, augmented humans, apes which had learned to use power tools, dogs which could carry on a rudimentary conversation, and so on and so forth. You could boil off the most insane of those rumours and still be left with enough credible tales to make the fears of North Korea's nuclear capability earlier in the century seem like an idle and passing worry. It was said that every nuclear power on Earth had at least one warhead targeted on Pyongyang.

'How did it come into our hands?' he asked.

His Father sighed and tipped his head to one side.

'If this is true…' Da'uud gestured with the tablet. 'I think I have a right to ask, don't you?'

'It was stolen,' his Uncle said.

'Well, patently.'

'Several times,' his Father added.

'Our information is that it was taken, originally, from a facility near Kanggye, up near the Chinese border,' his Uncle went on. 'How it was taken, we do not know. There is anecdotal information that it was offered for sale to the Chinese intelligence services, but the sale never took place and the item dropped out of sight. Some months later, it reappeared in Japan, where it seems the North Korean intelligence services made an attempt to retrieve it.'

'There was a firefight,' his Father said. 'Many casualties.' He shook his head. In their world, gunfire was the mark of a catastrophic failure of tradecraft. The whole point of espionage was that no one should know you had been there.

His Uncle shrugged. 'The next thing we know, it's in

Damascus.' He let the name of the city hang in the air for a moment. 'Several different groups of jihadists are bidding to buy it, then someone gets impatient and the representative of the vendors turns up in one part of the city and his head turns up elsewhere.'

'After that, we don't know,' his Father went on. 'We do know that it finally passed into the hands of a jihadi cell, and we suspect they stole it, because they certainly did not have the funds to buy it.'

'And we stole it from them,' Da'uud said.

'We did.'

'This thing is cursed,' his Uncle said. 'Everyone who has ever touched it has died violently.'

'I'm more inclined to put that down to human greed and stupidity than supernatural agency,' his Father mused. 'We are not greedy, and neither are we stupid. We will be more careful.'

>•<

Da'uud opened his eyes. Without moving, he scanned the area. It was late afternoon, and the sun beat down on the hillside. Far below, one of the great white cruise ships was sailing away in the general direction of Turkey, inscribing a white crease on the surface of the sea. A little further down the slope, a solitary scrawny goat was standing looking at him. Da'uud's watch buzzed; he turned off the alarm.

Turning his head, he saw a ragged hole in the ground where he had buried the seed. Looking carefully, he searched for signs of vapour rising from the hole, but he saw none.

He got up stiffly and walked over to the hole. It was easily large enough to put his head and shoulders into, the stones and rocks around it seemingly half-melted, almost vitrified. He dropped the rucksack down the hole, heard it fall a considerable distance before it hit bottom, then he sat down with his legs dangling over the edge and slipped inside.

The walls of the hole were smooth to the touch; by bracing and relaxing his knees and elbows he was able to let himself fall by degrees until, all of a sudden, his legs swung out into thin air and he lost his purchase and fell several metres. He landed on a level surface, absorbing the impact easily like a parachutist, and looked around him.

He was in a hemispherical chamber about ten metres across and five high at its highest point. The floor and walls were smooth and lustrous and gave off a low, pale blue luminescence. Above his head, the hole opened into the chamber's ceiling. Looking up, he could see a tiny circle of sky. He judged that he was almost 20 metres underground.

In the very centre of the chamber, the seed had germinated into a fat teardrop about the height of a six-year-old child. It was the perfect blue of a cloudless Mediterranean summer sky, and leaning down close Da'uud could see that its surface was covered in a network of fine black lines, like the craquelure on a piece of ancient porcelain. The surface was, he realised, also moving, very slowly. Or perhaps it was just the black lines – it was hard to tell.

He sat down beside the teardrop and looked around the chamber. *I am not afraid*, he had said. But now he was. He thought his Uncle would approve.

'It is called,' his Uncle had said, '*nanotechnology*. I am too old to understand these things; I do not know how a machine can be too small to see and yet still function.'

'Whoever developed it has, apparently, made unbelievable advances,' his Father added. 'There is, in fact, a rumour that it comes from a crashed spacecraft belonging to an alien civilisation.' And they had all laughed at that, but now, sitting here beside the machine, Da'uud did not feel inclined to laugh. To their knowledge, this machine had never been tested; all they knew was what it had been designed to do. The Western intelligence agencies, if they knew of this thing – and he assumed they did – must be going out of their minds trying to find it. It was, in its way, the most dangerous thing on Earth.

Moving quickly, Da'uud removed his clothes and sat beside the machine again. He took a deep breath, put his hand on the smooth surface of the teardrop, and pushed gently. There was a momentary resistance, and then his hand sank into it up to the elbow. He stirred his hand in a warm substance that seemed at once wet and dry. The skin of his arm tingled briefly, then went numb. The numbness welled up his arm until it reached his shoulder, and then surged across his body. He fought panic, fought the atavistic urge to pull free of the machine, and then the numbness filled his head and he slumped backwards on the floor of the chamber.

>•<

They had told him he would not dream, but somehow he did. He dreamed of his mother, who had died in a suicide bomb attack in Mogadishu when he was four. He dreamed of his brothers and sisters. He dreamed of his Father and Uncle, who had spent much of their lives theorising this operation, never realising that one day they would be in possession of something which would actually make it work.

In time, his breathing slowed, then stopped altogether. His heartbeat stilled. The machine built fine tendrils into his body, feeding oxygen to his brain. His skin hardened, became leathery, thickened and thickened again until his features disappeared. After two days, he lay in a featureless black cocoon. Within the cocoon, tiny machines worked busily to disassemble him, piece by microscopic piece. While he dreamed of his Uncle telling him about Europe and its decades-long war against people who were not *of* Europe, his brain floated in a thick soup of cells and furiously busy nanotechnology.

'The caterpillar does not dream of being a butterfly,' his Uncle had told him, 'any more than the butterfly remembers being a caterpillar.'

Above him, the hole to the outside world gradually closed itself.

>•<

Da'uud opened his eyes and took a deep breath. Without moving, he took stock. He felt warm and comfortable and well rested. No aches or pains. He flexed his fingers and toes and everything seemed to work. At some point, his arm had been ejected by the machine.

Very slowly, he sat up, and experienced a sudden wave of disorientation. The legs stretched out in front of him were white. He wiggled his toes, and, yes, they seemed to be controlled by him, but they were not his toes. He raised his arms and held his hands in front of his face. They were slender and white, their nails neat and pink. He turned them over and looked at his palms.

'They will not admit us,' his Uncle had told him, 'because we are other. We are not them. We do not look like them. They will overlook our colour if we have enough money or we have something they want, but we will always be different; we will never walk down their streets without someone attacking us or suspecting us of wearing a suicide vest.'

'The device is an infiltration weapon,' his Father said. 'It is the ultimate disguise for a deep-cover agent. We think the North Koreans may have intended to use it to flood the West with operatives – indeed, if there is more than one prototype they may already be doing so. For us, it is our doorway into Europe. For you, for your brothers and sisters. For our people.'

Da'uud stood unsteadily – his viewpoint seemed several centimetres too low – and walked carefully over to the rucksack on those alien white feet. He took from the pack a small mirror and held it up in front of his face, and a stranger's face looked back. A blue-eyed face topped by a shock of blond hair. He blinked, and those blue eyes blinked back. This was going to take some getting used to.

The machine sat in the middle of the floor, quiescent now, its job done for the moment. He thought perhaps it was fractionally smaller, but he couldn't be sure.

Da'uud dressed. For a moment, tying the laces of his training shoes, he became so hypnotised by the sight of his hands that he forgot what he was doing. *I am the same person, he told himself. This is cosmetic. Like having a haircut.*

But it was not like having a haircut. If the information he had been given was accurate, quite a substantial amount of his genetic code had been rewritten. He was no longer what he had been.

'If you were to approach the border looking as you do now,' his Uncle had said, 'you would be turned away. All of us would. The Europeans talk about jobs and economic pressure and population growth, but the truth is that they don't want us because we are *different*. They were content to rule us for a century, two centuries, but now we rule ourselves they do not want us among them.'

Though the hole in the ceiling had closed up, while he slept an opening had appeared in one side of the chamber. It was just high enough for him to step into it if he crouched. It led to a narrow, low tunnel which angled gently upward and opened on the hillside some distance away.

Da'uud stepped out and found that it was raining. Squalls, dancing in a strong wind, obscured the view. He checked his watch and discovered that four months had passed since he had put his arm into the machine. The season had changed. It was as if he had travelled in time.

'Go to the edge of Europe and establish an embassy for us,' his Father had told him. 'We will send someone by a different route to prepare new identity documents for you when you have undergone the procedure. When you are ready, we will send others. One, two, three at a time. If we look like them, we can walk among them. And if we walk among them, we can find our way into positions of authority.'

'We will effect change,' his Uncle had said. 'A great wrong has been done to the peoples of the South, and now the peoples of the North have walled themselves up against us. We will redress that wrong. It may take a generation, or two generations, or three. But we will open the borders again and our people will be free.'

Da'uud took a phone from his rucksack and sent a text message to tell his Uncle that the embassy was open and ready for business. Then he walked down the hillside, through the rain, to look for a job in this new world.

# HERE COMES THE FLOOD

**DESIRINA BOSKOVICH**

Gran's trial summons arrives the first week in March. We've been expecting this, but it still feels like a big deal.

Gran is eighty-one. She doesn't always understand what's going on, but she understands the trials. That's all she likes to do: sit in her rocking chair and watch the trials. Sometimes she yells or curses or mutters at the screen. Mostly she just rocks and watches. She likes the stories the defendants tell. She says they remind her of better days.

The summons flashes simultaneously on every screen in the flat: *The People vs. Hailey Wilson, for crimes against humanity.*

'It'll be a good one,' Gran blusters. 'You'll see. They'll all see! The bastards. I'll tell 'em.'

My mom rolls her eyes, touches 'accept,' and flicks away the summons. 'Right, Mom. You'll tell 'em.' She goes back to her game.

Mom's been living with Gran for fifty-four years. She probably can't wait to have her gone.

'I'll be famous!' Gran says. 'You'll see!'

'Probably not, Gran,' I say. 'Most people don't get on the popular shows. Most courtrooms just have a few viewers at a time.'

'Why the hell not? I'm as important as anyone, you know. I did just as many whatever-they-call-ems.'

'Crimes against humanity?' my husband Arnav suggests from the kitchenette behind us, where he's prepping dinner for the family.

'Yeah, crime against humanities. I did my part to keep the DPs out, you know. I even shot a few. We still had our AR-15s back then!'

'I just don't want you to get your hopes up,' I say. 'Most of the courtrooms are boring. They're not like what you see on TV.'

Gran harrumphs and then proceeds to completely ignore me as she searches for her favourite trial show.

Arnav and I glance at each other and roll our eyes. *Why do we even try?*

Here's the thing about living in a 1,000-square-foot apartment with four generations of your family: if you started a fight every time you got frustrated, you'd never stop screaming. So you end up rolling your eyes, a lot.

'Get it, girl,' Gran mutters at the screen as another octogenarian rambles to the courtroom about the things her children will never understand.

>•<

A few days later there's another DisPer attack.

The DisPers wriggled their way into the city through one of the waste tunnels and set off a bomb in a power substation. The blast radius is small and the DisPers only manage to cut power to one narrow sector of the city, but at those low levels any structural damage can be incredibly dangerous. The smallest fault lines can lead to collapse.

Leave those cracks un-mended, those fault lines unchecked, and a generation later we'll be buried beneath six storeys of rubble.

Like my father before me, I'm an engineer.

My team gets called down to the substation to inspect the damage. Eventually, if the city can free up the funds, we'll be tasked with patching it up.

In the meantime – make notations, snap pics, feed data

into our devices and assess which harms we can most safely ignore.

Most of the foundations are in terrible shape. The walls aren't secure. The waste tunnels are eroding in critical spots. The water damage sustained during high tides and hurricane events grows worse every year. There are too many holes.

Of course, it's only because of the existing damage that the DisPers could find a way in. When my dad was young, the engineers didn't have to deal with these kinds of things.

My dad retired early from the crew. Now, he mostly just drinks.

The DisPers meant to kill themselves in the attack, but failed. Security captured them: a young woman and a young man, about my age and Arnav's.

Their trial will begin soon too.

>•<

When I get home that night, reeking of waste and mildew, Arnav is in the brightest mood he's been in months.

The DisPer attack is all over the news. The anchors offer breathless commentary on this latest act of terrorist sabotage. They endlessly flash pictures of the DisPers: both brown-haired and blue-eyed, with crazed, gap-toothed grins and skin tanned by the punishing sun.

'Guess what, Natalia?' Arnav demands, and then answers before I can guess. 'We're getting them! My court lucked out. This is huge!'

Arnav does social PR and mindshare advocacy for one of the up-and-coming courtroom shows. Finally, he's got something exciting – this could make their judge a star.

'Way to go!' I high-five my guy. I'm exhausted and drained, but the news cheers me up. Arnav could even get a promotion, if he plays this right…

Gran and Mom don't notice our celebrating, they're so busy lapping up every sordid detail of the news. My four-year-old nephew is watching too.

'I'll give the DPs one thing,' Gran says. 'Those sons of bitches are scrappy. Thought for sure they'd all be dead by now, but they're still going strong.'

'For fuck's sake, Mom, language! Can you stop calling them DPs?' my mom exclaims. 'You sound like a damn trog.'

My nephew giggles. 'Trog! Trog!'

'What, I'm gonna call them DisPers like the rest of you brainwashed proles?' Gran demands. 'I've been calling them DPs since before you were born. I don't give a damn if suddenly people think that's *offensive*.'

'DP,' my nephew says and laughs hysterically. 'We hate the DPs.'

'Shh, Joey,' my mom says. 'That's not nice. We call them DisPers now.'

'We hate the *DisPers*,' Joey corrects himself, with hyperbolic joy. 'Gonna kill them. Gonna shoot all the DisPers with my AR-15.'

I've got to get the hell out of here. I look at Arnav. He looks at me.

'We're going for a walk,' I say, but Mom and Gran don't even hear; they're too busy staring at the screen.

>•<

The park where Arnav and I escape is actually pretty nice.

We sit by the fountain, listening to the soundtrack of chirping birds and gazing up at the simulated sky, the 3D clouds that drift there. The sky is just a ceiling – there are more city levels above – but it's better than nothing.

We lost our streams, our birds, our skies, for the shelter of the walls.

We don't remember a world with weather. We're safe inside, and the weather's out: the floods, the fires, the scorching sun. The ash-charred forests, the raging hurricanes, the desiccated hills. The displaced persons, hungry, thirsty, needy, sick.

When Gran was young this city took in the first wave of climate migrants (floods) and the second wave (droughts). Then a third wave began, fleeing the never-ending fires that burnt up north, and people said *Enough is enough.* They built the walls, they built the dome, they sealed the borders.

Except.

This city was built on a coast. Not on the water's edge like so many others. Not right at sea level like the great cities before it that were already gone. But close enough that, in previous centuries, the ships could come and go with the wealth that turned the world into what it was.

The globe is still getting hotter. The waters are still getting higher.

Every year the ocean laps a little bit closer, takes bigger and hungrier bites from our city's water-logged walls, and outside those walls are all the displaced persons our parents and grandparents abandoned to die.

'What are you thinking about?' Arnav asks me.

He's gazing across the park to where two small children

play with a RoboPup and two sets of parents sit on the emerald turf, laughing over the antics of their lil' tykes.

'Oh, nothing. You?'

'We'll find out soon,' he says, and squeezes my hand. 'They announce the lottery winners before the end of the month.'

'Yes,' I say. 'Yes. We will.' I try to keep myself from thinking about it. I don't want to get my hopes up again.

We've been entering the baby lottery every year since I was twenty-two. You want to start early; better too early than too late.

'You nervous?'

'Of course.'

I've been waiting for five years and I want it so bad I can't bear to think about it. My brother and his wife, they got it on the first try. Luck of the draw. That was all.

Arnav pulls me close and kisses my hair. 'Don't worry. We'll get it. If not this year, next year. Soon.'

The king tide comes in and another substation goes down, ancient equipment sizzling and creaking as dampened electric circuits crackle and pop. This time, the water rises to seven inches. They'll wait for it to recede before they can bring the substation back online. They've done this before.

This time, the water recedes to three inches and stops. It's still too wet. They can't risk it – not the equipment, not the workers – so decide to take this node off the grid for good.

My team is sent to scout out alternate locations, or find a way to add additional capacity to another already overloaded substation.

There are solar panels all over the outside surface of the dome. But the power's all still routed through the main stations.

My co-workers and I explore the grid, searching for ways to get more capacity from frayed systems. Everything is overextended. Everything is beyond capacity. Nothing can handle any more than it already holds.

In the meantime, the policymakers – the public faces of city infrastructure, who give lowly engineers like me a bad name – announce they have to tighten power rations until a lasting solution can be found.

Tighter power rations mean less screen time. Which means I have to hear about it at home.

I walk into a fight. Mom and Gran are arguing about which trial show to watch. They have different favourites. Now they only have time to watch one.

Mom thinks the limited power rations are because of the terrorists and the sabotage they did last week. 'I just don't understand why we keep putting up with this kind of thing!' she's complaining to the neighbour, who stopped in for a bitch session about the injustice of it all. 'The DisPers are getting bolder every year! It's getting out of hand.'

'It's not the DisPers,' I start, for what surely must be the 100th time. 'They didn't have anything to do with this. It's the water...'

'It *was* the DisPers,' Mom insists. One of her singular qualities as my mother is that she's always convinced she knows more about every single topic than I do, even – for instance – something I do professionally, such as my actual job. 'I heard about it on the news. They said the DisPers sabotaged the power station. With their bombs. I guess we're just going to let them destroy our civilisation. Someone has *got* to do something!'

'I'll tell you what you oughta do…' Gran starts in. 'When we still had AR-15s…'

'That was another substation,' I explain as patiently as possible. 'We got that fixed. This is because of the tides. The water damages the equipment and it becomes very dangerous, because—'

'Trust me,' Mom says. 'It was on the news. Some of us like to stay informed.'

Gran's taken the opportunity to seize control of the screen, where a female judge with statement hair is berating a flustered eighty-something. Did he eat meat? He did?

*Yes, well, but…*

Did he enjoy gorging himself on the Earth's last crumbs, the greedy, filthy pig? Did he buy goods shipped halfway across the world?

*You don't understand, we just went to the store, that was what…*

So he did. Never a moment's consideration for future generations as he enjoyed the spoils, savoured the loot: the belching, farting jet planes; the human greed-machines on their hoard of ill-gotten treasures, their water-gulping industry, their cheap plastic trash. Did he own a vehicle? *Yes?* Disgusting.

'When's *my* trial?' Gran asks again, for the half-a-dozenth time.

'Soon, Mom,' my mom says. 'Next week. Friday. For the love of God, get a goddamn calendar or something.'

>•<

After the shitty day, all I want to do is vent to Arnav, or maybe escape to the park for a few minutes as the simulated sky models the setting of an artificial sun. He's the only one who listens to me. About the rising waters. About the crumbling walls. About the fault lines that won't stop spreading.

But Arnav's not here. He's working late again, his team prepping feverishly for the mindshare campaign they'll launch for the DisPer trial. This melodrama is their shot at greatness. On energy breaks, he dispatches me token kisses.

Instead, I go to my brother Chris's room. He and his son are sardined side-by-side in the bottom bunk, both absorbed in their games. My sister-in-law's at work.

The bed's the only place to sit, so I crawl in and hunch against the wall, toe-to-toe with Joey. 'Uh, so... how's it going?'

It takes Chris a moment to break his focus and shift his attention to me. In that unguarded moment, I notice how old he looks; we're not children any more.

'It's bad,' he says.

'What is?' I ask. 'Your... uh... game?'

'It's not just a game,' he sighs. 'Christ, how many times have I explained... OK. Listen...' And for what, admittedly, is not the first time, he launches into an explanation of this virtual world he's participated in for years. How the VR outposts link the real-world cities. The mapping he and his pals have done. The knowledge they've shared. How this network has become the backbone of a nation long since disintegrated.

Ostensibly, we still live in the United States of America. The country was never officially dispersed, the federal structure never formally disbanded. But that doesn't mean anything. In the face of unending crisis, federalism was impossible. There were too many people. You couldn't take care of them all. You didn't *want* to take care of them all. It was sink together or swim alone, so the cities broke off, one by one.

A city could save itself. A state, maybe. A nation, no way.

But in the virtual world, there are still connections, there is still communication. Apparently, Chris is kind of a big deal in this arena.

Chris doesn't work much; he just pulls his basic income credits and does whatever it is he does in the game.

'But here's the thing,' he says, glancing at his son, Joey, who's oblivious; I can hear the upbeat music spilling over from his headphones. 'A bunch of outposts have been going dark. Cutting off communications. We can't connect to them any more.'

'They're falling?' I ask. 'Failed cities?'

'That's what we thought at first. When it was just a few.'

'But now?'

'It's a lot. They aren't all falling. Not at once.'

'So what is it? The network is going down?'

'No. They're cutting us off.'

'What does that mean?'

'It's intentional. They're doing it on purpose. They don't want to communicate with us any more. They're isolating us. Every day, the grid gets darker for us.'

'But why? What did we do?'

'It's not what we did. It's what's about to happen. It's the same thing the rest of us did to DFW after the coup. They were about to become like the DisPers. We had to focus on saving the cities that could still survive. So we went dark to them. We cut them off.'

I've known for a while things are bad. But even so, I'm shocked. I can't think what to say.

'They won't tell you that shit on the news,' my brother says. 'It's all about the trials.'

'So the cities across the network already know what people here won't admit. This city is falling. The floods won't stop. We're done.'

'Why do you think they started the trials to begin with?'

I shrug. I still can't think of anything to say.

'Dad knew. He knew for a while. Before he quit.'

Ostensibly, my father still lives with us. He and my mother never officially disbanded their union either. But we haven't seen him in months.

The city has a solution for people like him – banks of bunks like coffins you can rent by the hour, credit-operated showers. He draws his UBI credits, eats at the cafeteria, lives in the cracks.

I gave up on him a long time ago, as I've given up on so many things already.

But tomorrow I'm going to look for him.

>•<

I find him in a cafeteria two sectors away, sitting at one of the long narrow tables, sipping something neon green that smells like honeydew and rocket fuel. He's mellow and distracted, fuzzy around the edges. He looks and smells like shit.

I sit across from him. He gazes at me without surprise, as if I've been sitting here all day. 'Natalia,' he says. 'You wanna drink?'

'Why not.'

Dad flicks some button on the table and a moment later a robot server appears with my beverage. I unfold the straw and sip. It tastes like ass.

'So, uh, how's everyone,' Dad slurs.

'Well, Gran's trial is next week.'

'So we've got that going for us. And Joey?'

'He's a little brat.'

'That's my boy. Joe-Joey-Joseph.' Dad laughs to himself at some elusive joke. 'Did you come to invite me to Gran's trial? It's gonna be a grand ol' show...'

'No,' I say. 'I came to ask you why you retired.'

'What? A man can't enjoy his cups in his old age?'

'You're not even old, Dad. Why did you quit engineering? The city's a mess. The foundations won't hold much longer. We need all the help we can get.'

'No shit... Why do you think I quit?'

All my rage bubbles to the surface. My chest is tight; my mouth is dry. And I just want to scream forever: How could you abandon us? Why didn't you fight for us? Why didn't you try harder? And at this moment I don't even know what, exactly, I'm referring to. Our messed-up family. Our falling city. Our broken society. Our poisoned world.

It's too much and it's all too far gone and I'm too young

and helpless to fix anything at all.

'They're holding skyscrapers together with glue and chewing gum,' Dad mumbles. 'Repairing rocket ships with duct tape. You think I didn't try to tell them? We all tried.'

'You couldn't try harder?'

'Me? I'm just one guy. What could I do? Stop the fucking ocean from rising? This city was dead two decades ago. It just doesn't know it yet. Not everyone knows it. We know it,' he says, and makes a sweeping gesture across the cafeteria, hundreds of people like him – men, women, all like him, all given up.

'I've spent hours running simulations,' I insist. 'There are ways to fix it. We need to fortify the foundations, install high-capacity pumps in a bunch of spots, apply water-proofing materials in a consistent way, move the power stations to top levels where they'll be safe from moisture, add more solar panels to power the pumps… It's a lot of work. But it's totally doable. We have the technology. We can assemble the resources. We can still save the city.'

'It's never the science. It's the people. You don't have those. You never will.'

'But we just have to make them understand. What's at stake. Their children…'

Dad chuckles into his toxic beverage. 'You'll see.' He says. 'You'll see. I hope I'm dead by that time, but if not, I'll say I told you so…'

'Thanks, Dad. As ever, you've been a huge fucking help.'

'You'll see.'

>•<

Arnav scores me a ticket to the big DisPer trial and I take two days off work to attend. My co-workers are all jealous. Suddenly everyone's asking me about Arnav, about the show. His career is finally beginning to have its perks.

But it's different, being in the actual courtroom. No sound effects. No cutaways. No recaps. No dramatic music as the camera pans in.

There's the judge, and the jury, and the prosecution. Of course, the defendants, sitting side-by-side in their yellow jumpsuits, wrists bound, ankles chained. A small audience, myself included. There are screens embedded in the backs of the chairs that tell us how to react at any given moment, what sounds we should emit, what expressions to make. Servers ply us with intoxicants and stimulants, which makes for better TV.

These key figures of the courtroom seem forlorn surrounded by the army of camera operators, data wranglers, photographers, PR people, script writers, lighting technicians, make-up artists, producers, boom operators, errand boys, caterers. This is big business; something has to be.

Every time I glance at Arnav in his spot among that sea of crew, he's frantically flicking through screens, analysing ratings, polls, audience reactions, mentions and reactions on the social web. He tweaks the algorithms so they're running the best moments on the highlight reel.

The prosecutor is gunning for a promotion too. 'So what did you hope to accomplish,' he demands of the DisPers as he warms to his role, 'when you infiltrated the safety of our city and set off those bombs? This courtroom is filled with people who could have lost their dearest loved ones in the destruction. What do you have to say to them?'

He paces around the courtroom. He leans in so close he's almost spitting in their faces. They don't flinch away. 'Why do you feel so entitled to destroy this city you did nothing to help build? When I was young, my parents told me that people like you don't know how to do anything except destroy. I hate to believe they were right.'

Cued by the screens, the rest of the audience voices their disappointment.

>•<

On the last day, just before the sentencing, the judge invites the DisPers to make a statement.

The man passes on his opportunity to speak. He shakes his head. He'll be silent to the end. But the woman stands and addresses the court.

The DisPers speak English, but they're hard to understand. In two generations their pronunciations shifted and their vernacular changed. They speak slowly. They're not educated. They aren't elegant, they aren't articulate, and they can't express themselves as easily as the judge and the prosecutor, reading from their scripts.

'You're inside,' she says. 'We're outside. We don't have enough water. We don't have enough food. We don't have medicine. Our children are sick. We can't do anything but try to stay alive.'

Her voice is halting but her eyes are blue fire and I feel like I can't move, I can't breathe, I'm squeezing my hands into balled fists, just like the night I tried to speak to my father, maybe for the last time.

I look around the courtroom, the audience who probably

all won some lottery or pulled some favour, the jury handpicked to look good on television. I want to know what they think. Here, face to face with a DisPer, is she more or less than they imagined?

No one's paying attention. They're whispering to each other, fiddling with their devices, interacting with the screens on the backs of the chairs. The jury, too. While the camera crew scurries around getting everything just so.

I'm the only one watching, and the DisPer woman looks straight at me. Our gazes meet.

'We hang on by our fingernails,' she says. 'Most of our children die. But the ones who live? They know all about how their grandparents fought to make it to this place where they thought they would survive, only to be shut out. We tell them what you did. We teach them to be angry. We raise them to fight. Sooner or later, they'll tear these walls down. The flood will come. You'll be like us.'

After the statement, the jury moves to another room to deliberate; their discussion is broadcast over huge screens to the waiting courtroom.

The case is open and shut: the DisPers are sentenced to die.

Every screen in the city is playing three lines on repeat: *Our children... We teach them to be angry. We raise them to fight. They'll tear these walls down.*

'It's sick, really,' the news commentators say. 'The DisPers are psychopaths. They've created a culture of death.'

The court's mentions are off the charts and Arnav is jubilant. They've increased the ratings tenfold. The whole crew goes out to celebrate, and I tag along, as they get rip-roaring drunk and watch their social graph rise with every refresh.

He catches me by the bathroom and kisses me all over with sloppy drunk love. 'I'm definitely getting a promotion after this!' he whispers in my ear. 'Maybe we can even get our own place. I can't wait for the lottery...'

'I'm proud of you, babe.'

>•<

Gran's trial comes on Friday. It's nothing like the DisPers' trial, of course. She's not some famous terrorist, just one among the millions who got us into this mess.

The show is run by a skeleton crew, just a couple camera people and a lighting guy and a gal doing sound. The audience is mostly our family, plus a few professional audience members the show always hires just in case.

'This is my moment!' Gran says with glee, and then they whisk her away to make-up. I'm pretty sure they also shoot her up with some kind of amphetamine because when she approaches the stand she's spitting fire.

The charges against her are lengthy.

First there was the era of late capitalism; Gran only enjoyed the tail end of that herself, but she still devoured plenty of spoils.

'You ate meat?' demands the judge.

'I did, your honour,' screams Gran, 'and I would again if someone would just get me a goddamn hamburger!'

'You drove a vehicle? With gasoline? You used electricity that burned coal? You owned plastic items? And many other possessions?'

A series of images the facial recognition bots mined from the deep web now flash across the screens – pictures of Gran when she was young. Playing in her childhood bedroom. Sixteen years old and sitting in the driver seat of her first car. Eating fast food with her friends.

'That's just the way it was!' Gran shouts. 'It's not a crime to buy stuff! Or at least it didn't use to be...'

Then there was the era of climate catastrophe. 'Did you march on the capitals? Did you write your senator? Did you switch out your light bulbs? Did you protest in Helsinki in 2021?'

The floods came. The droughts came. The fires came. The displaced persons came in wave after wave.

Gran is flagging now. This is the most excitement she's had in at least a couple decades. And it's really not a good idea to feed old people amphetamines.

'There wasn't enough for anyone,' she says. 'Not enough food. Not enough water. Not enough houses. We had to build the wall, and the DPs kept coming through it, and sabotaging it the whole time, just like now, they'd blow stuff up. The cops handed out rifles to anyone who wanted them. They liked having our help.'

'Did you murder displaced persons?'

'It wasn't murder. Just self-defence.'

'How many did you kill? Three? Four? Six? Ten? Any children?'

'We did it for you,' Gran says. 'Fuck me, we thought you entitled little pricks would be *grateful*.'

Hailey Wilson, aka Gran, is found guilty of criminal negligence, accessory to global manslaughter, and climate destruction in the fourth degree, plus an unspecified number of crimes against humanity. (They weren't able to pin down the exact number of refugees she killed.)

'For these crimes, you are sentenced to live out the rest of your days in the Facility for the Elderly. All your remaining assets will be confiscated by the state. Defendant Hailey Wilson dismissed. *Next!*'

>•<

Last year, when they announced the results of the baby lottery, I got in a huge screaming fight with my mom. She said don't worry, it will happen, just keep trying. Your brother got it on the first try! It's all luck of the draw.

She always does that. Acts like she's an expert. But she's not. They didn't have the baby lottery when she was my age. She had two children, which was honestly at least one child too many, and here we are, the city is falling, the city is full. There isn't enough for everyone.

And so I said that: *This is your mess. This is your mistake. You were selfish. And now I'm suffering.*

Obviously, that didn't go over too well.

This time, Arnav and I plan ahead to avoid any such altercations. We slink off together to the park, where we can sit quietly by the fountain, sneaking sips from our flask, gripping sweaty hands together and awaiting the results.

When the message flashes onto our devices, my heart is in my throat and I'm too nervous to look at it. 'You open it,' I tell Arnav. 'Tell me what it says.'

I squeeze my eyes closed and wait for his voice.

Instead, he's kissing me, and I can feel his tears wet against my cheeks. 'We got it,' he says. 'We're up. Let's go make a baby.'

We laugh a little and we cry a little. Then we go to tell my family the news.

# FLY AWAY, PETER

## IAN HOCKING

Frau Goeth left for the old water-processing plant in the centre of the forest every day at 4 p.m. Today it was raining, and her usual half-hour walk had stretched to forty minutes. She had a clockwork repeater timepiece that had been her grandfather's. It worked as well as ever. She could see that she was late.

Many years would have to pass before the plant, an L-shaped arrangement of three buildings with corrugated roofs and sagging walls, could serve water to Recklinghausen. Its water channel had dried up years before Frau Goeth was born, then backfilled with rubble and wood to prevent people falling in; despite this, at least two children from the Home had strayed onto the debris the previous spring, when the ice pockets had melted to voids, and been swallowed. It was too dangerous to dig for the bodies, so the men did nothing more than erect crosses.

The forest road to the plant was a now a muddy track. It broke up ten metres from the entrance where two small birds were washing themselves in a puddle. Each twitch was followed by a pause, like they were a series of pictures, laid quickly on a table by a practised hand.

Snow had been falling steadily during May, but now, in early June, rain had washed it away. Rain from the east. That meant falling black dirt. Nobody knew much about what was happening in the east; some said it was depopulated, others that something dark was rallying there. Frau Goeth dismissed the latter as the old fear of the Germans, that when something wicked came, it would come from the east.

She lifted her grey skirt clear of the mud, being careful not to get any on her stockings, and did a little march on the slab before the doorway. The slab was a headstone from the graveyard that had once served the aristocrats in the *schloss* north of the processing plant; the *schloss*, like the name of the baron on the gravestone, had been long since trampled out.

She noticed that the water bucket used for washing the feet of the children was scummed over with ice. It would need breaking up. A job for Fräulein Sigrid, that.

The door always needed a little shove. Inside was a space hardly illuminated by a gallery of high, dirty windows. But a third of the solar panels on the roof still worked, and because there was a battery in one of the processing plant buildings, she could put on the electric lights when the children arrived. She noted, with a nod, that the flags were still hanging and the pinboards were in place and appropriately festooned. The little cage at the back of the letterbox contained an envelope. As she took it, Frau Goeth felt her heart momentarily lose its rhythm.

The next fifteen minutes were spent on a routine twenty years old, from when, new to the area, she had volunteered at the Home. In those days the Home had been well heated and bright, and the green paint on the walls had given the place a plump, forested look.

Her office was a high-ceilinged room with a circular window and a little folding desk. A wall calendar showed the summer schedule; each week, the Pups would work towards their badges, their progress marked with red slashes. Last week the topic had been aeroplanes. This week, it was hygiene. Next, it was marksmanship. She expected nine Pups today: Ben, Luis, Paul, Lukas, Emma, Mia, Hanna, Harold and Sofia. Little Sofia had only attended twice before, but the others were old hands of a few months' standing. She had State cards for all of them, indicating such things as household income, siblings, health issues, and – because she was a Home Leader – reports from informers about anti-State activities associated with their households. It was rare for her to read anything incriminating, because the children of troublemakers were rarely afforded the privilege of Home membership. And it was a privilege.

Frau Goeth had a mnemonic system for remembering her twenty children. Mueller was, of course, the miller; Richter was the judge. She even had a Lukas Hartmann, the tough man – a curious name for a grey, stooped boy prone to nosebleeds. The surnames were more orthodox than they had any right to be. Most had been adopted in the chaotic years following the Brightness where records had been destroyed or misplaced, when Germany had become a crossroads for migrants moving to and from every point on the compass, worn down like the headstone in front of the Home. A good German name had been a way of staking a good German identity, holding the hand of the past while reaching for the future. It protected the bearer from the charge of outsiderhood. Nowadays, things were more relaxed. Unless, for example, you were an outsider whose country sided with enemies of the State.

These thoughts of foreigners led her to the Spanish child (Spanish grandparents, at any rate) Florian, who had just this week left for Barcelona. She separated his card from the rest and put it next to the stove before turning to the envelope. Inside was, as she had suspected, a letter from the State. The middle paragraph was a gibberish of four-letter groups arranged in neat columns. She took out her repeater. She was going to be late for sure now, but there was no use worrying. She went to a locked cabinet at the rear of the office and took out her decoding wheel. She did not write down the plaintext; she remembered as she went along. When she was done, she composed a coded reply and placed this in her out tray. Then she put the decoding wheel away in the locker.

It was twenty, perhaps thirty seconds later that she realised that she was still standing at the locker, holding her handkerchief in her hands like a garrote.

There had been a little boy called Harry.

Except, that wasn't quite it. Not at all.

The little boy had been *her* little boy. Harry. Long ago now. She had been living in Berlin with Philip, a man from the north of England.

>•<

When Harry was born, England had been a staunch ally of the State and an important part of the war against the North. She couldn't quite remember when England betrayed the State, but it was before she left the hospital with Harry. The fortunes of Philip had changed so quickly. One moment he was a liaison between the English air force and the State; the next he was a glaring absence, gone like a front tooth. The door to their house had been broken, every picture of Philip destroyed. They took out his vinyl records and stamped on them. The police inspector who had come that evening, as Frau Goeth nursed Harry, had given her two messages.

The first, delivered verbally, was this: 'We think it is a burglary and there is, frankly, very little that can be done.

There are wider concerns for the State at the moment, as you will understand.'

The second, which he delivered by taking a piece of vinyl and holding it up to the light, and then looking once at her baby, was, 'You must accept what has happened and move on with your life.'

Harry took up all her time after that, for which she was grateful. Things could have been worse. The disappearance of menfolk was so commonplace that plans had been at the back of her mind for years. Many other women in her block had suffered the same fate and they tended to get together over ersatz coffee to build the State within the State, a community for the child who comes home to find his home destroyed, in name if not brick, or for the wife whose husband is taken, liquidated, or, as was the case with her and Harry, both.

In time, she thought of marrying one Elias Goeth who worked in the State archives and had, since their schooling together in a Home in Charlottenberg, been baldly, urgently in love with her. Even now, looking at the tumbler on the locker in the Home, thinking of Goeth made her shudder. Her mistake had not been to refuse marriage. Her mistake had been to wait too long. After all, she was a young mother with a child relying on a fragile tangle of friendships – no family, not since her sister was murdered – and she was lucky to have the attention of even so dark a man as Goeth. If she had married him earlier, he might have been more attached to Harry.

She knew something was wrong as she came home one night, with Harry, from the factory where she helped make soap: hard, hurting soap that nobody but the richest in the

State had any chance of avoiding. She had been walking in the centre of the road where it was safest, holding little Harry by the hand. He had spent the day under her workbench with the other children, returning lost moulds and tools and charming the rest of the workers.

As mother and son passed a tower block, she saw Frau Dienes look up from her step, where she was brushing away the dark streaks left by the rain. Frau Dienes saw Harry's wave but, instead of waving back, stepped inside.

'Is Aunty Malis OK?' asked Harry.

Her mouth was tight. 'Aunty Dienes looks busy.'

They passed three other acquaintances on the way home and were ignored each time. She had a hard feeling in her gut that only intensified when they turned onto their home block and saw Elias Goeth, her new husband, smoking a pipe alongside a policeman. The policeman had the decency to look sadly at the child. Elias was all smiles. Elias exclaimed he had finally managed to enrol Harry in a school for enemy children where he'd be safe from all the bullying.

There was no bullying; this was the first she had heard of the matter.

Her hatred for this man overwhelmed her. She let go of Harry and whirled her arms at Elias, but it was all too late. Children had been taken too many times for the authorities to be unprepared for her reaction. A second policeman appeared from the shadows and punched a hypodermic through her coat, skirt and underwear, into her rump. The mixture stung as it spread and she fell onto her back screaming, punching at her dead leg, as the neighbouring windows slammed shut and her husband apologised to anyone who would listen on behalf of his wife, who would soon be as right as rain.

She never saw Harry again.

A year later, after the funeral of her husband, Frau Dienes – now Malis – invited her for coffee and cake. As they sat there among the drab decorations of a State Christmas, Malis passed Frau Goeth a blurred photograph of a report. Frau Goeth read it. Then Malis burned it. Frau Goeth thanked her, went to the grave of her husband and stared at the wooden cross as black rain fell. When it was dark, she took the cross away and, in the corner of the graveyard, broke it over her knee.

Frau Dienes' stolen report had claimed her son's tissues had gone to help State sailors burned in the Skagerrak campaign. At the bottom of the blurry last page a note had been added that Harry had been caught singing English nursery rhymes – 'foreign memetic agents' – to the other children in the soap factory. As she read this, Frau Goeth asked herself: *Who makes these decisions? What is the threshold for disobedience? Where is the innocence? What is punishment?* Eventually, after all the hours in a year, she stopped asking herself.

Frau Goeth, now the Home Leader, used her handkerchief to dry her tears. There was a fashion among young woman to use the black residue of rain as eyeliner, but Frau Goeth had never done this; when she was a girl, contact with the residue had led to open sores, often around the tear ducts. 'We weep as we weep,' her father had said. Many claimed the after-effects of the Brightness had gone, but she would never take the risk. She wore no make-up. There were no black marks on her cyan handkerchief and no tell-tale smudges around her eyes.

The main hall needed dusting, but Fräulein Sigrid would see to it. Frau Goeth wanted to make sure the instructions in the encrypted State letter were carried out before the children arrived. In the main hall was the pinboard where eight sheets of paper represented the eight best ideas of eight children for what Peter Hoskins, the subject of the letter, could do during his new life in Germany. As she tore them off, Frau Goeth looked at them for a second time, the first being when she had inspected them over little shoulders the previous week. One showed a sandy-haired, diagrammatical boy eating an ice cream. In another picture, a similar-looking boy danced in dark rain. Frau Goeth took them all down until there was no trace of young Peter Hoskins.

She didn't think of him as the 'English boy', or the 'quiet one' any more. She didn't think of him at all.

It was twenty minutes later that Fräulein Sigrid knocked on the office door. She was a dumpy teenager who always wore a thick scarlet headscarf. She was sometimes wilful but Frau Goeth liked her, give or take.

Immediately, Sigrid's eyes turned to the stove. 'Toasty in here with that thing.'

Frau Goeth wasn't a big fan of small talk at the best of times. She tended to award it like a gold star on student work. She did not respond, but if the other woman noticed this, she didn't react.

'Our newest recruit will no longer be attending.'

Fräulein Sigrid's dopey expression vanished. She looked alive. 'Peter?'

'No Peter, no nothing, young lady.'

Fräulein Sigrid's eyes locked onto Frau Goeth's for a moment longer. Was this rebellion? Surprise? Or the very human need for detail? But the detail didn't matter. Because they never changed. The abductors, nice enough men, would have kept him calm with stories about ice cream or a zoo trip all the way to the ruined industrial area where they had the clinics.

Fräulein Sigrid reversed into the corridor. Frau Goeth finished composing her letter to the leader of one of the Youth groups in Dortmund – there was going to be an Away Day – and found herself, to her bewilderment and shame, humming the last few notes of an English nursery rhyme.

Soon, she heard the first of the children arrive, and their parents. Feet thundered in the hallway: fast patters and slow clomps. As the children passed her door – little Ben opening it briefly to wave, Paul to bow – Frau Goeth greeted them formally, all the while remaining in her seat. The parents did not say hello and did not linger once the children were delivered.

Frau Goeth was very clear about not entering the hall until 5 p.m. Until that time, she relied on Fräulein Sigrid to keep them occupied with games and wear them out as much as possible so they would sit still during the edification.

At 4.55 p.m., just as Frau Goeth was reaching to refill her pen, Fräulein Sigrid put her head back in. 'Sofia asked if they could play cricket. The English game. I wasn't sure what to say. Now might be a good time to...' In lieu of a predicate, she raised her eyebrows.

Frau Goeth would not be supplying the predicate. She let the moment stretch out to an uncomfortable degree. It seemed to work on Fräulein Sigrid. Finally, she said, 'A good time for what?'

The girl floundered. 'To tell them about…'

She almost said '*Peter*'. Frau Goeth could tell.

Frau Goeth simply raised her eyebrows. Like most lessons, and like the lessons Frau Goeth had learned herself, it was better for the pupil to wend their own way to the conclusion. To supply, as it were, their own predicate.

Fräulein Sigrid nodded. 'I see.'

Hard on six o'clock, when the electric light took over from the dirty sunlight, Frau Goeth strode into the hall. Immediately, the Pups, who had been running circles and yipping, fell silent. Frau Goeth counted them – nine in all. Ben, Luis, Paul, Lukas, Emma, Mia, Hanna, Harold and Sofia. The previous helper, Godrun, had given them what she called 'dwarf names' to help her remember them: sneezy, scratchy, skinny. Frau Goeth had no need of this.

The children watched her approach like sailors might watch an iceberg.

Frau Goeth clapped her hands twice and asked the children to make sure that the toys and games had been returned to the games cupboard. When this was done – silently, with Fräulein Sigrid in attendance by the cupboard, accepting the bits of string, spinning tops and balls as reverently as an armourer – Frau Goeth walked to the great pinboard and turned. She held out her hands with her palms down, waiting for the children to heel in a semicircle. When they did, she lowered her arms and the children sat.

Sofia had not been in the Home long, and she lagged behind with the sitting just as she had lagged behind putting her toys away. Frau Goeth said, 'Sofia, is there something wrong with your dress?'

Sofia, fidgeting, frowned at Frau Goeth. She turned to her neighbour in her troop, Ben, and stage whispered, 'Why does she think there's something wrong with my dress?'

Ben looked at Sofia; not in horror, exactly, but in confusion. Like all the children here, he was too young to fully appreciate why his parents were so anxious for them to attend the Home, but he knew that it was very important to them, and meant things like more food and greater safety. So he sat and did as he was told, even when he didn't know why; he simply knew that it was better to do what Frau Goeth asked.

'Sit down quietly,' he whispered back. Some of the others giggled.

To show that she wasn't without heart entirely, Frau Goeth smiled, but she knew her teeth were dark, and the effect was not always disarming.

Sofia shook her head to show that she didn't hold with all this business, but she did quieten.

'Good evening, children,' began Frau Goeth.

'Good evening, Frau Goeth,' they replied.

Sofia put up her hand. 'Can I dance a bit?'

'You *can* but you *may* not,' said Frau Goeth. She did hope that the child wasn't retarded. That would make Sofia's life much harder, and much shorter. 'We're going to say our promise. Do you remember the promise?'

The other children were sitting rock still, but Sofia leant forward and stretched her arms out like a cat. She giggled to herself, then said, 'So where's Peter?'

Frau Goeth said, 'Who?'

Sofia laughed innocently, as though she anticipated liking the game that Frau Goeth was about to play. But the other children didn't laugh with her, and they ignored her when she looked at them, to see what they thought of the game. 'Peter,' she said, as though they were deaf. 'From *England*.' To Ben, she said in her stage whisper, 'Peter is going to show us how to play cricket this week.'

Nobody said anything. Ben looked fearfully at his dirty feet.

Eventually, Frau Goeth said, 'Does anyone remember a Peter?'

The children shook their heads. Ben shook his most vigorously. Sofia thumped Ben on the arm. 'You're all playing a trick on me and it isn't very nice.' She folded her arms but looked at Ben sideways, ready to be included.

Frau Goeth said, 'Sofia, this is a place without violence. If you do that again, you'll go into the cupboard.'

Sofia laughed at that, then put a hand over her mouth.

Frau Goeth began the promise.

'In the presence of this blood banner...'

The children, apart from Sofia, spoke the words as one with Frau Goeth. The oldest among them were confident and clear, and the voices thinned out and became clumsy as they got younger, all the way down to Sofia, who mouthed along in a distracted but game way.

When the oath was over, Frau Goeth looked at them.

They were so young. Almost too young to concentrate on proper badge work. Though she had mapped out the schedule week-by-week, she decided a change was in order. She clapped her hands once and said, 'Fräulein Sigrid, I believe we'll show them Godrun's video.'

Frau Goeth had a teacher's sense of the dramatic, and she was pleased by the reaction from both Fräulein Sigrid and the children. Sigrid, who had been standing on the outside of the semicircle with her arms folded, shook her head as though to clear it, to shake herself free of what she must surely have misheard. The reactions from the children were more varied. The older ones were quiet; the younger ones excited. Ben said, 'But we aren't supposed to talk about Godrun. She was naughty.'

'Naughty?' said Frau Goeth.

Ben looked panicked for a moment, as though he'd lost something valuable. He patted himself to find it. Then his eyes cleared. 'She was... Wasn't anything.'

Frau Goeth nodded. 'Quite right.'

Emma raised her hand.

'Yes, Emma?'

'Aren't we going to learn about hygiene?'

Frau Goeth shook her head. She raised her eyebrows at Fräulein Sigrid.

Sigrid said, 'Frau Goeth, perhaps we can speak for a moment.'

'No, Fräulein Sigrid, we will have the video,' said Frau Goeth. She had seen people like Fräulein Sigrid come and go. Godrun had been like her: young, well meaning, able to spout State lines, but never quite to a convincing degree. 'You'll find the recording on my desk. The projector is on top of the toy cupboard. We can wait for you, can't we, children?'

Mostly together, they said, 'Yes, Frau Goeth.'

Fräulein Sigrid walked away with her eyes down. In a moment, she had the projector on a chair behind the children so that its picture fell on the wall beside the pinboard. She wound the handle for a full minute.

When she looked at Frau Goeth for the nod, the Home Leader gave it.

The moving image was black and white, and shaky, as though shot in secret, but the scene was starkly lit and clear. In the foreground was a table upon which had been placed a large card. It read: 'Execution of Godrun Mala'.

Some of the children made anticipatory coos.

Godrun, who, until a few weeks ago, had been a helper at the Home, walked into frame wearing a dress with a narrow waist and a full, wide skirt, not much different to that worn by Fräulein Sigrid. She was considerably thinner than she had been the last time Frau Goeth saw her. The projection cut to a group of stern men in trench coats, all of whom were gathered around her. One was taller than the others and wore a tricorn hat. He was reading from a piece of paper. It might have been the last rites, but there was no sound to convey his words, only the clacks and whirs of the projector. The men started to shake hands with each other, as though a difficult negotiation was complete.

The projection cut to Godrun being led up the two steps to a low scaffold. A breeze tugged at the hem of her skirt, which was just visible at the bottom of the frame, and at her hair, which had been inexpertly tied back. The whole time, her expression was not blank, exactly, but unconcerned.

It might have been what a dentist sees before he asks his patient to open wide.

Frau Goeth looked at the children. They were watching quietly enough now. Sofia was transfixed.

Two men moved alongside Godrun. One of them was holding her shoulder, as though she might fall, and the other was reaching up for the noose. It was clearly too high, and needed to be tugged down. There was another man in the foreground. He was looking lost, as though he had been told to stand there but didn't know what to do.

The man pulling down the noose was taking a long time. Eventually, the man holding Godrun gave up and moved to help him. Together, they pulled the noose down over Godrun's head, and secured it snug with her throat. They spent a great deal of time tugging and adjusting, making sure that it was low enough to fit but not so low that the rope sagged. All the while, Godrun stared off into the distance. Frau Goeth wondered what she could see. Frau Goeth would never know, because the camera was never turned.

The projection cut to Godrun standing on the gallows.

The men around her were now wearing black masks. They weren't full hoods, as Frau Goeth had expected the first time she saw this projection, but masks that covered only the top half of the face.

The guard nearest the gallows pulled a lever and the panel beneath Godrun opened. She dropped. However, something had gone wrong. The rope was too loose and she landed in a stumble, perfectly unharmed, only halfway swallowed by the hole. Frau Goeth put a hand to her mouth, stifling a laugh. For the first time, Godrun's face contorted with irritation. But she did not cry. Soon the expression passed and she looked around at the men patiently.

'She's going to dance!' shouted Luis. At the sound of this, Frau Goeth snapped her eyes to him. But he wasn't looking. He leaned back and waggled his legs in the air. Fräulein Sigrid swooped and roughly sat him up straight. Luis was quiet after that.

The projection cut to a later time. The apparatus had been reset and Godrun was back on the trapdoor. When the man pressed the lever, she dropped cleanly, though only a few centimetres. The knot in the rope was slightly to the side, and her head was tipped the other way. There was something fake about her closed eyes. Frau Goeth thought of a wakeful person trying to sleep, to bring on the darkness as quickly as possible. Her rotation, as the slight twist in the knot straightened out, made her turn more fully towards the camera.

Fräulein Sigrid moved forward to stop the projection, but Frau Goeth held up her hand.

Godrun had started to shake her head. She opened her eyes. They were dark.

No, no, no.

A minute later, after some twitches that recalled the birds washing themselves in the puddle outside the Home, Godrun was dead.

Frau Goeth turned to the children and took a full intake of breath.

'What did you see?' she asked them.

'Nothing,' they replied.

'About whom?'

'No one.'

Frau Goeth nodded. 'Very good.'

Frau Goeth was most interested in the reaction of Sofia. The video had been put on to teach her a lesson, and it did seem to have calmed her down a little. Her expression was blank. Ben, meanwhile, was trembling. It would pass. This experience was an important part of the deadening, something like strength training, a thing Frau Goeth had experienced and was duty-bound to visit upon these children.

'We've seen enough,' said Frau Goeth. 'Fräulein Sigrid, will you please take the projector away?'

Luis blurted, 'But she's still dancing!' and some of the other children laughed. Even Ben. That was good.

Sofia said something. Frau Goeth didn't quite catch it, but the pause in Sigrid's packing away of the projector told her it was something to be followed up. She asked, 'What did you say, Sofia?'

Sofia looked up at Frau Goeth quite confidently. Without a trace of challenge, she said, 'She should have flown away. Like in the nursery rhyme.'

Frau Goeth's mouth twitched. 'Quite.' She cleared her throat and clapped her hands to the room at large. 'Today, then, hygiene.'

›•‹

Frau Goeth was attending to her papers, and enjoying her hot stove, when Fräulein Sigrid knocked on her door and opened it. Frau Goeth waited a moment before looking up. Few assistants had ever been this rude. 'Presumably this is important, Fräulein Sigrid?'

'We're looking for Sofia.'

Frau Goeth said, patiently, 'Fräulein Sigrid, you need to see to it that no child leaves without their parents arriving.'

'I've looked everywhere, including the garden.'

Garden was a cruel word to describe the ash yard between the water plant and the old railway line.

'Fräulein Sigrid,' Frau Goeth said quietly, as though this hardly needed explaining, 'Sofia has only been with us three weeks, but she's run home by herself on at least two occasions. Could it be that she's done this again?'

Fräulein Sigrid's face reddened. 'I'll keep looking. I'm sure they'll both turn up.'

Frau Goeth put down her pen. 'Both?'

'Yes, little Ben is missing as well.'

Over the next hour, Frau Goeth and Fräulein Sigrid looked for the two children everywhere, in the store rooms and even the long attic. There was no sign of them. Frau Goeth wasn't unduly concerned. Although children were never meant to leave by themselves, they were wont to do so routinely, since their houses were mostly to be found at the end of the forest path. When the time of darkness came fully later that evening, Frau Goeth told Fräulein Sigrid she should go home, while Frau Goeth herself would lock up and have one last look around. Reluctantly, the woman departed.

Fifteen minutes later, Frau Goeth was standing on the doorstep with her key in the door, about to lock it, when she had a flash of inspiration. She went to the back of the hall and put her ear to the large grey toy cupboard. Inside, she could hear someone whisper, 'Fly away, Peter, fly away, Paul. Come back, Peter.' A pause. 'Now you.'

In a low voice, almost so low it was wolf-like, Frau Goeth said, 'Come back Paul.'

'It's Frau Goeth,' said Sofia, with a gasp.

'I want to get out now,' said Ben. 'I want to get out.'

He struck the cupboard. Little gong sounds. It was, of course, impossible to open from the inside.

Frau Goeth said, dreamily, 'Fly away.'

She found she could not remember the face of her own child, little Harry, the German child with the English name.

She put her palm to the cool metal. Ben struck again and again, like a heartbeat.

'I want to get out!' he shouted. 'Let me out! Please.'

As Frau Goeth walked away, she remembered the sounds of her own Harry as he was carried from her. She remembered his screams, how animal they sounded – gargling, throaty, chokey – mixing with the screams of both Sofia and Ben. Sofia, in particular, was only now losing that precocious edge. Finally learning a lesson.

Frau Goeth locked the door to the water plant and walked down the path until she was lost in the trees. Without removing her hand from the pocket of her skirt, she squeezed the button on her repeater timepiece. She was going to be late home. Her next visit to the water plant would be in one week. She would not be late. There would, no doubt, be a cleaning job for Fräulein Sigrid.

# A GOOD CITIZEN

## ANNE CHARNOCK

Like a massive heart attack. That's how it felt. Woken from the depths by a *chud chud chud* in my chest as the neighbour's washing machine launched its spin cycle. I checked the time. Ten past three in the morning. Again. A full, unbalanced load of hand towels and tablecloths. I know that for a fact because when I first complained, eleven months ago, she told me the restaurant linen had to be washed overnight. Since then, six nights a week, I've heard the rattle of cooking tins and bottles as the machine barges side to side against her stove and fridge.

I've told Verity, the neighbour, that her washing machine might as well be screwed to the back of my bed's headboard. Our shared wall is paper thin. But she's unreachable. She has that shoulder-shrugging, well-that's-the-way-it-is attitude. Hard-faced. I mean, *I'm* a straight talker myself – put that down to my northern roots if you like – but there's no going back once you've tripped into outright rudeness.

In pitch darkness, I lie with my eyes open. The spin cycle reaches its top speed. I'm trapped in a black box of white noise. And I'm thirsty. I'll never get back to sleep.

Maybe I should bang on the wall? After all, we're beyond the point of reasoned argument. I want her to know I'm still angry, that she's still waking me up. But then, *my* banging on the wall may disturb someone else in this labyrinth of a building. I punch my pillow. Not so clever – last week's shoulder strain flares up.

Once again, I rehearse a spat with Verity because I can't stop myself. It's all whipping around in my head. I'm telling her: you're not the only person with a job, some of us have to be up early, and don't be ridiculous – of course I can't move my bed, you should see the size of my place.

I check the time; I've been awake for nine minutes. I switch on my bedside lamp and shuffle across the bed, reach up and open the window inwards by a few inches. Slipping my hand through the gap – rain licks my warm skin – I lift the metal cup and funnel off the windowsill. Rainwater tastes much better than tap.

Slow sips. I sit up in a half lotus and wait for the click of the washing machine, the end of the full cycle, the start of *my* wind down.

I should take up meditation – as I keep promising myself – because the God's honest truth is this: I wouldn't feel so angry about the noise if I could convince myself that I like my neighbour. That would change everything. I'd be saying to myself: poor Verity, doesn't she work hard? Home late from the restaurant, washing the linen, back to work mid-morning, determined to make something of herself. She isn't taking the easy route like so many people. She could volunteer for unemployment, take the universal wage, earn a bit on the side – like they're allowed to. But that doesn't interest Verity. She's prepared to work hard. Maybe she'll start her own restaurant, take the risk of falling flat on her face.

The easy route isn't for me either; we've that in common. By rights, we could become soul mates.

*Click.*

Thank Christ for that.

Poised to switch off my lamp, I hesitate and stare up at the ceiling. Roly is walking around upstairs. I hadn't heard him over the noise of the washing machine. He pads around his flat all night making the floorboards creak. You see, I don't find Roly annoying. He's an insomniac. Or, at least, he prefers to work when everyone else is asleep. He refers to his song-writing as his work, but it isn't *work* as such. It's how he keeps himself occupied. The point is this: he's a lovely guy, and I like the idea of him pacing his room thinking up brilliant lyrics. He's considerate, too; he stopped wearing his shoes at night when I mentioned I could hear him. Now and then, he gets carried away – bangs out a rhythm by smacking his desk. That's how it sounds to me, down here in the middle of the night. Even that doesn't actually irritate me. Roly's a sweetie.

For the sake of good karma, I need to tell myself that Verity, underneath it all, is conscientious, someone I should admire. I'll persuade myself that she isn't a don't-give-a-shit-about-anyone sort of person. When I hear her washing machine tomorrow night, I'll recite… I need a new mantra. I know. I'll say… it's great to live close to all her energy. She's an inspiration.

I make a final check on all my classes – age groups, indoor activities versus outdoor field sports. It's a real mix today ending with an afternoon session of cross-country running. Even if the weather improves through the day, I'll come home muddy thanks to last night's downpour. I've packed coloured vests for two teams, plastic cones for running and dribbling skills, five balls and, for me, a change of running shoes and trackies. I'm kneeling down, jiggling the zip to close the bulging kit bag, when my wristband vibrates. The message reads: *Voting closes in four hours.* Damn. I still haven't decided.

The weather forecast is for light rain sometime during the next hour, so I make an early dash to the bus stop. I stride out along the path through our communal garden. I'm lopsided – hampered by the over-sized though not-so-heavy kit bag – and I feel gawky, as I always do when I walk across the front of our opulent mansion block. Of course, it's a sham. At one time, the entire building was home to a handful of wealthy families living in grand style in a row of tall terraced houses. But the innards are now diced and spliced into 255 studio flats. For the odd moment when I walk along the path, I see the edifice and luxuriate in my association with such a handsome building – the neighbours cast far from my mind.

Roly stands at the end of the garden path, hands in pockets, looking up into the sky. I follow his gaze but there's nothing to see.

I call to him, 'Roly? Aren't you allergic to mornings?'

He takes three steps towards the garden boundary and stands under the bough of a cherry tree, stares up into the crown. Without looking at me, he says, 'Oh, you know… I'm stuck with a few lyrics. Want to write about rain falling on leaves. How it sounds when a raincloud passes over. How you hear the first raindrop, and the next, and then the raindrops start to fall quickly until *all* you hear is one continuous sound. Yeah?'

'How it sounds? I'll tell you, Roly. When I'm running around with the kids, getting drenched, it sounds like this: squelch squelch.'

He smiles but concentrates on the tree, on the leaves.

I ask, 'How did you vote? I can't decide this week.'

'Option one. I always vote for option one.'

I stare at him as if clapping eyes on him for the first time. He *always* votes the same way? Whatever the referendum question? He's deranged. Who'd have guessed?

'But why would you do that, Roly?' I hear the sadness in my own voice.

He's not listening. I take a short step towards the garden gate but rock back and forth on my feet, juddering. I ask, 'You only *ever* vote for option one? What's that going to achieve?' I laugh, almost incredulous. But truly I'm embarrassed. Doesn't he realise that I've caught a glimpse of the real *him*?

He looks at me and frowns. 'Saves time. Don't want those shitty pointless arguments in my head. Anyway, it's one vote. What does it matter?' His head jerks back. 'Wait. May be starting – the rain. What d'you think?'

'Don't you want to make a difference, Roly?'

His shoulders shake in a lazy effort at laughter. 'It doesn't though, does it? That landslide vote to re-open the Channel Tunnel? Three years ago? Well, it's still closed, isn't it?'

'But you shouldn't vote at all if you don't take it seriously.'

'And lose the benefits?'

I step onto the bus and grab a seat that gives me a clear view of the news screen. I'll make a decision before I reach the school. A scrolling ticker tape repeats: *Vote by 1300 hours today. New options for voter benefits.* I'm quite happy with the free travel pass. Most voters choose that.

A panel of four pundits is mid-flow presenting their opinions on the referendum.

Option One: Prisoners receiving a whole-life sentence will be offered euthanasia.

Option Two: Prisoners receiving a whole-life sentence will not be offered euthanasia.

I could convince myself either way. I've done so several times, back and forth, during the past week. I've found myself surprisingly comfortable in both mind-sets. Which means… I'll end up voting on a whim. How I feel in the moment. I slump down in my seat. Some people really care about this, and I owe it to them to make a wise, ethical decision. It's my civic responsibility. The broadcast cuts to an advertising jingle. My wristband is vibrating. Prompting, prompting.

Roly is so… feckless. I bet he votes as soon as the referendum options are released. I blink at my app, HandsUp, and vote for option two. I need to nullify Roly's cynicism. I receive the automatic response: *Thanks for making a difference!*

It's not fair. Every Sunday evening, I put aside one hour to consider the arguments for and against. And I listen to the late-night debates. If Roly doesn't participate properly, he damn well shouldn't receive a free travel pass. I know his true colours now and imagine him laughing at me, mocking my commitment. But what's *he* doing with his life? What's *he* doing for the people, for our nation?

I should ask him: have any of your songs ever been recorded? Has any singer ever sung your lyrics? Bet not.

That's the trouble when people decide against work, real paid work. They take the universal *easy* wage and look down on people like me. As though we're greedy money-grubbers. They like to imagine they're somehow above it all. I'm sick of their pretensions. It's laughable. I wish I had a quid for every time I've heard, *it's the only way I can make time for my art.* They're pissing about like Roly.

Listening to raindrops! Jeez, you couldn't make it up.

><

The indoor sports hall is double booked. Although I arrived first, the other teacher gets priority because his kids are younger. I remind myself: if you're given a choice, always work with the younger kids. And don't assume the automated booking system is free of human error.

My mum says that when she was a girl the month of June always kept its promise of sunny weather. She should know because her birthday falls in June. You remember the weather on your birthday. Don't you? Anyway, here I am. Another wet day in June and I'm soaking wet, with a class of drenched ten-year-olds. They don't seem to care if they're having real fun, playing tag games and the like. Personally, I don't think the kids need competitive sports – athletics, ball games, swimming. As long as they're running around, that's all that matters. Keep them active for five half-days a week – healthy body, healthy mind et cetera – and the National Health Service will fix itself. Why did it take so long for the penny to drop? Why drill information into children, in subjects they'll never *ever* apply in adult life?

In fact, I read online last week that for most office workers in the old days, the only time they experienced an elevated heartbeat was during sex. Only sex was keeping them alive. Completely believable because my mum, a call-centre operator until she took the universal wage, is forever whinging about the compulsory exercise classes. She does the absolute minimum and gripes if a session overruns by even five minutes. And she's not in the least apologetic about her ailments. No sense of shame. She just doesn't see it.

As for teaching her age group, I avoid those classes like the plague.

My shoulder strain starts to play up. I won't mention it to Mum when I visit this weekend. She'd make her usual dig about fitness fascism. Last weekend, she warned me, 'You'll be an invalid within ten years.' She hates seeing me in running gear.

I step on board the bus heading home, feeling super-healthy-tired, and an alert flashes on the news screen: *Release of new referendum options at midnight!* A second-by-second countdown begins. The anchor cuts in with breaking news. 'The first live debate tomorrow evening at 1900 hours will feature last year's top-rated public protagonists.' I'm all aflutter! Belinda of Barrow is brilliant. She tells it *like it is* without being rude, and Solihull Pete can lift the mood with a killer joke. So dry; he's hilarious. I hope it's an easier question this week.

As the bus glides past my block of flats, I hoist my kit bag on my shoulder. I spot Roly. He's standing, surrounded by stacks of boxes, outside the building's main entrance gate. Though I'm worn out, I squeeze through the doors the moment they open and walk quickly towards him. I don't understand it; he didn't say anything about moving out. I mean, I know he's a midnight prowler, but a new tenant...

It's a terrifying prospect. As I approach, he half-heartedly raises a hand, and I mouth, 'What? What?'

I drop my bag by his stack of boxes, and he says, 'I'm out. Summary eviction. The whole block's been re-designated. Workers only.'

'That's awful.' I look past him at three other piles of boxes on the pavement. 'You're not the only one leaving by the looks of it.'

'I guess we're the first batch. They'll stagger it.'

I don't know what to say.

He adds, 'At least they've provided packing boxes.'

'But where are you going?'

'Dormitory accommodation up in Northumberland. On the coast. Transport's on the way right now.' He turns and meets my eyes. 'I pushed a note under your door. I thought I'd have to leave before you…' He's blinking, rapidly.

I blurt, 'I didn't know the Housing Office could do this without warning. We haven't taken a vote. I mean… they really should consult the people.' My heart's beating hard. 'Roly, you shouldn't have to live in a dormitory, not with your writing and—'

'Look, it's here already.' He points down the road.

It's too sudden. I'm shaking. 'Promise me, you'll drop by if you're ever visiting.'

He gives me a look that says, fat chance of that.

The transport pulls in; Roly's name is displayed on the destination panel. He places his palm alongside his name. The door slides open.

'Here, I'll help,' I say to him. I pick up a box – it's heavy – and slide it inside. The top of the box has a handwritten scrawl: 'Notebooks and Submissions.'

So he *is* trying to sell his songs.

'There's an upside to the move,' he says. 'I hear the countryside is stunning up there. Dramatic weather, storms.'

'Yes, you'll write your best songs. I'm sure of it.'

>•<

I waved him off and felt glum all evening. That is, until Verity knocked on my door at eleven o'clock. Still wearing her restaurant uniform, she apologised for calling so late, said she'd seen my light was still on. She handed me an invite to her restaurant's first birthday celebration and said, 'Free drinks.' More to the point, she told me she'd arranged for a fellow waiter to do the overnight laundry, that he'd take over the chore in a week's time.

Suddenly, things were looking up. I took a beer from the fridge to celebrate and decided to stay up until midnight for the new referendum.

I'm glad I did because the referendum turns out to be an easy one. Such a relief. I won't need to watch the debates this week.

Option One: Compulsory exercise should be increased by one hour a week for citizens on the universal wage.

Option Two: Compulsory exercise should be decreased by one hour a week for citizens on the universal wage.

As the options are announced, the polls open online, and I vote for option one. At that very moment, I imagine Roly casting his own vote. My vote, his vote, the first two raindrops. That makes me smile. It feels sweet to show solidarity with my absent friend. What's more, I can see his point now. Because, having made a quick decision, I've set my mind free. Free for my own thoughts, at least for the next seven days.

# THE ENDLING MARKET

## E.J. SWIFT

Welcome to our exclusive marketplace, where you will find animal assets with remarkable powers. Congratulations on your recommendation.

Whether through ingestion, transdermal application, wearing the part of the animal against your skin or keeping it in the place where you sleep, in endlings or near-endlings, these attributes are multiplied. As the owner of an endling asset you may benefit from all kinds of good fortune: you may attain unexpected prosperity, or become extremely powerful within your sphere of influence.

The Endling Market trades exclusively in commodities where the listed species is known to have dropped to fewer than ten individuals in the wild. With the Endling Market you are secure in the knowledge you are purchasing a <10 wild species article, no other agency gives this guarantee.

For assets currently on auction, visit LISTINGS. Starting prices for APEX PREDATOR assets are available on request.

›•‹

We didn't leave him behind, whatever you might have heard.

I'm not saying we liked the guy – frankly, he was a pain in the arse – but we would never have abandoned him. That's not why you've come? It's usually the first thing people ask. Yes, I am Junaya Bowman, who else would I be? The monks haven't converted me yet.

My apologies. I've been over this so many times already. You've come a long way to meet me, I understand. It is very peaceful here, perhaps you will enjoy the change of scenery. And the views, you must admit, are spectacular. But don't be fooled: it can all change within the blink of an eye. Tomorrow everything you see may be obscured by fog.

You haven't come for the views either.

You're here for the leopards, then. Do you know that in Kyrgyzstan the snow leopard is a sacred animal, a guardian of great warriors? It's only appropriate for such a majestic creature. You'd think with all the technology at our disposal we would have learned more about them, but they remain the most elusive of the big cats, truly the ghosts of the mountains.

Before I begin, at least allow me to pour you some of this excellent tea.

It was the usual expedition team: myself, Nihal and Simone. I've been researching snow leopards for over thirty years, so I was the veteran, though Nihal and I go way back. Simone is ten years younger but she's better versed in drone tech and analysis. We make – we made – a good team. And we should have stuck to that. The Himalaya is unforgiving territory; the last thing you want is to be trapped up here with a rookie. There are just too many things that can kill you, and I'm not talking about the leopards.

I assume you know the extraction was financed by Xander's father's company. That put our backs up straight away, having to rely on private funding. But the cost of the extraction skyrocketed when we lost the chip, and we wouldn't have got far without New Horizons stepping in – at least, not fast enough.

I was born in the thirties, when studies suggested a slight, surprising jump in the leopards' numbers. More likely researchers were getting better at tracking them; pattern recognition software was a game changer back then. I grew up in a world that was transforming irrevocably. Every week there was something new: the coral reefs, the West Antarctic ice cap, advancing malaria lines or viruses emerging from the permafrost. Biologists were recording shifts in migration routes that were millions of years old.

Things in the mountains move more slowly, but they move. Over the years I've watched the glaciers of the Himalaya retreating, the tree line rise. With the tree line came farmers and their livestock, and the livestock brought further conflict between leopards and people. Year on year, the cats were being pushed higher up the mountains, to the most remote and inaccessible parts of the range.

Even so, they weren't doing so badly up until 2070. Protections were strong, the corridor between the two populations was clinging on, and the Tibetan monasteries had a lot of success with their programmes of conservation. We relied on the monks for news of sightings to tag and track more cats. Strange now, to think of this as a time of optimism, even while numbers continued to decline. It was the epidemic that finally did for them – that viral strain that ripped across Asia in 2071. It was bad news for the bharal but fatal for the cats. The monks began finding cats all over the range, dead or near death. The virus affects the brain, so the cats would get confused and wander down into human territory where they'd die.

I saw more wild cats in that time than I'd seen in twenty years. And while all that was going on, poachers were getting bolder.

I don't think a single government agency's got close to tackling the Endling Market. The server moves every few months. Species appear on the site when their numbers have dropped to about ten individuals in the wild. It was amphibians at first. Reptiles and marine life followed (don't ask me how these people "guarantee" marine life numbers), then mammals started appearing. I lived in dread of seeing snow leopards on the market. I had dreams where my scanner matched the markings of a cat we'd tagged, its skin splayed on a filthy wall, its blood being drained into rows of medicinal vials. I'd wake up sweating, check the market. No leopards. Just a dream. I told myself it would never become a reality. The snow leopard was too iconic; like so many apex predators, it had the advantage of having caught the public's imagination. That, if nothing else, would keep it safe.

I was wrong.

NEW LISTING***__Pseudophryne corroboree__
(Corroboree frog)***
Wild#<4
Entire specimen. Gold and black skin.
Bidding opens at $800,000 or equivalent
Amphibia are a symbol of fertility and are renowned
for their aphrodisiac qualities. The frog is known to
bring exceptionally good fortune in business.

Fifteen months ago, the snow leopard population had declined to five individuals in the wild. Two males, one female, and her two cubs, which we believed were the offspring of the older male. Poachers got him with poison. With his chip still active we managed to locate the body before the endling contractors did, which was the sole consolation of a catastrophic day. We found the male on the riverbank below the cliff face, as though he'd been trying to drink, perhaps wishing to ease the pain of that drawn-out death. It had snowed overnight and his fur was stiff with frost. His eyes, now dull, would not be removed and sold: this was the best we could do.

Nihal and I wanted to act then and helicopter the rest of them to safety, but we couldn't get the license organised in time. I won't bore you with the legalities around relocating endlings. It's complicated. All we could do was monitor, and hope the security on our chips was strong enough. With the crash in population we'd finally been granted an International Space Station hook-up a few years back, so our signals were much more reliable. If these four leopards could hold out, and if the younger male didn't find the cubs before they were grown, the female would be ready to breed again in a couple of years.

The younger male was killed two months after that, with darts – we found out later our camera traps had been hacked. I couldn't bring myself to look at the Endling Market, so Simone looked for me. They sold his fur, his bones, his claws, his blood. His eyes went for five million apiece. In a backstreet slaughterhouse, that beautiful cat was being dissected, parcelled up, shipped to the homes of eager buyers.

The eyes of a snow leopard are very pale, quite unlike any other cat. I wondered if they had been bought as a pair, or separately. I wondered who had bought them, and I imagined what might happen if I ever met that person.

The repercussions of the male's death were immediate. An undercover agent warned us there were adverts for our female and her two cubs, offering obscene rewards for their capture. We had to get to them before someone else did. With our ISS connection, the extraction should have been straightforward – GPS, helicopter us in, track on foot, dart and recover. We were all set when, two days before we flew out, the female leopard's chip went inexplicably dark.

Our first thought was that the poachers had found her.

I don't know how to describe the bleakness of that night. Refreshing the Market every minute, terrified of what we would find. None of us could sleep. Each hour that passed was a reprieve. We allowed ourselves a modicum of hope. As the night went on, that expanded to belief. Our leopard was alive. We just didn't know where. We were back to twentieth century tracking, searching for the animal kingdom's greatest magician.

It was almost as if she knew we were coming for her.

NEW LISTING*****Squatina aculeata**
(Sawback angel shark)***
Wild#<3
Formaldehyde specimen
Bidding opens at $950,000 or equivalent
A preserved sawback will give the buyer eternal
protection. Sawbacks are particularly effective against
vengeful spirits, coastal inundations and drownings.

The New Horizons bargain was simple: they would meet the expedition costs on the condition we let baby boy Xander make his ludicrous VR film. I was hoping he would get fed up before the first day was out. He could have holed up at one of the monasteries until daddy could copter him out.

Prejudiced? All right, I'll give you that. I'd set against him before we'd even met. It didn't help that he turned up wearing the most expensive kit money can buy. He looked the part – a very shiny version of it – but it wasn't more than fibre-deep. His kit contained the latest cell regeneration facial-care but there wasn't a grappling hook in sight. We quickly discovered he didn't know how to work the heater, and his camera gear was going to slow us down, when we wanted to be covering as much ground in a day as we could.

Xander's intention was to capture a virtual reality experience of a leopard encounter. The word *encounter* left me deeply uneasy. Don't get me wrong, there's been some wonderful work with nature and VR, right from the experiments pioneered by Attenborough back in the 2010s. New Horizons is not one of those companies. New Horizons is about the extremities of fear: their most successful franchise is *Shark Attack*, and in a world that only recently managed an international ban on finning, that tells you everything you need to know. I'm told having a limb bitten off is optional.

My antipathy must have been evident, because the night before we set out, Nihal took me aside and told me to be nicer to Xander. His film was irrelevant, said Nihal. We were here for the leopards and we couldn't afford to piss off Xander's dad. Anyway, it was doubtful the kid would get any footage, because as soon as we got a glimpse of the cats we'd need to tranq them. But I was fuming. I said Xander would compromise the entire expedition.

Nihal said he understood why I was upset, but we didn't have a choice.

He was right. I was upset, and I was taking it out on this idiot.

I have dedicated my life to working with snow leopards, and I was facing their possible extinction in the wild. I had perhaps one chance to save them. I hated what we had to do. Not every relocation is a success story. Sometimes the animals don't settle. You can die of homesickness, I believe that.

Nihal has always been more pragmatic. One day, he said, we would be able to repopulate these mountains. He said our leopards were making the sacrifice of all captive animals: their freedom for the survival of the gene pool. But I saw the rising tree line, the melting snowcaps, and that didn't feel like pragmatism to me - it felt like a terrible delusion.

On the first day our New Horizons friends dropped us by helicopter, unloading us and our gear on a plateau at thirteen thousand feet, about two days' trek from the outskirts of the female leopard's known range. It was early autumn, there were berries on the juniper bushes and the midday sun gleamed on the snowfields of the surrounding peaks. I spotted the distinctive outline of a golden eagle overhead, soaring in lazy circles. Our route by land would be far more convoluted. We had agreed a rota to babysit Xander, who couldn't be trusted not to tranq himself.

Nihal, Simone and I were used to long stretches of silence, broken only by words of caution. Each of us concentrating on where we placed our feet, our poles, the width or extreme narrowness of the path ahead, acutely attuned to the presence of the other two, ahead or behind. In this labyrinthine country I never lose the sense of how brittle we are. Everything comes under siege: lung capacity, muscle endurance, mental acuity too.

Xander wouldn't stop talking.

He wanted to know how many leopards we'd tagged. What it was like to handle them. If we'd witnessed a hunt, if we'd witnessed a kill, how the cats slaughtered their prey, everything they ate, how fast they could run, how high they could climb, if they'd ever attacked us.

Nihal attempted to defuse the situation, explaining patiently to Xander that these weren't common leopards, that they were shyer and much more elusive. You could pass within metres of the cat and never see it. Snow leopards can live at heights of nineteen thousand feet, Nihal told him. They can drag their prey up a vertical cliff face, their jaws clamped around a victim three times their size. They can vanish in the gap between two heartbeats. The leopard may see you, but you may never see the leopard. Xander listened, or made the pretence of listening, but the questions didn't stop. How close had we got to a leopard without the leopard knowing we were there? When had it become aware of us? At what point had it known?

It wasn't long before he was struggling for breath and struggling to keep up. Simone lost it then. Save your oxygen, she told him.

When the time came to pitch camp I could have cried with relief. Xander, mercifully, had his own tent, as did Nihal. Simone and I were sharing, as we usually did to save on gear. Nobody offered to help Xander and it took him twice as long to pitch as the rest of us, but he had to learn or he wouldn't have lasted two minutes. Following a short, terse supper, we hunkered down for the night.

Simone fell asleep at once but I lay in the darkness for a long time, listening to her breathing, aware of the dim glow from Xander's tent as he drained the batteries of his field pad. Eventually that too went out. Even then I lay awake, my mind turning with thoughts of the leopards. If they were hidden, if they were safe. If we would find them in time.

NEW LISTING\*\*\****Abronia frosti***
(Frost's Arboreal Alligator Lizard)\*\*\*
Wild#<5
Skin (azure blue, black, pebbled texture),
Partial skeleton (spine/skull), Heart
Bidding opens at $1,500,000 or equivalent
Lizards herald regeneration. Lizard assets
are particularly valued for their traits of
adaptability, overcoming adversity and
resilience in the face of great odds. Lizard
hearts are known to cure terminal illness.

The next morning we reached one of the camera traps which had stopped triggering. Some intrepid animal had worked its way inside. We argued over whether to reconnect the batteries. Simone thought it was worth doing and Xander jumped at any chance to get footage for his film, but Nihal and I were wary. What we could use, the poachers could use too. We felt our best chance was to go off radar, use the knowledge we had of the female's range, and try not to advertise our presence to hunter or cat.

That afternoon we climbed another thousand feet, and by the end of the day we were just beneath the snow line, deep in leopard country. Around us, the shoulders of the mountains reflected back whiteness to a pale sky. With a couple of hours' light before sundown, Simone fired up our sparrow, working the little drone in a grid pattern, checking her pad for evidence of prints or – if we were very lucky – of a recent kill. Xander peered over her shoulder, eager for a sighting, but all the drone showed was rocks and lichens and snow.

The temperature that night dropped to minus ten Celsius. Simone and I slept back to back, making the most of each other's body heat through our sleeping bags. Again, I was aware of the glow from Xander's pad, but this time I was too tired to stay awake.

Our mood on day three had brightened. There was a feeling that we had made it: the camp was established, the real work started now. We each had our tasks. Simone would continue to operate the drones, searching for herds of bharal that might draw the leopard. On the ground, Nihal and I were looking for scat, urine, any signs that the female had passed by her usual marking stones in the area. We'd been working our way around the camera traps, a monotonous but methodical circuit. For the first week our optimism remained high, although the cameras revealed nothing but the occasional marmot or hare. Xander's enthusiasm did not wane, but he filmed more and talked less, and it felt as though we'd reached a detente. Nihal took him painstakingly through our maps of the area. Leopards like patrol lines, he told Xander. Mountain ridges and old riverbeds; they're creatures of habit.

Each morning we got up, melted pans of snow for our calorie-packed instant porridge, shared our plans for the day's work and promised one another today would be the day.

We remained at that base camp for four months.

It was how I imagined the shoots of stoic photographers

in the previous century, staking out hides for weeks and months on location, the concessions being that we carried ISS trackers and received food drops by New Horizons drones. Xander, the least accustomed to the climate, needed constant reminders to wear his goggles, and as the winter came on to keep his nose and hands covered. I'll say this for Xander: he didn't complain, and he didn't leave. Temperatures at night plummeted to minus twenty and some days we were camp bound by blizzards. The altitude played havoc with our tempers. We were beginning to doubt our leopard's survival.

The first evidence came over a hundred days after setting up camp. Nihal, out alone on a four-day round trek to check the farthest camera trap, found fresh scratches on a marking stone. The claw marks were sheer, evenly spaced and unmistakeable; a swab of the rock face gave us a urine sample and a timeframe. The female had passed by within the last week.

Nihal uploaded the camera's files to the ISS, and at the base camp we waited for Simone to transfer the footage to her field pad. Xander and I gathered round as she scanned through the last two weeks of footage. The trap had been triggered by smaller mammals, as well as the occasional bird. Each new appearance brought a flash of disappointment. I began to doubt Nihal's evidence.

A leopard came into view. Simone froze the screen and ran pattern recognition on her markings, but I knew it was her before the software beeped a match. We watched as the leopard moved across the frame, her motion tentative, great paws placed upon the ground with care. She paid no attention to the camera, went to the cliff wall, lifted her tail and sprayed. One of the cubs appeared. I heard our collective intake of breath.

We watched the footage play out. The mother and the cub remained in frame for a full minute, before moving on. There was no sign of the other cub. We stared at the empty landscape, felt the heaviness of despair. Then the second cub arrived, chasing after them.

I asked Simone to replay the footage. My voice sounded strange to me, stiff with the effort not to cry or shout with relief. We watched the footage a second time, a third. We could have watched all day.

I looked at Xander. He was gazing at the pad, something close to awe in his face. I remember thinking, perhaps I've misjudged him.

Simone and I discussed our next move. The footage was three days old, and by the time we caught up with Nihal, the leopards could be five days ahead of us. The odds of finding them remained slim. Xander had no such doubts, and went to pack his film kit in readiness. I watched him going about his tasks, wondering if I resented his optimism or simply envied it.

After four months without a sighting, I couldn't quite believe what we had seen. But it occurred to me that Xander could, because Xander believed in miracles. He couldn't conceive that the miracle might be what we had just witnessed, that it might not come again, on this expedition or on any other. That what we were embarking upon was an act of faith. That was the problem, I thought: Xander wanted the close-up shot, the stench of leopard saliva, the heavy drag of the tail through the snow. He wanted the glory of the leopard, not the ghost. I wanted to tell him that nature isn't like that, it doesn't oblige and it owes you nothing. But I didn't think he'd listen.

Perhaps I should have told him anyway. Perhaps I should have tried.

NEW LISTING***__Alcedo euryzona__
(Javan Blue-banded Kingfisher)***
#<3 last breeding pair
Two specimens, full taxidermy:
Beautiful blue/orange plumage
Bidding opens at $2m or equivalent
Kingfishers are emblems of prosperity. The blue of its colouring is associated with historical concepts of royalty. Kingfisher assets have been known to bring great wealth in a time of peace.

What I'm about to tell you isn't in the official report.

We moved our base camp to join up with Nihal. With a blizzard chasing us, the trek was an excruciating exercise in folly. Instead of relief at our arrival we all retired in a foul mood, aware we had put ourselves at risk and nervous for what the morning would bring.

I woke in the night with the certainty that I was being watched. My heart was pounding as it would in the wake of a nightmare, although I was sure I hadn't been dreaming. Slowly the drum of my pulse in my ears subsided, and I could hear Simone's breathing, regular in sleep. The sensation of being watched remained.

Leaving the tent at night was a last resort – we had a pee bottle in the outer compartment for emergencies – but I didn't think, didn't question what I was doing. I squeezed into the outer compartment of the tent, felt around for my gear and pulled it on as quietly as I could. My eyes were adjusting to a deep grey so I knew the skies must have finally cleared; the darkness wasn't absolute.

The tranq gun was in its usual place. Night vision goggles next: I activated the infrared as a backup. The warm mound of Simone's body was illuminated through the inner compartment. I exited the tent and stood outside in silence. It was a night for gods. The mountains were as quiet and still, the skies as clear as I'd seen in thirty years, a state I knew from experience would not endure. I removed my goggles to observe the canopy above, the pale spires that surrounded our camp rising starkly against a proliferation of stars. I was tempted to wake Xander, to tell him here was something worth filming. I felt the chill of the night air through my bulky arctic gear, my body slowing to accommodate the cold. I snapped back to alertness as, once again, I became aware of the sensation of being watched.

I pulled the goggles on again and checked the other tents. Red glows marked Xander and Nihal in their sleeping bags.

I walked a short distance along the trail. It was a stupid thing to do, the sort of thing I would have shouted at Xander for. Yes, it was a clear night, but that could change in an instant, and in these environments you can die ten metres from your tent. I kept walking, the feeling of observation intensifying with each pace. People talk about gut instinct. The monks here insist that all things are connected. However you choose to explain it, I knew what I was about to find.

The leopard was waiting for me at a curve in the track. On the far side, the path dropped away into a ravine.

There was ten metres between us, a distance the leopard

could cover in two bounds. Her heat signature was a blaze in an empty world. Very slowly, I reached to turn off the infrared. Now I could see the detail. The leopard had her back to me, but I didn't doubt she knew I was there. I saw the great sweep of tail, her haunches, the curve of the spine, the back of the head with the rounded ears, those familiar rosettes rendered faintly green through the imperfect vision of the night goggles. I didn't need an algorithm to tell me it was her. Those patterns were etched in my memory.

You're alive, I thought.

*You're alive.*

Neither of us moved. I should have been, if not afraid, then at least extremely wary. The leopard had a choice: to turn and face me, or retreat. If her cubs were near and she considered me a threat, she might attack. More likely she would slink away, or freeze where she was and hope that her stillness made her invisible and I would leave. The tranq gun was in my arms. I lifted it. The rustle of my wind-jacket was electric in the night. I had a clean shot. It was the perfect opportunity; her cubs would not be far. The leopard's tail twitched. I had to act. This was it, the one chance we'd get. Any moment she might turn. Any moment she might run. My finger rested on the trigger.

The leopard lifted one great paw, frozen in momentary indecision. The paw lowered. She flattened herself against the ground, and began to creep away, belly pressed to snow. My finger was on the trigger. I still had the shot. For several seconds, I had the shot. My hands were frozen but my aim was solid, I knew I wouldn't miss.

I didn't take it.

I watched her glide away. On that clearest of nights, she

blended into her environment so quickly, so completely, I couldn't tell you the moment I saw fur and the moment I was watching rocks and snow. After she'd gone, the cold hit me very fast. All at once I was aware of my tingling feet, my hands losing sensation. I stood a little longer, stunned by what I had done – or rather, what I hadn't. At last I turned and hurried back towards the camp.

Someone said my name.

It was Xander. I'd had my head down, utterly absorbed in what I had witnessed, and even with the goggles I hadn't noticed him approaching. He backed away, hands raised, apologising for startling me. He asked if I had heard anything, because he thought he had. I told him I had scouted the area. There was nothing for him to worry about.

I saw his gaze drop to the tranquiliser gun under my arm. He didn't comment on it, so neither did I. Instead I told him to get back to the warmth of his tent, as I was going to do myself.

I waited until Xander was safely inside his tent before returning to mine. I gently replaced both goggles and gun in the porch of the tent before squeezing into the sleeping compartment. Simone shifted in her sleeping bag, but didn't wake.

I thought about rousing her and Nihal and telling them what I had seen. If we went out now, we could track the leopard to her cubs. I thought of the leopards in a green sanctuary, the two cubs growing to adulthood within safety, within borders, a triple flare of hope for the future. I thought of the leopards in captivity. I thought of the leopards on the Endling Market. I thought of the leopard dissolving into the night, and I knew I could never betray her.

I slid into my sleeping bag and closed my eyes.

In the morning, Xander's tent was empty.

NEW LISTING\*\*\***Panthera tigris sumatrae**

(Sumatran tiger)\*\*\*

Wild#<1

Pelt by private enquiry only

Medicinal: Blood, Bone parts including

Humerus, Claws, Tail, Eyeballs

Tiger parts are renowned for their powers of
healing. Tigers are also wardens against evil
spirits and a tiger asset has the unique ability to
absorb and destroy a malevolent spirit or ghost.

Xander's father threw everything he had at the search: there was mountain rescue; there were air ambulances; there was private security; there were drones; there were seasoned explorers and mountaineers. Anyone who knew the region, New Horizons would pay up. The search went on for months.

I told Nihal and Simone the truth: that I'd seen Xander when I came back to the tent, that I'd waited until he'd got back into his tent. I'd deliberately put the goggles back on to check he'd gone inside. I didn't tell them what else I'd seen, or that I'd had the gun out.

Nothing of Xander was ever found. Not a scrap of clothing or a bit of camera kit. The Himalaya vanished him completely. That must have been the hardest thing for Xander's father, the realisation that the mountains do not give up their secrets, do not bend to any will. The three of us helped where we could. Nihal and Simone thought with all the technology deployed to find Xander, we were bound to find the cats too. I gave them no reason to believe otherwise.

I don't know what happened to Xander. All I know is, at some point in the night, he left that tent and never came back. He took his camera but left his tracker behind. I have to suppose he was looking for the leopard.

Things turned sour, the way they always do. Accusations, speculation. New Horizons wanted nothing more to do with leopards, or with us. There was talk that Xander's father would try to sue us. Nihal and Simone returned to the research base in India, but I stayed. I didn't plan to stay this long, but the longer I stay the more frightening the prospect of leaving. What's the word? Institutionalised, thank you.

Here's a question for you. *Panthera uncia*, the snow leopard. Does it merit its name when the snow is gone? It's hard to imagine, I know, but one day this extraordinary vista of snow-capped peaks will be replaced by bare rock. Lichens and moss will colonise the uppermost reaches of the mountains. It'll take decades, maybe even centuries, but it is happening. And I can't help wondering, if my leopards survive that long, will they be the same or something different, detached from the habitat in which they evolved? Could they breed with common leopards? Will their paws and tails become smaller, their coats turn to gold? Or will they become true ghosts of the mountains: a symbol of what we used to have, and what we might have conserved.

I don't expect I'll see a snow leopard in the wild again. The monks would advise acceptance, perhaps tell me it's enough to know they are out there, somewhere. That is the truth of the natural world: unimaginable wonders existing just beyond the peripheries of our lives. Most of us will experience it only through the medium of film or VR, although the urge to protect – to save – remains. The leopards have taught me that this is rarely a straightforward act.

You've finished your tea, I see. You won't mind if I leave you here? I tend to head out around this time of day. Or come with me, if you like, though you'll understand I can make no promises for what we'll find.

I go out looking for them every day, and when I get back to the monastery I check the Endling Market. There are regular claims from poachers. With each new listing I feel the weight of responsibility, like suffocation under snow, and I wonder if I can ever forgive myself for what I didn't do. But the claims have always turned out to be fake. So I keep searching.

Thank you for visiting the Endling Market – we hope you found what you were looking for. Before you go, make sure you've signed up to our alerts for NEW LISTINGS. Remember, once it's gone, it's gone!

# GLITTERATI

## OLIVER LANGMEAD

Wednesday. Or was it Tuesday?

'Darling?'

'What is it, dear heart?'

'Is it Wednesday, or Tuesday?'

'It's Tuesday today.'

'Did we not have a Tuesday yesterday?'

'No, dearest. We had a Monday yesterday. I recall it being Monday quite clearly, in fact, because Gabrielle was wearing that blue Savinchay dress with the sequinned trim, which she only ever wears on Mondays because it would be outrageous to wear Savinchay on any other day of the week.'

That settled it, then.

Simone unpeeled his face from the pink leather chaise-longue. Last night had been a rainbow of cocktails, resulting in the headache now threatening to impinge on his usually immaculate poise. He went to the gold-plated Manchodroi dresser, which he only ever used on Tuesdays, and was astonished to find his usual dose of painkillers gone.

'Darling!' he cried.

'What is it, Simone?'

'My medicine is missing!'

'Have you checked the Manchodroi dresser?'

'I have opened the very drawer in which my Tuesday dose is stored, and that drawer is quite empty. Might you have accidentally taken them?'

'Certainly not.'

'And you're absolutely sure that today is Tuesday?'

'I'm positive, dearest Simone. I have just this minute remembered that Galvin was wearing his red Crostay suit last night, which he only ever wears on Mondays, because, as everyone knows, red Crostay is a delight which should only ever be savoured on the first day of the week. I am absolutely, 100-per-cent certain that today is Tuesday. Could it be that you've misplaced your medication?'

'Well,' said Simone, uncertainly. 'It could be. I remember very little of last night.'

'Use the supply we set aside in the upper left cupboard of the guest wardrobe. And do get ready. You have work in two hours, and it would be simply awful were you to arrive too late.'

This was true. It being a Tuesday, it would be the talk of the office were Simone to arrive at work anything more than twenty minutes late. Simone quickly rushed through to the guest bedroom and rooted around in the wardrobe until he located the spare painkillers. In the guest bathroom, he spread the white powder across the shining surface of the chrome sink and proceeded to snort it all up in one go. The drugs fizzed in his brain, and his headache began to recede.

'Superb,' he said, to his ruffled reflection. 'Most delightful.'

Tuesday, then, which meant wearing white to work. Simone searched through his walk-in wardrobes and located his white suits. The first, a close-fitting number from Messr Messr, the second, a looser, but tastefully trimmed alternative from Saint Darcington, and last, his brand-new white suit, made with a newly invented meta-material infused with light-emitting micro-LEDs from Karpa Fishh, which was at the very forefront of fashion technology. Still not feeling himself, Simone settled on the tastefully understated Messr Messr suit, and laid it out while he got to work on his face.

Tuesday was a pale day, which meant bringing out his cheekbones. He began with a three-point washing formula from Karrat, and moved on to some moisturiser from Stringham, before clearing that away with body-temperature water sourced, purified and heated to perfection by Dracington Lord. Then, he moved on to his Flaystay foundation, applied with his perfectly softened Karrat brush set, and finished up with a layer of ivory-white Flaystay powder. The powdering done, he blended his grey Stringham blushers together and began to highlight the shape of his skull with perfect precision, applying liberal shadows to the space beneath his cheekbones. Then, once his face seemed perfectly skull-like, he began to draw out his eyes with his collection of Dramaskil complementary eyeliners and eye shadows, until they were quite the centrepiece of his face. Running his fingers along his collection of Dramaskil false eyelashes, he selected a brilliant-white pair speckled with tastefully dusted black powder, and delicately affixed them to his eyelids using Dramaskil's gentle false-eyelash glue. These, he finished off with a little of Stringham's excellent mascara to bring them out. Finally, he settled on a light grey Seleseal lipstick, to contrast with his perfectly whitened teeth, and lined it with some black Seleseal lip liner, to give his lips some real definition.

Pouting to make certain that all was in place, Simone sealed it with Grantis Grato make-up fixer, spraying liberally to make certain nothing would slide off during his busy day ahead.

Face affixed, Simone pulled on his Messr Messr suit and tightened his tie.

Two forty-five, already? Simone hastened through, air-kissed his wife, and struck a pose before the hallway mirror, which was framed with bright bulbs in order to reveal every single possible flaw in the beholder. Feeling satisfied, he left for work.

>•<

Unfortunately, Simone's route to work took him above the streets of the city suburbs, where the poor unfashionables lived.

The windows of the pristine vibro-rail carriage revealed the depths below, where the houses were made for practicality instead of design. They looked, to Simone, like terrible parodies of the packaging that some of his cheapest items of clothing came in. Simone stared down at the suburbs, his mouth curled in contempt.

The uglies. The unwashed, unmanicured masses. The unfashionables.

It pained him to see them down there, milling around without the first idea of how dreadful they appeared; how their untrained aesthetic senses were so underdeveloped that they could barely comprehend their own hideousnesses. To think, they did actual labour! To think, they used things like shovels and wrenches and drills! Simone shuddered, but found himself unable to look away. The horror of it drew him in completely.

It was unfathomable that people existed like that.

The carriage slipped through a tunnel, and suddenly they were there, at the heart of the horror, where beyond the unornamented fences the unfashionables lumbered around. If only Simone's tear ducts hadn't been removed – why, he would have wept for them. Feeling his gut squirm inside him, he watched them go by, bumping into each other, smiling their ugly, unpainted smiles, staring open-mouthed and lustily at the vibro-rail carriage as it swept past: at its contents – the beautiful glitterati.

To think that they were the same species. It boggled the mind.

Simone secretly hoped that the unfashionables would all catch a disease and die. Of course, it wasn't fashionable to think such thoughts. The fashion was that the uglies were to be pitied, and that charity in the form of discarded past-season wardrobes was a sign of good character. But Simone only said that he sent his old wardrobes down to the unfashionables. In reality, he burned his clothes when he was done with them. The mere thought of his discarded suits touching the skin of any of those aesthetically impaired imbeciles made him feel ill.

So caught up in horror he was, that Simone barely noticed the vibro-rail carriage gliding to a halt. He was the last to leave.

The vast and crystalline Tremptor Tower rose ahead, and Simone felt his heart lift. Surrounding the square were offices built to be aesthetically brilliant, but none compared to the mighty beauty of Tremptor Tower. It was like working in Heaven – the fluted glass cylinders which made the whole building look like an enormous celestial organ always made him smile. He was careful with his smile, of course. It simply wouldn't do to affect his face before making his entrance.

He checked his watch. Precisely twenty minutes late. Perfect.

There was a queue at the front entrance, and the instant that Simone set his eyes upon it he felt his heart stop. Every single man and woman in the queue was wearing purple.

What could it mean? Had he missed an issue of one of the 116 different fashion magazines he was subscribed to? Holding a hand delicately to his chest, Simone felt as if he must flee – he must go home this instant and feign illness. But it was too late. He was already caught up in the queue. And those behind him…

Simone risked a glance backwards. Perfectly painted open mouths and wide eyes. Horror.

Maybe it was a joke, and everyone in Tremptor Tower was in on it. Maybe he would make his entrance and everyone would clap and applause and laugh, and he would laugh with them, and they would all drink champagne and reminisce for years to come about how delightful the jest had been.

Slowly, the queue moved forwards. Then, it was Simone's turn.

Striking his best pose, Simone sashayed inside.

Absolute silence. The hands poised mid-clap to receive him were completely still. The long red runway yawned out endlessly before him, but still he sashayed on – eyes on the horizon, lips pursed. Not a single camera flashed. But there, at last, his salvation: the steps leading off the entrance runway and across to the lifts. He would have run the last few metres, but not a single drop of sweat had been shed in Tremptor Tower since its construction, and he certainly wouldn't be the first to desecrate the hallowed ground.

Inside the lift, Simone pressed the button for the tenth floor with one shaking finger. Everyone around him was wearing purple. They kept glancing at him, but he kept his eyes down, studying the tastefully designed Tremptor elevator carpet.

Eventually, the elevator arrived at the tenth floor.

Simone power-walked the final few steps into his office, and shut the door. He crystallised the walls so that they were opaque, and sat down behind his three-tier desk.

What could have happened? What had gone wrong? Unless… Simone's eyes grew wide.

What if it wasn't Tuesday after all? What if it was actually *Wednesday*?

The implications were unbearable. Was he to spend the entire day unfashionable? Wearing all white when it was a complete faux pas to be in monochrome on a Wednesday? But what could he do? He could phone his wife and get her to bring a spare suit. But then – what about his face? The Grantis Grato make-up fixer was already in place. His make-up would be solid for at least the next eight hours.

Simone resolved to hide in his office all day. If anybody came knocking, he would claim to be in a meeting. It was the done thing, after all. An actual meeting had not occurred in Tremptor Tower since its creation, but to use being in a meeting as an excuse was to be considered polite.

There wasn't anything of any real substance in Simone's office. He would have to get creative in order to bide his time. There were artfully piled stacks of blank paper, and aesthetically pleasing towers of electronic equipment that he had no idea how to use. Nobody in Tremptor Tower did any work, after all. That would have been a hideous use of the mind. Actual work was for the dreadful unfashionables below, who could afford the brain-power.

Simone took a deep breath. It would be all right. He would simply read magazines all day. Drawing out the latest *Gentlemen's Art* from his desk, he began reading – admiring the models wearing the best in avant garde designs – and eventually began to relax. It would be fine. Only a few people had seen him, after all. He would laugh it off tomorrow. They would all laugh it off, and drink champagne, and it would be a funny anecdote.

There came a knock at the door. 'Simone?' It was Darlington.

'I'm in a meeting!' he cried, hiding behind his magazine.

'But Simone, you simply must come out! It's Trevor Tremptor. He's come to see us.'

How utterly dreadful! Simone had forgotten. Today was the day that Trevor Tremptor, fashion icon and head of the Tremptor Company, was coming around to mingle with those on the tenth floor of his tower. Simone was mortified. This could mean embarrassment before the whole company. Worse – this could mean demotion.

Trembling, Simone stepped out into the corridor and stood before his door.

Everyone else was lined up, all dressed in purple. As soon as they set eyes on him, there were gasps. Monochrome? On a Wednesday? It was outrageous.

There was Trevor Tremptor now, air-kissing each of his co-workers, and offering little compliments. Everyone blushed the correct amount, and struck a little pose. Trevor himself was an Adonis – so incredible to look upon that it hurt Simone's eyes. Had ever a more fashionable being existed? Simone wanted to disappear into the carpet.

At last, Trevor Tremptor arrived before Simone. There was a long silence. Everyone was holding their breath.

'Simone…' said Trevor, carefully, but Simone couldn't meet his eyes. He kept his head down, so ashamed of what he was wearing. He knew he was letting everyone down. 'Simone…' said Trevor again, and Simone closed his eyes, waiting for the guillotine to drop. 'That… is… *fabulous.*'

>•<

The rest of the day passed in a magnificent whirl.

Simone was promoted not just to the eleventh floor, but all the way up to the nineteenth, where some of the most beautiful people in the company worked. The offices were dazzling with their array of poised statuaries and intricate pieces of useless electronic equipment. Even the stacks of blank paper were of top quality – a creamy white, displaying this month's Tremptor logo.

Everyone applauded him, and he was surrounded on all sides by remarkable fashionistas, who each praised him for his daring. 'Monochrome on a Wednesday?' they said, 'it's simply incredible! Unheard of. It's so *subversive.* The irony of it, and the *precision* of it.'

Invited on a tour of the offices, Simone was overwhelmed. It felt like his brain was on fire. The people on the 19th floor made those down on the tenth look like snivelling uglies, but now, here, Simone knew he could realise his full potential – his place as a true innovator in the art of fashion. He had never considered himself an innovator before, but now that he was here it was obvious.

After work, everyone treated him to drinks at the bars. Beneath the neon lights, Simone himself felt neon. He drank endless bottles of champagne, and beautiful rainbow cocktails, and inhaled so much white powder that it felt as if he was breathing drugs instead of air. He was on top of the world. He was brilliant, and he knew it. Everyone slapped him on the back, and called him remarkable, and gave him their business cards, and no less than three magazines wanted to take his picture.

In a whirling, frothing, state of absolute euphoria, Simone submerged in neon. For the first time in his life, he felt as if he really knew that he was beautiful.

When Simone awoke, he was still buzzing. 'Darling! Did you hear about my promotion?'

'I heard everything, Simone! But we have no time to chat this morning. You simply must ready yourself for work. After all, it being Thursday, you must be ten minutes early.'

Of course she was right. But something was tugging at Simone's bubbling brain. Something had happened to him. Something was different.

He unfurled from the pink chaise-longue and felt like a beautiful butterfly, emerging from its ugly cocoon. Today was the first day of his life that he was truly fashionable. Today he would dare to go against the trend again. He would show them all how brilliant he was.

And there was his first moment of inspiration, courtesy of his wife. He wouldn't be early, nor would he be late. Simone would arrive at work *precisely on time.*

But what to wear? What to wear?

Thursday usually meant flowers: organic greens, brilliant yellows and every colour of the rainbow. It was a day in the fashion world devoted to life. But Simone was a fashion prodigy now, and he knew that he must represent that. He must show them all that he was worthy of the nineteenth floor of Tremptor Tower.

Death, then. He would spit in the face of life and all would love him for it.

Grey. It must be grey. He threw open the doors to his walk-in wardrobes and swept his hands along his suits, before coming to the grey section. There was his darling Sarcross suit – a desirable classic – and his thick ungainly Redrad suit, which was only to be worn on the third Sunday of each month. But instead of either of these, Simone tore open the boxes containing his slate-grey Dan Chopin suit, which he had been saving for a special occasion. It was made of an experimental material which was considered capable of drawing out the dullest, least-vibrant shade imaginable.

He would be the opposite of life. He would be a void of unlife.

But what about his face? What would he do?

Simone emptied his cupboards, searching for anything grey. But none of it was good enough. How was he meant to represent absolute nothingness with a bit of eyeliner? Some false eyelashes? A grey lipstick? Frustrated and trembling, he threw powders at the walls, and shattered glass bottles.

'Simone?' His wife. 'What's happening?'

'I simply must...' he hissed, at his reflection.

But there – another moment of inspiration. The walls in the pool-house were being repainted in shades of grey. Normally, of course, Simone would avoid the unfashionables while they were at work – to behold them so close would make him nauseous – but today he must be brave. He would face them, for the sake of his art.

Running through the house, he flung open the pool-house doors. Water reflected across the half-painted walls, and a dozen pairs of unornamented eyes stared at him in wonder. Simone hated them. Waves of hate rolled over him. But he persevered. He burbled some nonsense gibberish at them and grabbed one of the buckets of paint.

CAUTION, it read on the side. TOXIC FUMES.

Simone upended the bucket over his head. The paint was cold, and a little slipped down his throat, but the fumes shot up his nose, making him sure of himself.

Running back to his mirror, he saw that he had done right. His skin was perfectly grey. It was brilliant. He grinned, and the whiteness of his teeth sent shocks through him. They weren't good enough. Dipping his fingers into the still-wet paint covering his neck, he rubbed at the white until it was dulled. Then, he washed his hands in the paint. Grey skin, grey teeth, grey everything. Only his eyes would emerge – the wild ever-watchful eyes of death.

Finally, he put on his Dan Chopin suit.

Grey nothingness: death. He was ready to face them.

Laughter tumbling from his lips, he entered his wife's dressing room.

'I'm ready!' he cried.

Her eyes widened and she let out a shriek, but Simone paid it no attention. He knew that he was beautiful. Even as she fainted, he air-kissed her and ran for the door, tapping at his paint-encrusted watch. If he left now, he would be exactly on time for work. Just as planned. He could already hear the applause thundering in his ears.

>•<

The vibro-rail carriage was empty, because everyone else had arrived at work early.

Simone felt the excitement growing in his gut. Or maybe it was illness. It was difficult to tell. The fumes wafted into his nose from the paint covering his face and made bubbles in his brain that weren't grey, like the paint, but neon, like the clubs of last night.

As the carriage passed over the suburbs where the uglies tramped around on their worn shoes, a stream of bright pink vomit shot out of Simone's mouth and coated the window. Instead of being disgusted by the sight, Simone became fascinated by it. Through the lens of his pink vomit, the dull realm of the unfashionables below became a thing of beauty. Suddenly, the regular shapes became organic, lumpy things, enhanced by chunks of undigested food, and the uglies were like brilliant pink beetles, their unkempt features bright.

*But of course this should happen*, Simone thought. He was becoming so fashionable that his very effluence was making the world beautiful.

Beyond the suburbs, the carriage smoothly sailed on past the streets where the unfashionables walked. Another jet of vomit soared majestically from between Simone's grey lips, splattering all over the windows, this time in bright orange. 'You're welcome,' he said at the uglies, admiring the way that the streaks of red through the orange made pretty kaleidoscopic whirls to mask their hideousness.

By the time the carriage came to a halt, Simone felt euphoric. Stumbling from the vibro-rail, he beheld the way that Tremptor Tower wafted around in his vision as if it was a flag in a gale. He inhaled deeply, huffing great gouts of paint fumes into his lungs, and his euphoria heightened, killing any doubts he might have had. The pain in his gut was getting worse, but of course it wasn't actual pain. It was only the transformation occurring – his transformation from tenth floor fashionista to nineteenth floor fashion innovator and icon.

Wrapping his hands around his collar to hold himself upright, Simone swanned up to the Tower entrance. There was no queue. He was the last to arrive today. But it was perfect, so perfect – they would all have a chance to see his brilliant daring.

Throwing the doors aside, he swaggered down the red carpet, letting his hips lead him. The carpet wormed perilously beneath him, but he kept his stride. There was no applause to greet him, and no cameras flashed, but that was fine. Simone knew that his audience were too awed to respond. He shot glances to the left and the right, and saw members of the press fainting – falling from their chairs as if life had left them.

'Today,' he announced, swinging his arms wide. 'I am death!'

There was a shriek from an unknown source. Simone leapt heroically from the end of the red carpet, fell to his knees, and then dragged himself standing again. The shriek continued. The whole lobby whirled around in his vision, as if it was all caught up in a storm and he was the eye of it, and he couldn't locate the source of the scream. It was only as he managed to summon a lift that he realised that the shriek was tearing its way out of his own lungs. He let it happen for a while longer – screaming out the last of his ugliness, no doubt – and then inhaled sharply through his nostrils. Paint fumes powered their way into his brain and everything suddenly stopped whirling around.

The lift rose and rose, and Simone felt a great itching across his shoulder blades. He scratched weakly at the place, feeling a pair of strange lumps there, and for a moment he worried that something was terribly wrong. Breathing heavily fixed that worry – soothing his thoughts and reminding him that this was just another part of his transformation. By becoming death, he was becoming art.

By the time the lift arrived at the nineteenth floor, Simone's legs were no longer working. The doors pinged open, and a stream of red vomit erupted volcanically from between his lips, showering the perfectly white carpet. A dozen colourfully painted faces peered out from office doors as Simone hauled himself along, towards the distant conference room. Bodies dropped as he passed by – fainting spells affecting his jealous colleagues, no doubt – and he laughed at them. He laughed at their clownish faces, painted to worship life. He was death! Come among them!

The fact that he could no longer walk was fine, because he knew now what the lumps on his back were. Why, he wouldn't need to walk ever again. His transformation was nearing completion – he would be a bright grey butterfly of unlife. There was a sharp, stabbing pain in his gut, which he knew were the last throes of his metamorphosis, and he grinned, spitting blood from between his teeth.

Pulling himself up using the conference table, Simone lounged in the chair, awaiting his flock. They would all worship him, he knew. Worship him in his capacity as the most fashionable being to ever grace them. For he knew now that his transformation was alchemical – that he was transcending the mere human form and becoming fashion incarnate.

There was an uproar, but Simone couldn't tell if it was inside his head or not. The room spun, blurred, become unreal, and then suddenly stopped. There were faces at the door, and among them was Trevor Tremptor himself, gripping hold of the doorframe. His nostrils were splayed, his eyes were wide, and the ends of some of his hairs were split. *Ugly*, thought Simone.

'*What*,' demanded Trevor Tremptor, seething, '*is the meaning of this?*'

'Behold!' burbled Simone. He tried to stand, but only succeeded at slipping from his chair onto the floor. 'I—' he managed, coughing. 'I am death.'

'Hideous!' screamed Trevor Tremptor, lancing at Simone with one outstretched finger. '*You're fired!*'

Wiping at his nose temporarily cleared it, and Simone felt the paint fumes as they wrapped themselves around his brain and rolled around inside his hollow body like a thick mist. Filled with renewed strength, he leapt to his feet and tore at his jacket and shirt. 'I am death!' he howled, at the top of his lungs.

Two security guards rushed into the room. They were uglies from below, built for strength instead of beauty, and Simone loathed them. He wouldn't let them touch him. To do so would be to desecrate his perfect transformed state of absolute fabulousness. So, he darted from between their grasping hands and swung himself clear over the conference table. Ahead there was only the window, but that was fine. It was time to reveal his true form.

Simone smashed through the window and unfurled his wings.

>•<

It was generally agreed that Simone was a fashion genius, after all. The way his body lay splayed on the ground, blood leaking out of every part of him – why, it was a masterpiece. His image made the front cover of several magazines, and for a few weeks afterwards fashionable people killed themselves on Thursdays. Then a new fashion came in, for sequins, and Simone was forgotten.

# ROOM 149

## JEFF NOON

The day's work: corridors twelve to fourteen. Still bleary. Gritty eyes, dry mouth. That dream again last night: no sleep after that.

I set off walking, opening one door after another and looking into the rooms.

Examinations at the threshold: empty, empty, empty, wreathed with smoke, empty, empty, empty, empty, empty, angled by thin beams of moonlight as though from an open window, empty, dark, silent, empty. As always the air in room twenty-four was musty, waxy, as though someone had just that second snuffed out a candle; every time the same effect. I lingered over my fantasy, of one day finding the person responsible. I will know them by their burned fingertips smeared with ash.

We moved on, room by room.

Empty, empty, dark, empty, silent, hushed breath, empty, dark, silent, empty.

Beatrice marked the vacant rooms as *Void*.

Void, dark, silent, a cat meowing, empty, silent, dark, a man's wordless cry for help, cut off even as I opened the door.

It made me shiver, just to hear it.

Of course there was nobody there, only the weeping's last echo. It was a dreadful sound. Beatrice was puzzled, her fingers hovering over the pad. Her face was pale from the sickness.

'What shall I put down?'

I thought for a second. 'Wordless cry of pain.'

Then we hurried on, hoping to complete the morning's rounds without too much delay. But the dream returned, with the poor woman's face turning to look at me from far away, up close, and the thought of it made me stop where I was, just outside room forty-two.

Beatrice waited without saying a word.

I shrugged off her hand.

'Just keep working.'

The hours passed. We found the usual array of minor items: a tiny fragment of paper torn from a book, a strand of brown hair, a silver coin spinning to a standstill.

Only one room, number 157, held anything of real promise: a white envelope lying on the floor. It seemed to glow in the light of my torch. I glanced back to call in Beatrice, only to see her leaning against the doorframe for support. She was still uneasy on her feet and often I heard her throwing up in the night. Just two weeks on board. I shook my head in sympathy; it had taken me more than six months to become fully adjusted, but still, there was a job to do. I called her again and she looked at me with weary red-rimmed eyes.

'Yes, anything?' she drawled. 'Anything special?'

I wasn't sure, to be honest. But knowing this room, knowing its history…

She came forward with the pincers and together we picked up the letter and sealed it in a sterile carrier for later analysis. It was, I think, the very first envelope I'd ever found in all my years on board the archive satellite.

Back in the office I examined the few snippets we'd retrieved. I tested them for psychic contamination: all were clean. After that, they were quickly catalogued and tagged for storage. Only the envelope concerned me. I read the name of the person it was addressed to: *Adelaide*. That was all, no address, no postcode, just a woman's first name in a beautiful cursive script. I imagined the dark blue ink flowing from the nib of a fountain pen. Carefully, using the blade of a penknife, I slit open the top of the envelope and pulled out the folded sheet of paper it contained. It was a short handwritten letter.

*My dearest Addie,*

*I write this knowing that soon I will be taken away. I will never see you again, nor speak with you, nor kiss you. How my heart breaks at the thought. But we must be strong. There are more important things than love, I fear. The struggle must go on, even if I myself can no longer participate. Think of me always, as I think of you now, my dearest, in these the last few days of my life.*

*Yours in faith, Leonard.*

Beatrice appeared at my side. 'What is it?' she asked. 'What does it say?'

I showed her and waited as she read it.

'That's it?'

'Yes.'

I could see that she was unimpressed.

'It's important, Bea.' I took the letter back from her. 'You do understand?'

'Sure, sure. But when do we get to meet the people?'

'I'm sorry?'

'People. You know. Ghosts. Whatever you call them. The lost ones. I mean, we are going to find some people, right?'

'It's not like…'

She stared at me. 'What is it like?'

It was the first time she'd raised her voice to me.

Beatrice was twenty-two years old, still existing on Earth time, still using the mindset of someone who lives in a house on a street, in a city with roads and prisons and churches and office blocks filled with cubicles and noise and people rushing here and there in their endless pursuit of work and money and pleasure.

'It's simple,' I told her. 'We don't see people. Not any more.'

'You used to, though?'

I nodded and put on a kind face. 'Yes, of course, in the early years. Many were found, many returned to Earth. But not these days.'

'No?' Her face crinkled with disappointment.

'Only the objects they owned and loved, the movements they made, little actions, gestures, shadows, reflections, breaths, a spoken word maybe...'

'A word? You heard a word? What did they say?'

I took a breath. 'Never mind. Take this to Mr Peterson. Go on.' I handed her the day's collection all safely bound in the carry-all.

'What about the love letter? Aren't you going to include that?'

'Not just yet. I need to make a decision about its value.'

She looked doubtful, and waited for further explanation, but at last she nodded and left the office. A moment after she'd gone, once my heart had slowed a little, I picked up the letter and read through it a second time.

It stirred such memories in me, memories of the last ghost I ever saw on board, that of a woman, a young woman. It was a little over a year ago. Her form trembled in the room, in room 157 on corridor fourteen. The same room where the envelope had been found.

It never leaves me, that moment.

I reached out. Far away. Up close. My hand touched hers…

Cold, then hot.

A shiver. A tingle of nerves.

We looked at each other. Across space, across time.

She smiled, and then frowned. Her emotions were mixed up, I could see that. Her confusion. Her loss. Her eyes blinked on the edge of tears.

Seeds in her hair, flower petals.

'Who are you?' I asked. 'What's your name?'

There was no answer. Only the slow fade of the human shape as the room returned to full darkness. To the dust, the damp air. And something else. Her perfume lingering. Freshly mown hay. She had been in the countryside, I thought.

Birdsong: distant, barely heard. Then silence.

The room folding itself around me, in all its gathered loneliness.

I stood up from my desk in shock at the memory, at its power even now to take me over. And last night I had dreamed of her again. Was it a kind of pre-echo, or even a premonition?

At least now I had a name for her, this dispossessed body, this ghost.

*My dearest Addie…*

><•<

Beatrice came back with the requisite paperwork, which I signed and sealed with the wax stamp. She went back to her studies, while I decided to walk over to the cafeteria for coffee. Finding the letter had troubled me and I needed time to think, but on the way I could sense that something was wrong; people were rushing along Circle Nine Boulevard, either alone with their heads down, or in pairs whispering to each other. I stopped Tom Underwood as he came out of the elevator on floor seven and asked him what the problem was. He frowned in reply, and his eyes closed up tight.

'What is it?'

Then he looked at me. 'Kara, haven't you heard?'

'No. What?'

'They're shutting us down. The whole project…'

A wave of panic surged through me. I could hardly breathe.

Of course, I'd always feared such an event. It was coming up on ten years since 2084, the year the regime had collapsed, and there were constant complaints of the lack of results, or of too much funding being wasted, funding that was desperately needed back on Earth, for the *real* problems affecting *real* people. Not ghosts. Not mirages, illusions.

'How long do we have, do you know?'

Underwood shook his head. 'I don't know. They're saying less than six months. Maybe four months. I don't know. I heard…'

'Yes?'

'Connelly in General Admin said for sure we'd be out of here in four weeks.'

And with that he hurried off, muttering to himself the whole time.

I stepped into the elevator and went to press the button for the cafeteria, but my finger hovered over the panel.

What now? What would I do now? I'd been here for so long, for so many years, refusing all Earthbound leave. This was my home. *I can't go back. Not now.* How the hell would I live? *Down there.* In the dust, the grime, the sweat, the crush of bodies, the heat and the misery.

No. It would not happen. There had to be a mistake.

I pressed the button for floor 101.

The conjuring engine could be heard as soon as I exited the elevator, sounding as it always did to my ears like so many thousands of human beings – men, women, children – all whispering their secrets to each other. Pure fancy, for no ghosts had been caught since the last projector on Earth had been dismantled in '85. But there it was; the beam took me over every time. I was alone, thankfully, as I walked over to the viewing rail. The other side of the funnel could barely be seen, so wide the chasm was, so filled with vapour, and I had to steel myself before I dared to look down.

The great swirl of black and grey mist spun around and around in the vast chamber like the eddy of a monstrous whirlpool.

As always I felt myself being pulled forward in fascination. Only the wire netting of the barrier prevented my willing fall. It was a common desire: there were stitched-up apertures here and there in the wire from those occasions when the conjuring spell had proved too powerful. What were they thinking, that the beam would offer them immortality?

I pictured the many rooftop projectors back on Earth, each one mounted on a Ministry of Justice building. The law had been forced on the government by the faction that would later lead the revolt.

*All stolen, adjusted, edited, or vanished people, attributes, objects and images must be stored safely in case of any future law that might be passed, relating to the re-establishment of the human rights of the individual or group concerned.*

In other words: the regime can steal your property, your assets, your papers, we can even make your bodily image vanish, as long as we preserve it in a form suitable for future retrieval, if such an action becomes a necessity. Hence the archive satellite was launched, a vast warehouse where all the people's images transmitted from the planet's surface could be kept for safekeeping. Really, it was a kind of floating prison in space, a version of the old transport ships that had carried criminals to the far-flung colonies on Earth. But instead of sending actual people, we sent their virtual forms, their avatars, all the poor unfortunate faces and bodies that had been removed from the newscasts, official documents, and history books and films. For a couple of years after the regime's fall the satellite felt like a haunted house in orbit. That's when we started to use the word 'ghosts' to describe the beings that manifested in the rooms. Now I see it more as the deep subconscious mind of the home planet, a place where our shameful or disavowed memories were stored.

I took the folded letter from my pocket.

*I write this knowing that soon I will be taken away.*

My hands trembled. At some unknown point in time this letter had been projected here as evidence of rebellion, or illegal thoughts. What had happened to the letter's author, to Leonard, I wondered? Had his image also been transported, after his death? Did his spirit wander lost through the rooms, along the endless corridors of the vessel? And his love, Adelaide? Would I ever see her again? For there was too little time left on board. I feared that with the satellite being closed down, she would be stranded here, left behind, disregarded.

So many people lost, so many.

I wondered what their story was. He, the rebel, she the loyal lover? Or he the follower to her leader? Or perhaps they moved as one, fighting for the cause in the shadows, finding their love where they may, on the run, or hidden in dirty hotel rooms or basements, away from the All-Seeing Eye. I imagined his capture, his refusal to give her name away, even under torture. I pictured her reading his letters every night, over and over, especially this final one. *Think of me always, as I think of you now, my dearest, in these the last few days of my life.* And later on she also was arrested, found guilty, killed most probably, and her image transported to this prison in the sky.

I folded the letter once more and replaced it in my pocket. *Retrieval is all.* Those were the words spoken to us by the overseer on the first morning of the new order. Retrieval is our new task: the people's spirits must be found, and sent back to their families.

Stepping away from the chasm, I felt the touch of a hand on my skin. A singular fragile knowing loving touch, on the nape of my neck. Her fingertips moving gently, causing the hairs to stand erect and my whole body to shiver.

*Adelaide...*

I turned to face her, to plead with her that I was sorry, sorry for being an active part of the regime that cast her image adrift from her body in the first place, and for not taking proper action that time when I saw her in room 157, for not delivering her safely back to her home. But most of all I felt the need to apologise for being composed of flesh and bone and blood, when all the many thousands of victims had been reduced to nothing more than emptiness inside a moving frame.

*Adelaide. My darling…*

The walkway was empty. I sighed and was bitterly cursing myself for falling prey to fantasies when I heard a noise along the gantry and looked up to see Beatrice moving towards me with unsteady steps.

'Be careful,' I called. 'You've never been up here before.'

She drew close. Her eyes were wide open as she took nervous glances through the barrier, down into the whirlpool. 'Oh Christ. That's incredible.'

'Yes.'

'They said you might be here.'

'Is there a problem?'

'Kara, you've heard the news, right?'

I nodded. There was little more to say.

We both turned to look down onto the chasm, the great hollow centre of the satellite, where the conjuring beam spun and spun relentlessly.

'I don't get it,' Beatrice asked. 'Why is it still turning?'

'It will always turn. The same mechanism that once gathered ghosts from the Earth also drives the ship. It's the centrifugal force that keeps us spinning, that gives us gravity.'

I had calmed down a little now, although the back of my neck still felt cold and tingly.

'One day it will come to a standstill.'

'That will be…' She hesitated. 'That will be very sad.'

I was surprised at my assistant's reaction; it was the first time I'd heard such a sentiment from her.

'You know, Beatrice, I've been here for fifteen years now.'

'That long?'

'Yes. I was stationed here during the regime, and I stayed on voluntarily after the fall. I've seen the conjuring beam in action, swirling feverishly, filled with the gathered spirits of the lost. I have heard their voices in the whirlwind, seen their ravaged faces.'

Beatrice murmured at my side. Perhaps she too was spellbound by the mechanism.

'Fleeting glimpses, nothing more.'

'And now…'

'And now we pack up and return to Earth, to our old homes, if we still have them, to our families, our loved ones.'

'Kara?'

'Yes?'

'Do you have anyone waiting for you, Earthside?'

I shook my head. 'No. Nobody.'

This is my sanctuary, my prison.

And my only family: the wandering spirits.

>•<

A meeting had been called in the main hall, where Overseer Benedict would address us about the fate of the satellite, our personal and professional worries, and about our lives back on the planet's surface. In all truth, I could not face his mawkish platitudes. Instead, I split away from the crowd and took the elevator to corridor fourteen, and along to room 157. The small enclosed space was dark, darker even than usual. Nothing stirred. Not a sound could be heard. Had she disappeared already, moved on elsewhere?

'Adelaide…'

I called her name softly. Surely now, with so little time left, she would make her presence known.

'Are you here? Adelaide, show yourself.'

I waited, and the room answered at last. It breathed. The air moved towards me, away, towards me, away once more; I felt it against my face, soft, caressing.

I spoke her name a third time, a mere whisper, and the room trembled with the scent of freshly mown grass.

Adelaide's eyes appeared first, pale, and then growing more blue and icy until they shone as jewels. Her face and body followed. Her long auburn hair was covered as before in grass seeds and pollen grains and flower petals and specks of hay.

Now she stood before me.

Here, in the moment. Fully present.

She reached out.

I mirrored her.

And even though her lips did not move, I seemed to hear her speak, quite clearly.

*Where is he? Where is my Leo? You took him away from me.*

But as our hands met her whole body shivered and immediately began to fade. Her power was too weak, her phantom state too fragile. Had she been damaged in some way, during the transport? It happened on occasions: the violence of the conjuring beam might fray images at the edges, or even tear them into pieces. These wounded entities were always the most difficult to retrieve.

I reached forward as though to grasp her, to pull her back, but my hands closed on empty air. Only her voice remained.

*You stole him from me...*

And now I stood alone in an empty room. Perhaps I had always been alone, subject to fancies and vain hopes. Perhaps I was conjuring my own desired spirits into existence, nothing more. And yet those final words echoed still. And I realised then that Adelaide wasn't pining for Earth at all, or her old life of freedom, but for the return of her beloved, of Leonard. We had taken his ghost from her, returned him to the planet.

Now she wandered, searching the rooms for his spirit, as I wandered and searched in my own appointed task.

How close we were; how far apart.

I placed the folded letter on the floor and walked out into the corridor.

As I got back to the central hub I could see a small group of people hurrying along towards me. They were carrying someone on a stretcher. Perhaps someone had collapsed in a moment of stress, thinking of the forced return to Earth, of gravity at its proper strength, life's untold pressures, cacophony. But no, it wasn't that. It wasn't an old-timer that had been taken ill. It was Beatrice, the youngest of us. She had fainted at the end of the overseer's speech.

I followed the group towards sickbay and waited anxiously as the doctor made his examination. The patient was out cold for more than two hours, lost in a deep coma. But at last she came round and I was allowed to visit her in her bed on the ward. Her eyes were closed and she barely nodded as I took hold of her hand. There was little response; she was still very weak. The doctor told me it was a sickness brought on by her metabolism and psyche still adjusting to the satellite's artificial gravitational field. But when Beatrice opened her eyes at last, and when she looked at me, I knew different.

>•<

After three days and nights back on Earth, I finally climbed out of bed. My body was still unused to the new environment. I felt that great tree roots were wrapping themselves around my ankles and pulling me down, wanting to bury me. It was a over a week before I could venture outside. I'd been given an apartment by the Retrieval Board, with six months' rent paid in advance, as had all the satellite's staff. I had also managed to save a high percentage of my salary; there wasn't that much to spend it on 400 kilometres above the planet's surface. So I had no urgent need to find a new job: no plans, no dreams. Very few friends. There was a social club and therapy group for ex-retrievers, but one meeting in a cold church basement had been enough. The blank eyes and jittery hands disgusted me. It was one of the reasons I avoided as much as possible the mirror's gaze.

I had seen and heard nothing of Beatrice.

In a way I blamed myself for what had happened to her. It was this feeling of guilt that held me back from seeking her out, of talking to her, or sending a message even. Guilt, and fear. But now I was ready.

The documentary report on the wall-screen triggered me. Slow-moving shots of the satellite's interior corridors, the thousands of empty rooms where the ghosts of the lost had once teemed, a potted history of the regime and its fall, the giant image projector fixed to the roof of the central branch of the Ministry of Justice. The programme told the story of one particular dissenter, a middle-aged man – from first suspicions, his capture and interrogation, imprisonment, disappearance, his animated image sent into space to be collected by the satellite's conjuring beam. And years later, this same image wandering as a ghost from one room to another. Being retrieved, and returned to his family's home back on Earth. The doddering parents seemed happy to receive and dote over this transparent semblance of their long-lost son, while the rebel's wife and thirteen-year-old daughter were more hesitant. What was this strange apparition that hovered before them in the living room, fluttering around a central energy lamp? I felt they were seeking instructions that never came: precisely how were they supposed to behave towards him?

How do you love a ghost?

I decided to look into the background of Adelaide. All the relevant information was easy to find now that the National Archives of the Lost had been opened to the public. I did a search connecting the names Adelaide with Leonard and whittled the nine possible results down to one: Leonard Hawkins had been arrested in 2076 for crimes against the state. His lover and fiancée, Adelaide Palmer, had followed two years later. Her simple crime: speaking seditious words in public. A further search told me that Leonard's image had been retrieved four years ago, and sent back to Earth. Having no known associates or family, his image was currently being kept in storage, awaiting adoption if he was lucky. Or termination, if not.

Poor Adelaide Palmer, of course, had never been retrieved.

As far as the records went, she was still up there with the other lost ones, still orbiting the Earth in the dying satellite, awaiting the moment the conjuring beam would finally give in to entropy. The lights would go out, the systems fail. And then at last this final remnant of her life would die. Well, that was her official outcome.

I knew otherwise.

I went back to the draughty church basement and sat through the tiresome stories patiently. I saw Tom Underwood's eyes staring at mine across the circle, as I knew they would. I nodded and smiled, and afterwards we chatted awkwardly of this and that. Then I asked the one question that mattered. Tom had always been the satellite's unofficial collector of gossip, and that skill had stayed with him back on Earth. He gave me the address of a friend who probably knew someone who would definitely have the information I desired. It took me a little over a week to find Beatrice. She was living in a bedsit in Muswell Hill, north London. It was dingy little place, smelling of incense, damp and rotten food. Her few weeks with the company had gained her little, but she greeted me with a blank smile and allowed me in without protest. She sat there in the armchair with her legs curled up beneath her, listening as I spoke. In many ways she was a pitiful sight, with no interest in cleanliness or personal hygiene. Her chair was surrounded by crumpled chocolate wrappers and empty orange juice bottles. Like myself, I knew she hadn't been outside much since the landing. Life closed in around her like a vice. Occasionally I would see the lively young woman she had once been underneath the mask of pain and doubt. Her brows creased with worry, yet her eyes lit up. She was drawn two ways; all I had to do was tip her over into acceptance. And then pray.

>•<

Two days later I waited outside the National Archives of the Lost at nine in the morning. A winter's mist was lifting across Hyde Park and the cold metallic sun glazed the clouds. Half past the hour came and went and I was ready to give up when I spotted a tiny figure half hidden among the stark black trees. It was her. She stepped into view. I watched as she crossed the road and came up the stone steps.

Nothing was said.

We walked together in silence through the entrance way, where I paid the fee. A lighted path led the way for us, through the echoing vaults, along the central chamber with its marble statues of the great and good of the Victorian and Edwardian eras. It was another part of the building we descended to, deep in the cellar. We were underneath Hyde Park by now. The air became oppressive and close. The corridor's end was lost in the dim light, and voices called to us from the doors on each side as we walked along. I could feel that Beatrice was nervous; at one point her hand clutched at mine for reassurance. I was anxious also, of course, but I tried my best not to show it.

And then we found Room 149.

From one dismal room to another; from far out in space, to the old tunnels of London. I could only wonder what the outcome of this journey would be.

I turned Beatrice to face me and looked into her eyes. I needed this last sight of the ghost that lived inside her. It took a moment only for the young woman's eyes to cloud over and be replaced with the eyes of Adelaide. From her hiding place deep within the flesh she rose up, and she looked at me with such yearning that I could neither move nor speak.

Instead, I opened the door with the key I'd been given at reception and entered, myself first, and then my companion.

One last examination at the threshold.

The room was more like a cell than any living quarters. The central lamp burned with a dull glow. It glimmered for a second, and then the shadows of the room stirred into life and a figure emerged from the corner. A figure of light and energy. A human image.

Leonard Hawkins.

His physical body was long dead, probably buried somewhere in an unmarked grave; yet his spirit had survived.

Beatrice stepped forward slowly.

Leonard shimmered, his body translucent, golden.

They met in the middle of the room.

They touched.

Without hesitation, Adelaide left her living host and joined with her lover; in spirit they tangled, in spirit they danced, they merged and separated, and merged together once more, endlessly. The small room glowed brightly around them as the lamp responded to the new arrival. The two bodies whispered against each other.

It was done.

I took Beatrice by the hand and led her away, back into the corridor. She came along quite easily, again without speaking. I felt that she had very little weight to her, and I knew that she would have to retrieve herself now, her own personality. It would take a while.

We walked back up the stairs, through the gallery of

silent eyeless statues, back outside, and across the road, into the park. Cold air refreshed our bodies. The world: how solid it had first seemed after my arrival, how concrete, how unyielding.

Now it trembled beneath each step I took, a fragile object. Myself as fragile. Beatrice, also.

Our bodies and the world, perfectly suited.

Sunlight gleamed on the frosted surface of the Serpentine, and a lone rook cawed from nearby, unseen, as we moved off through the trees.

# PERCEPI

## COURTTIA NEWLAND

We saw it after dinner nationwide on a weeknight. Between the celebrity dance competition and hit US soap *The Lanes*. Everybody had been buzzing for months, the rumour mills were in overdrive and when the media promised the Buddy 3000 would be unveiled that very evening, the whole town was talking. We all wanted to see what came next, and so we all made sure we were in front of the VS when the first ads aired.

They said the Buddy was the best of its kind, a new generation. That science had made the final leap and harnessed creation's power, there was nothing they couldn't grasp, the future was limitless. They were mostly Seneca supporters of course, usually the ones who stood to gain. Employees, the CEO, the Mayor. Others said mankind was heading for the fall, that playing God would only lead to death and destruction, but no one listened to them. They were the poor or the religious, which in our town pretty much amounted to the same thing. There were leaflets printed on flimsy paper you could see your hand through proclaiming mans' inhumanity, the final days. There were panel discussions and news items and petitions but nothing was going to stop Seneca from launching the Buddy, they must have known that.

We sat in the almost dark for some reason, the flicker of VS light crossing our faces, and we waited. The screen went blank for a long time, but we could still see because the eyes of our long-suffering 1250i were bright enough to bathe the room in a soft, golden glow, as though we'd been submerged in honey. It stood between the sofa and wall, facing the screen like the rest of us, silent apart from the hum of its workings. We ignored it, consumed by our wait for the most part, though we could feel it even then, the uncomfortable way in which we turned our backs, our collective guilt.

Brightness from the VS, blinding light. Celestial music. We covered our eyes. When the light grew piercing enough to feel on the back of our hands it faded and was replaced by the Seneca logo. We nudged each other, lowered arms. The logo became superimposed onto an image of green grass, a cliff edge, blue skies and white clouds. There was a figure, a man standing by the edge of the cliff, arms by his sides, looking out to sea. The camera, which had approached rapidly from high above and behind him, swooped just above the perfect grass, zoomed towards the man and when it got close, circled, rose and hovered.

Piercing blue eyes, high cheekbones, tousled blonde hair and a cleft chin. Tall and slim, beige slacks, blue shirt, sensible brown shoes. The man was tanned and unsmiling, rugged and good-looking, ignoring the camera and even us, the viewers watching nationwide, to look up into the sky at some distant place he perhaps hoped to travel one day. We held our breath.

*Welcome*, a female voiceover said, *to the world of Seneca, the world of the future, now. Welcome to the Buddy 3000.*

We couldn't believe it. We leant forward in our seats, jumped from the sofa, crowded the viewscreen. The man placed both hands on his hips, raised his chin. The celestial music reached a crescendo. We gasped, laughed, doubted.

A head and shoulders shot of Daniel Millhauser, Seneca president. We relaxed. That couldn't have been the Buddy, we reasoned, what a terrible ad. Very confusing. Some strained to hear what the president was saying over loud voices of denial. Someone turned the volume up. Millhauser was sitting in an austere leather chair talking to camera. He seemed matter of fact, as though he was explaining the company's financial position in the global economy via stock and shares. He spoke of the company's past innovations as if we didn't know them, as if we lived on the Outer Limits; its humble beginnings as a manufacturer of calculators and digital watches, his great grandfather Arthur Millhauser assembling circuit boards by hand until he made enough to buy his first shop. Subsequent Millhausers handing over the business like a relay baton. Green screen desktop computers, carryalls with video streaming, 1000 gigs of memory in your hand. The Seneca robotics division creating machines that rolled and served, machines that crawled like a spider and served, machines that eventually walked, haltingly at first and were unable to climb stairs, but soon even that innovation was past memory. The Seneca Communications Robot, a crowning glory; the 500, 1000, 1250, 1500, 2000. SCRs provided as standard with every house sold, more affluent families buying another; one to take care of the kids, one for them. Millhauser explaining just what made the Buddy so special – the ergonomic design – here, the company president allowed a wry smile. *More human than humankind,* he said. Greater intellectual capacity, the SNS-8748, a patented chip designed to collate and articulate cultural differences so the Buddy could function anywhere from New York to Papua New Guinea. Stronger, safer, more efficiency, the ability to self-repair, longer battery life, shorter charge time. Easy to assemble, the option to have the Buddy custom built by a tech for more credits. A child lock so the young couldn't order Buddy to do harm, even as much as swear. Additional teaching modules sold as downloadable content, thousands of subjects for the family who preferred home schooling. The Buddy could dive to 100 metres, climb to 50,000 feet and was already in service above our heads, on space stations and satellites and dry dock launch platforms.

While Millhauser pitched his miracle product to our houses, the nation, we sat forwards and listened. We swallowed every word as the camera tracked ever so slowly to the right, imperceptibly at first, until we realized the Seneca president's head was leaving the shot. We second-guessed ourselves; it was the shot leaving *Millhauser.* The camera kept tracking, first revealing nothing but a window overlooking clear green grass, a blue sky; the cliff, it was the same cliff! Then the edge of a large, tidy desk, pads and pens, a Manchester United coffee mug, the corner of a wafer thin viewscreen, a nameplate - *Daniel Millhauser, President* - and finally Millhauser behind the desk wearing a distant smile, the quiet trickster sat with his hands clasped.

And we jumped. Nationwide, probably the world over, we jumped at the realization. Millhauser got to his feet, placed a hand on his doppelganger's shoulder. He smiled at the Buddy and the Buddy smiled at him, though it was impossible to tell one from the other, and then, even though they both looked pretty jovial it became difficult to tell what was meant by such dubious humour, or who had told the actual joke.

They looked straight into camera, spoke as one.

*The Buddy 3000*, they repeated. *The world of the future, now.*

The Seneca logo, the Buddy 3000 logo, a black screen with details in white, the price, specifications, small print that outlined monthly repayments of 15% APR. Ten seconds or less and the information was gone. Dark screen. Opening credits of *The Lanes*.

Uproar in front rooms, houses, streets, towns and cities. The hit US soap discarded like a used battery. The next morning queues were a block long outside Seneca Showrooms all over the world, but there were no Buddies. There were TV interviews and chat show appearances by Seneca CEO Ravindra Mehta, more handsome and skilled in PR than his reclusive president. There were web trailers and Mall openings with men on stilts dressed in Buddy suits, a public appearance with the Prime Minister and no sign of a single Buddy. Speculation was rife. Mehta waved his hands a great deal, smiled with perfect white teeth and spoke of fine-tuning.

One night we went to bed and when we woke, emerging from the warm cocoons of our homes to leave for work, or school, they were stencilled everywhere, a numerical infestation on walls and street lights, road signs, pavements and kerbs, bollards, billboards, even some vehicles. Three paired numbers. A date, we soon realised. 12.10.84.

There was outrage in government circles over what was essentially vandalism. Seneca claimed no responsibility for the appearance of the numbers. Mehta went on live television to rubbish claims of an international graffiti campaign while confirming that yes, this was the official launch date. It must have leaked somehow, he smiled. We nodded, disbelieving, accepting his lies. We expected no better and that was the issue. It became easy to ignore what they did, to pretend it didn't matter.

It must have been the same everywhere, but in our town the Buddy was all anyone could speak about. It seemed to relate to any given subject. The battle for *Montes Pyrenaeus*, still raging, the dubious economy, the huge cost and fallout, both literal and figurative, of interplanetary travel. The rising temperature of the Earth, unemployment, immigration. We debated and disagreed and our raised voices filled the night in coffee shops, bars and restaurants, in pool halls, after hours clubs and back alleys, in factories and playgrounds and public spaces where people of all ages gathered in excitement, faces bright with the promise of a new age. It was our happiest time, we owed Seneca that much. They presented us with a dream made real, a figment of imagination made flesh and bone. We were elated at the chance to become hopeful, the opportunity to be something more than we were, the gift of idealism. After all, this could change everything. VS channel programmers, both cable and terrestrial, sensing this new hunger, this hope, began to screen old movies from the last century and more recent productions under the collective titles 'Android Week', or 'AI Night', or 'Cyborg Season'. There was a vast appetite for the films until people began to realize many of the plotlines came to pessimistic endings no one had dared think about, let alone speak of. It was rumoured Seneca stepped in at that point, and no one was conclusive about what happened, but one by one the runs of movies were cancelled, leaving us with a vague sense of disquiet no one dared to articulate.

The months passed without warning. The ads intensified, while the posters and online spots became unavoidable. Seneca threw a huge launch event, screened for free on all channels, attended by the world's biggest movie stars, models, singers, royalty, presidents and Prime Ministers. Our town, like many others, threw a street party with images of the launch projected onto a whitewashed wall. Everyone came. We watched a live news report where BBC anchorwoman Leticia Daley took us deep into Seneca's distribution centre to witness thousands of human-sized boxes rolling along interlinked conveyer belts resembling miniature highways, some dystopian automotive future, before being loaded into HGVs by 2000s with the gaze of the blind. We commented on her hushed delivery, her unflinching gaze to camera, how the whites of her eyes matched the pallor of her skin, the loss of her flirtatious smile. Then it was back to the launch, the celebrities and music, back to CEO Ravi Mehta's smile and Leticia Daley was forgotten.

We imagined a scenario replayed in homes worldwide, that what we experienced was reflected a million times, like a Seneca warehouse constructed of mirrors as tall as the moon shuttle. Buddy boxes wheeled into front doors by 2000s wearing specially designed khaki uniforms, families standing aside in awe, unable to keep excitement from their faces. The boxes drilled open, peeled like the husk of unworldly fruit to reveal a soft, translucent bubble, milk clouds floating above a sea of grey, a surface fluid as water yet able to hold its ovoid shape; the mass trembling, even before the 2000s produced cutting blades from the ends of claw-like fingers. The medical workers amongst us, doctors, nurses, pharmacists, could not fail to notice the ovoid resembled an amniotic sack. Some told our partners. Others kept their silence and simply watched the robots cleave into thick flesh, egg white jelly easing free and the mass collapsing to reveal our Buddies, naked apart from the minimal underwear to protect their modesty. No one thought to ask why machines needed modesty in the first place.

And simply as that, the new age dawned. The premier generation of Buddies went far beyond anything Seneca had promised, and within the first few weeks it was common to see machines everywhere. Though it was difficult to tell them from afar, especially when they were at rest, you always knew an android when you saw them up close. It was something in their eyes, their facial expressions. There was no emotions, no life, no *feeling*. It was like staring into the face of someone in a coma. They were warm to the touch, could laugh or cry, even bled if their skins were cut, but they responded to the world as though they were weary beyond measure, had lived a thousand years and grown attached to nothing at all.

There were problems, of course. Much like any new technology, there was failure, accident, human error. A batch of originals shipped to Melbourne developed a fault also found in Shanghai, Valencia, Cologne. The machines mysteriously shut down, and had to be recalled. Another batch shorted out and caught fire, levelling buildings in Bridgetown, Mumbai and Orange County. The owners sued Seneca, winning a hefty sum, and those who were insured claimed replacements. A machine was mistaken for a woman who'd had an affair with a human's husband, and was gunned down late one night walking through a park. The wife was arrested, later released without charge. Though machines were forbidden from harming humans there was no such law for us and even if there were, we knew it would be broken. The wife went back to her husband, who resumed his affairs within months. She followed him to a hotel on the outskirts of the town, kicked down the door, and shot the husband plus his girlfriend. She was given two consecutive counts of life.

For the most part Buddy owners had no complaints. The originals were trustworthy and strong, highly intelligent but docile. Buddies saved humans from car accidents, repaired broken machinery and stopped potential suicide victims from leaping in front of trains, even as violent crime hit a sharp decline. Nationwide, productivity was said to have risen by forty per cent. Daniel Millhauser was awarded the Nobel Prize. It was rumoured he'd used company profits to buy 400 acres on *Mare Frigoris*, the sea of cold, thousands of miles north of the troubles. The media claimed he planned to build a Seneca base to help strengthen the strike for Mars. Millhauser wouldn't grace the subject with an answer.

Affluent, middle-class consumers packed their varied SCRs into boxes, in some cases shipping them back to Seneca, or selling them to poorer families. We kept ours in the garage, just beyond the bonnet of our car, next to the lawnmower and a rusting tool cabinet, orange growth creeping its hinges. Within a few weeks the soft, golden glow of the SCR's eyes was no longer seen. It became commonplace to hear the high whine of inner mechanisms, to see Buddies stepping with a jerky, knee high, marionette tread that would have been painful for humans. On the streets, in parks and shopping malls, it was normal to see men and women with Buddy companions in tow like faithful dogs. Even those who had protested against the androids, still did, fell into silence when they saw them, stopped waving placards and chanting. There was something in the way the machines would regard the demonstrations that made it all seem wrong. No emotion, and yet maybe there was a flicker of something, an awareness that they were being spoken of, categorized maybe – that they were outside the boundaries of what it meant to be *us*.

Our tenuous peace was shattered by news of a moon base bomb attack. We breathed easier; things had been going too well for too long. One hundred and twenty-seven killed, thirty-one injured, much needed supplies and arms raided. A relatively small band of workers, recent descendants of the first lunar miners, had protested against unfair working conditions and absconded to the moon's dark side five years ago. For the last twenty-four months, led by a woman the authorities knew as Mika Cole, miners had attacked government interests, from the mines, to supply ships, to the communications networks, though it was unclear which particular government they were fighting against, or what their demands might be. The base on *Crater Goclenius* had been the home and workplace of Terraformers, those charged with transforming the harsh landscape from white rocks and dust into something more uniform, suitable for human habitation. They had been protected by two marine platoons who lived on the base, but many of the miners had been marine trained too, long before they were contracted to the moon, and taught their sons and daughters well. The fact that Mika Cole and her followers had survived five years of constant darkness spoke volumes about their resourcefulness. Even though the media wouldn't admit, it also made them all the more fearful.

We could see it coming. Some debated the morality. Others said it would never happen. Three weeks of silence, of nothing but media images of survivors wrapped in bloody rags being transported to Earth, of the shattered and bomb-blasted moon base X-2100, a spider-shaped construction with a vast hole in its abdomen, leaking valuable air into space. A plume like the exhaled breath of a whale, white continuous steam. Mika Cole's ID photo, black pitted eyes and blonde hair, the seven-figure price on her head. The pinched, furious expression of a Coalition delegate reading the damage report as if it were a eulogy; which in some ways, for them, it was. Live reports from the permanent boundary between night and day, Letitia Daley in a bulky spacesuit, even more sombre than the delegate before her, exposing the world below to the thin line no human had ever dared to cross before the miners, a stark exchange between the established and the unfathomable.

The silence was ended by a hurried, almost embarrassed announcement. Launch dates for Second Generation Buddies had been brought forward, the latest, much improved version enlisted to fight lunar terrorism, sent to the moon to test their capabilities against trained human soldiers. They would be rocketed three days and approximately 239,000 miles to perform a job most believed they were built for. Those first seeds of scepticism were sewn on furrowed ground.

Night after night for the next eighteen months, we came home to harrowing pictures on our viewscreens, of war and death and atrocities far worse. At first the casualties were all human, the victims all terrorists we were told. Maimed, blackened limbs like chargrilled meat. Cauterized stumps, gouged and missing eyes, flesh torn to reveal the glistening inner workings of the body. The War Buddies, as they had become unofficially known on Earth, were instructed to recover the dead and injured alike. Sometimes it was as difficult to tell one from the other as it was to tell an android from twenty feet. POWs were displayed like flesh and blood trophies, while a baby-faced Marine sergeant gave an emotionless progress report. The enemy was a worthy opponent, he said, and yet they were falling. The Buddies were fighting alongside humans and doing a commendable job.

We sent children to their rooms, watched the screens through our fingers. We sat forwards like when it all started, disgusted, wanting to know. Soon, we realized, as the nights went on to become weeks and months, that the cameras were catching glimpses of strange casualties and injuries we were unaccustomed to.

One night, it was a woman on a gurney, clutching below her knee. The camera moved on, bumped some unseen object, inadvertently dropped and filmed the severed leg. Jagged, black meat, the result of a bomb it seemed; the foot deleted, sagging tendons, muscles and pumping blood, gleaming metal protruding from the midst of all that flesh.

What stayed with us, what people repeated after that one, accidental image that would herald the most monumental change in world history since humans migrated from Africa, was the look on that android's face. The way she regarded her missing foot, with disbelief and horrified regret; her screams of pain. We hadn't imagined machines felt anything – in fact, thinking back, we were pretty sure the First Generation *didn't*. This was something new, something we'd hardly dared to consider. We wandered into back gardens and front lawns, stared out of windows and through telescopes at the chalk white satellite above our heads, thinking of all the things we hadn't known.

When Mika Cole and her followers faced heavy losses, they retreated into the mountains and caves of the lunar dark side. These vast, unmapped territories became their battleground. Coalition losses began to mount. Small, difficult to track teams sent raiding parties to government settlements, gathering supplies such as power lamps and generators, food, battlewear, weapons and ammunition. Terrorist sympathizers began to construct or buy their own ships, hide them well and blast off from the Earth's most desolate places: deserts, woodlands, jungles, arctic fields. At first, no one on the space stations did anything. They were not the army, weren't authorized to kill. Thousands of ships went on their way to the moon's dark side to support the terrorists. Many died making the journey, at many stages; ships would explode on take-off, break apart in the atmosphere; navigation systems failed and they would strike a communications satellite, or their equipment would mysteriously die halfway, freezing the occupants to death, their ship a slow spinning mausoleum grasped in cold orbit. Some would come in too fast, crash against the powder-grey surface. Even so, many others made it. What became of them, little is known. It's assumed they must have succeeded, because the violence began to intensify, earthbound politicians began to grow worried, and the effort to quell a minor insurrection, something that shouldn't have taken three months by governmental reckoning, started to look as though it wasn't going to end.

No one knew how, but Mika Cole was brought in alive. Rumours said the Coalition gained a lock of her hair, isolated the DNA and paid Seneca a vast sum to develop an android clone, much like the mechanical Millhauser who beguiled us from the beginning. The cloned Mika infiltrated dark side mountains, sent raiding teams on false missions, sewed dissention, captured the terrorist leader and brought her to the Coalition. The intention was apparently to have her returned to Earth to stand trial although, predictably enough some said, she never made it. Media reports claimed she took her own life, poisoning herself in her cell.

A new terrorist leader, who referred to their self only as Liberty and sent a digitally recorded message via a reprogrammed SCR, said Cole would never have done such a thing, that she was murdered. They told the Coalition the war would not be over until every last one of them was dead, or the lunar terrorists killed the government workers and army in retaliation, whichever came first. They named themselves – *Esse est Percepi* – to be is to be perceived. To this day, the battle goes on.

Yet as far as the Coalition, Seneca and the media were concerned, the war was over. They'd won. They held press conferences, broadcasted VS spots, even brought back the street parties to celebrate. Very few attended. The psychological fallout of the war, unintentional though it had been, was that nobody trusted the 'unholy Trinity' as they'd been dubbed. The physiological fallout was the Second Generation Buddies' return to Earth, recalled from a conflict many thought they shouldn't have been involved in. Public opinion swayed against the Buddies. We had seen what they could do to the human body, sometimes intimately. We had seen their pain, frustration and anger, human failings that caused the war to blossom in the first place. We had seen them built to resemble people, had been taken with the thought, but when we heard that power was used to forfeit our moral code, to take life, we considered the consequences. The almost empty street parties, long trestle tables packed with food, streamers and balloons, viewscreens and more machines than people, the adults drawing their young away from androids with open fear, was the worst advertising the world had ever known. The problem was this wasn't some faulty inanimate object that could be recalled from retailing shelves. These were powerful, highly intelligent beings with scars on their skin and the vision of an alien landscape in their eyes.

The 'android problem', as it was often referred to, was discussed in many circles but no one in power came up with any solutions. Some government ministers campaigned to scrap the Buddies, an idea that of course Seneca was highly against. Others said they should be kept busy, put to work. Human Rights groups were faced with a quandary; if the machines were made of flesh and blood, had nerves and DNA and analytical thought, how could one justify their mistreatment? The original protestors, the church groups, the unions and anti-AI campaigners renewed their zeal, taking to the streets and parliament once more. And the machines watched. Said nothing. The First Gens remained inscrutable, though it was possible to detect a curl in the lips of the Second Gens, if we ever caught sight of them.

For they had mostly relegated themselves to the night. Perhaps feeling an affinity with darkness, perhaps fearing the light, Second Gens were rarely seen, preferring to keep themselves apart. They frequented the after-hours bars, the strip clubs and casinos. They slept in empty warehouses on the edge of towns and cities, abandoned houses, or the few run down hotels that would take them. It quickly became apparent that no provisions had been made for their welfare. After all, they were only machines. When they appeared in daylight it was often to speak of their war experiences at Human Rights rallies, where they would maintain a neutral, quiet tone. They would cry. Few of the injured machines had been repaired, as the cost was deemed too expensive, and they displayed the full range of their horrific injuries. One who had repaired himself, replacing his facsimile arms with the claws of an SCR 2000, became a spokesmachine of some kind. The gifted orator, who told the world his name was X, was a poster boy for campaigners. He would not cry, repeatedly saying all he wanted was fair treatment. The liberals amongst us remarked that X sounded pretty much like the *Esse est Percepi*.

Those of us on the streets in early dawn, or coming home at that time, or those who were creatures of the night would see them. Small, huddled groups massed in the darkest corners as if for warmth: heads down, bodies close, sometimes shifting from foot to foot, most of the time impossibly still. An immobile state we could never hope to attain, all life departed. There would be talking from somewhere, someone, we could never tell who, but there was always one voice, a call and response, a deep murmur from the group like the throbbing hum of an idling motor. We'd draw closer and see the gatherings were entirely made up of machines. The one voice would fall silent, the hum recede into nothing. We would try and talk with First and Second Gens only for them to move away, marionette steps jostling against a smooth, almost human glide, leaving us sighing white clouds of breath into a space once occupied, alone in the darkness. We became afraid.

When the police tried to break up the gatherings, the machines ran. Often they were caught, arrested, kept in the cells until morning and released. First Gens were asked to produce papers and ID that detailed who had purchased them, but of course, no one purchased Second Gens. After months of being arrested, beaten even, one Second Gen fought back. His name was Titus and he hospitalized the police officer. The National Guard was called. Titus went underground. Ravindra Mehta appeared on VS, appealing for calm, side by side with X, who told the world machines meant humans no harm. The National Guard, perhaps afraid, perhaps a little over zealous, went after the Second Gens a mite harder than necessary. There were fierce battles. The machines began to break into armouries, rout enemy attacks. Machines were destroyed. Brave men and women with families were killed. Titus was destroyed. The

National Guard appealed for calm and still the machines fought on. There were sightings of larger android meetings, hundreds, thousands in one place. Soon our First Gens were gone when we woke in the mornings, and they returned with no explanation as to where they had been, what they had been doing. They were calm, logical in the face of our hysteria. The next night they were gone again. After a while, they never came back.

In their wake, the machines left an undecipherable message, much like Seneca's stencilled numbers back when we could hardly remember. Like the numerals, they appeared everywhere overnight. Our walls and houses, shopping malls and parks. No one knew what it meant, even Ravi Mehta was dumbfounded. It wasn't so much a word as a simple, common symbol:

Our governments declared Martial Law, but it was too late. The army flooded our towns and cities like dam water. A 9 p.m. curfew was imposed on humans and machines alike. Tanks and armoured vehicles rumbled along high streets, but the machines were gone. We watched the media and prayed. Human Rights campaigners appealed to our governments for a peaceful strategy to end the stalemate, but their efforts were not helped by X's disappearance with his machine brethren. Daniel Millhauser made a rare speech, a fifteen-minute recording where he quietly lamented all that had happened, telling us Seneca would do everything in its power to uphold peace, that they had no quarrel with humans or machines alike. We felt it sounded like an appeal for his life rather than calm, although it was confirmed he was holed up in his fully functional moon base, far from earthbound troubles, even though the lunar war was still as bitter and cold as solar winds.

Army scouts caught intelligence reports of a gathering deep in the countryside, close to 10,000 machines camped in a disused war bunker. They bombed them. Thousands were destroyed. The machines called it 'The Lancombe Massacre.' They waited seven days, and in the dead of night, they attacked.

We felt the ground shudder as bombs fell, and could see them bring light to dark skies. During the day we would go about our business, timid, scurrying from place to place like mice. The army assured us they had everything under control, but the images on the VS said different. They were sustaining heavy casualties, the list of dead and wounded growing. In some countries, those too poor to have any real technological army, humans were forced to flee, giving machines the advantage. We saw it on the pirate channels, how they invaded the streets and houses, set up camps and fortified roads with cars, tanks, sandbags. In our town, some would wake to strange noises and wander our homes, weapons in hand, to see the machines foraging through possessions, mostly from garages and workshops. If they saw us they would raise their guns, back away into the night. Shops were easy targets. The machines' stealth became legendary. We began to reboot our SCRs in an attempt to use them as guards, and although they were largely unsuccessful, they made us feel safe.

A security man in a home improvements warehouse disturbed a gang of machines while on night watch. He opened fire and was killed. Two days later a man was murdered when he discovered two machines ransacking his house. His wife, who survived, claimed she was raped. She said the machines had taunted her. They had no need to replicate; they just wanted to see how it felt. She'd heard them discuss their disillusion with X and his 'rules', justifying their crime as a legitimate rendering of what the machines had called for, the true meaning behind the symbol @.

Anarchy.

We humans rose to the challenge. People were upset, grief stricken, understandably. The army sent to protect us was questionable, barbaric. We took matters into our own hands. There were many among us who disagreed, pointing out that the machines had treated us as targets for the most part, uniformly expressing no regret for the deaths, or abuse of ordinary citizens, aside from X, now known as Xavier, who sent recordings steeped in dismay. Some argued that his sympathies seemed hollow, insincere. Their voices were drowned by those who said the machines were simply doing what had been done to them. How were they supposed to respond? Their lives, if you could call them that, had been threatened. We barricaded doors and windows, installed SCRs with weapons protocol, bought, created, traded guns and ammunition.

The foolhardy went on national VS and bragged of what they intended to do if the machines entered their homes. They were usually masked and armed, holding weapons above their heads like victory flags, like the war was over, had already been won. The cautious amongst us kept silent, had the good sense to weep as the night became alive with explosions and needle-sharp tracers. We knew what we had to do, what the true cost would be. We left our homes in search of rumoured android camps, rebels if you will, we crossed fields and entered forests and abandoned industrial estates, waving white flags even as corpses began to appear on our streets. The messages from our governments and Seneca came less frequently, and eventually ceased. We wept harder because the foolhardy would die.

We cannot say what took place within those camps. Suffice to say they accepted our solidarity. Although this account serves as a record of events and the stance we took, theoretically we are still at war so we omit details. Let it be known we are proud to have stood for the oppressed in a time of revolution, but we do not denigrate the humans or machines who stand against us. Any lost lives are lives worth grieving. Sacrifice is a part of any revolution and there is no revolution without bloodshed.

Prior to emancipation day, the sight of shuttles piercing clouds became as commonplace as the sound of heavy artillery. Tickets were costly. Many did as the lunar freedom fighters had, buying or building their own craft. Now materials were in short supply. People who owned ships were reluctant to sell in case they were needed. Predictably enough, people fought.

That final night the sky lit up as though the sun had changed its mind and returned. They might have been fooled into thinking they were witnessing an early dawn had the light not come from the west. It burned for hours, a blood orange that burst on the horizon and they came onto the streets, soldiers, civilians and SCRs alike. From then until the actual dawn, the darker side of the sky was drawn with the furious scribbles of hasty departure. Even when the sun rose, throbbing, sore with anger, the roar of rockets and engines, the rattling of windows, was constant accompaniment to all that we did.

We arrived in daylight, picking our way through litter and fresh dog excrement. Thousands of First and Second Gens, more than anyone had seen. Us, armed humans, walking alongside. People ran and were mowed down indiscriminately. The old, legs foal-weak, women clutching babies attempting to shield them from gunfire, infant children, sandals chattering against their feet. The rules had changed with that temporary dawn. They ran from truth, filled with a desperate self-preservation that caused vile acts we never would have imagined, let alone carried out. Husbands pushed wives into the line of fire, leaving them for dead. Friends stole weapons from the weak, rummaged in the pockets of broken bodies for ammunition, credits, food, anything they might need. The horrors we saw fuelled our justification, veiling our eyes until our expressions became as stoic as First Gens, and yet we were more alive than ever. They entered sewers and underground tunnels, war bunkers and maintenance systems. We followed, attempting to slow our body's vibrations so we might become machines, like those we fought beside.

# DEGREES OF ELISION

## CASSANDRA KHAW

Observe—

A man, stooped over a table, cigarette drooping from the edge of a downturned lip. He exhales, carcinogens and nanites, recent bio-history. Lung performance: circumstantially acceptable. Vascular integrity: good. Dopamine saturation: minimal, requires action.

The smoke tendrils diagonally into a vent. In the background, music: jazz from the '50s, alleyway wisdom told in saxophone and bass, pruned, of course, of inflammatory content.

Frameshift—

The table is a screen, gel-based. His fingers leave ripples in the plasma. The interface is nostalgic, recalling the two-column architecture of old newspapers. Light emissions savage the strong jaw, the cheekbones cut sharp as a government suit. Make him gaunt, strange, and hungry.

Pull back—

We see his office. Cubicle, really. Four walls. Slate-black. No ornamentation except for the carcass of a succulent in a corner, leaves shrivelled to brown. A backpack hangs like a corpse from a hook on the door.

'Huh.' His voice: a coarse tenor, ill-used, not pleasant but also not unpleasant. We see the silhouette of fingers steepling, a spine uncurled.

Observe—

His face, haloed in neon.

Observe—

His fingers – long, pleasingly shaped – skating across the screen, pulling up windows. His touch grazes a word: accept. Text disgorges onto the panel. We see him lean forward. The camera follows. Static. A recording begins.

Now listen—

Her voice: female, gorgeous. An erotic contralto, laced with something of the French. Not much. Enough. Too much and it risks becoming overpowering, unctuous, tawdry.

She propositions him with a duty, moans the last line: 'We trust you know what to do.'

He does.

>•<

History is reams of data points, each the sum of a billion snap decisions and considered actions, sustained by narrative, stitched together by those who survived. In eras past, society believed it was also inviolate, every recorded viewpoint sacrosanct.

We know this is a lie now.

There is no singular truth, no fact that cannot be altered, repositioned and resold to the world. This is what men like him do.

They change the world.

Observe—

There can be symphonic music. Wagner, or maybe Górecki, something dark, moody. The man lights a fresh cigarette, this one contraband, only tobacco and sweet clove. Breathes in, breathes out.

He takes it slow. This is not an action scene. Smoke tangles between his fingers as he navigates between conversations, looking for commonalities, places where an idea can be applied, removed. Subtlety is integral. Novices gouge at the past, leave it wounded, vulnerable to suspicion. But men like him, they understand restraint.

He finishes. Grunts. Satisfaction trilling in the lower registers, borderline sexual. This is his best work yet. The man rises. Hits send. Spares a moment to contemplate the woman in the recording. Wonders if she had been flirting with him. He does not recognise the voice, but the department is colossal. He has not spoken to everyone.

Maybe it's the new girl in Services, the one with the painted-on skirt, the blowjob lips. Could be her. She always has a smile for him, doesn't she? Brushstroke lashes over blue eyes, mouth slightly agape, tongue wet.

The man presses down on his erection, warns it to secrecy. He's married. Conjecture is not felonious, but he knows his spouse would disagree, would suffer umbrage at the notion he'd entertained fantasies of her on his mouth, a stranger on his cock, his world remade into sex and skin and salt.

He goes out. The lights follow, one minute and forty-eight seconds after.

>•<

'You're late.' Her voice: quiet, sweet, slightly nasal, but not unpleasantly so.

'Work.' Reply. Rote.

He shrugs off the backpack, lets it drop where he stands, and pours himself into the couch. Their apartment is government-issue. White on white: utilitarian furniture, mid-century-inspired. Sleek. He would never admit to her, but he loves it, enjoys the austerity, its implications of character. His wife – slender despite three pregnancies, wild-haired – crosses the room, folds herself into the chair opposite.

'We need to talk.'

'No, we don't. We've been through—'

'I know. But, I still – this still bothers me. A lot.' His wife pulls a knee to her chest, knuckles going white.

'We've spoken about this. I've said I'm sorry. And—' He lifts hands, spreads them. 'I don't know what you want me to do. What happened in the past? I can't change that. And we were on a break.'

She flinches, full-body. Her reply is acidic. 'Yes, and all bets were off and we could do anything we wanted during that time, but don't you think you should have had the courtesy to tell me?'

'I didn't ask you for any information from that time, did I?' Riposte. Tone even. 'And you didn't supply anything either. What I do value is our present—'

'I didn't do anything that needed to be explained.'

'Neither did I.'

Her jaw twitches. A contraction of muscles, like a finger squeezing the trigger. It fires off a light in her eyes: rage. 'Couldn't you have told me it was a colleague of yours?'

'Would that have changed anything? She meant nothing, means even less now.'

A flash of teeth. 'I don't know what to do with you, sometimes.'

She leaves, doesn't explain why. His analysis software posit nothing of value. He considers replacing them, even cancelling his subscription entirely. What's the point of keeping things as they are if they don't do what they're meant to do?

'Angel—'

Door slams. Hard.

The man sits, face in palms. He says nothing.

>•<

Observe—

It's late. Three in the morning. The sky is indigo-black. No constellations. A haze of orange wicks from the streets; the city never sleeps.

Frameshift—

We see the shot through a window, framed by tree boughs. A large bed. A figure on one end, tangled in white sheets. The man's wife. She is awake. The door opens, creaks on its hinges, exposes the man's gaunt silhouette. He hesitates, almost retreats when she turns and props herself up on an elbow, hair gleaming turquoise in the citylight. 'Come here.'

He complies, coils into the sheets, leg curling over hers. His grip is possessive, his voice bruised. He aches, and he aches, and he aches. 'I'm sorry.'

'I know you are. I know, baby. I know. '

Pull back—

It has been hours. Teal suffuses the horizon, cinematic. A few birds shriek welcome to the dawn. The man is asleep, arm draped over his wife, hand on her pelvis. She is not.

>•<

Observe—

The man at his desk. His shirt is rumpled. The top button is undone. This is not an easy assignment. Today, he is rewriting the living.

Listen—

Recordings, garbled, a single voice layered over itself, slightly out-of-sync: a politician's voice. Stentorian. Old. The noise resolves into a single speech, impassioned, a call to arms. It is not rehearsed. It quakes with emotion. He means this.

But it is not acceptable. Dripping light from his fingertips, the man maps phrases to phonation, text to audio; checks, rechecks, checks again for every opportunity to minimise modification. He has decided. The original soliloquy stays. Mostly. A line here, a line there, omitted, or restructured; shortened, stretched, strung with nothing words, so that there is space for suspicion. Pitch and phrasing, the man changes too. These are vital.

Hours pass. Then:

Listen—

He plays the new recording: conviction has become fiction, a salesman's solo. Briefly, regret palpates his chest. The man thinks: this one could have changed the world. But he has his orders, his salaried task. Besides, if the minister had meant what he said, if he had truly believed, there would be no room for misinterpretation.

Observe—

The man clutching his world view.

Observe—

The frown that pits his brow, brackets his mouth in fine lines, old age's first vanguard.

Observe—

The breath that convulses in the hollow of his throat, the tremor that says I do not believe.

Observe—

The man does not flee. He walks, struts; lets arrogance

winnow his misgivings to dust, to nothing, to specks of memory, molecule-small, too small to matter, like a handful of weekends spent with a girl who never mattered at all.

>•<

This is a flashback. We know this because of the sepia overlay, the camera-haze that transforms every plane of skin, turns every face poreless, unreal. This is meant to invoke nostalgia.

Observe—

A beach. Stars in the sky, too many to itemise. It is cold here, the breeze dragging salt-scent from the north. The man and the girl sit at the periphery of a campfire. Their friends smile. They understand.

Observe—

Their fingers coil together, patterns of want.

'I thought you were interested in, you know.' She is young, too young, and so beautiful in this moment, tawny-skinned and silver-eyed. Her hair burns copper in the firelight.

'That was a mistake.' The man drinks the sight of her, the brandy-gold lines of her legs, her face. She is close enough to kiss. He leans in. 'I know what I want.'

Her smile is so bright it hurts.

>•<

'Do you love me?'

His answer is immediate.

'No.'

>•<

We return to the present.

The man is mapping his apartment in frantic strides. The lights are dim. It is too late, too quiet, too empty.

His wife is gone.

The epiphany develops in increments, in bursts, glass-edge sawing slowly between his ribs. Shock becomes grief.

His wife is gone.

The man makes circuits through every room, riffles through drawers, looks beneath beds. He leafs through her books, hoping to augur an explanation, or a note pencilled in the margins. Anything to say *why*.

His wife is gone.

The thought pounds like a hangover. It is too massive to cup in his skull, so it spills from him in wracking sobs.

His wife is gone.

The man weeps.

>•<

Listen—

'Where is my wife?'

The girl's voice: glacial, sibilant with spite. 'Nice to hear from you too. First call in ten months, and you're already making demands—'

'I— I don't have any time for this. I need you to tell me if you've seen my wife.'

'Last week. We had coffee.'

'Why—' He strangles the question. 'What did you tell her?'

Defensive: 'I didn't tell her anything. She asked questions. I answered.'

'I—' He chokes the words down, squeezes them until they snap. 'I don't understand.'

'What part? The fact that your ex-fling and your wife might get along? Or that women talk?'

'I ended things with you *cleanly*. There was never any confusion as to what was going on between us. I told you that, and—'

'You didn't tell me you were married.'

'*Because it didn't matter*—' Slam. The man beats a fist on the table. 'We were separated. We— there was an agreement between us. We— we acknowledged the possibility of casual sex with people outside of the marriage. That is how breaks *work*. It. I— For all intents and purposes, I was a single man and you were a single woman, and—'

Her voice is a hiss. 'I fell in love with you, anyway. You knew that. You had to have known that.'

'It isn't my fault that you couldn't read the signals, then.'

'And it's not my fault that she has my memory-cache.'

Slam.

The line is dead.

>•<

Observe—

The man in his office, pale, hunched, his bones laser-cut-sharp. A stubble infests his cheeks, his jaw. He has not shaved in days.

Observe—

Light drooling from the spider-bones of his hands,

crusting his nails. He digs into data banks, surveillance footage, phone conversations. Everything and anything he can find.

Observe—

The man. He breathes deep, recites a throwaway conversation for the fifth time; adjusts timbre, changes pitch, elides that misguided fondness, pheromone-driven, so far from the truth.

Observe—

The man dissecting a photograph. He blurs her face, twists the set of his limbs, makes them into strangers, a lunch into a coincidence.

Observe—

The man cutting into a video, splicing it with another, another.

Observe—

The man will not give up. Truth is subjective, reality interpreted with degrees of elision. All he needs to do is find the right one. All he has to do is show her, and she will come back. She has to. She needs to.

Observe—

The man turning a page. He plunges on.

# THE INFINITE EYE

## JP SMYTHE

We all saw the signs, all of us, stuck to walls in ways that seemed wilfully ignorant of the rules, but labelled with government stripes; that felt like a reason to pay attention to them. *Work*, the sign said, under a picture of what looked like a bird, but we all knew wouldn't be, or couldn't be. Slick with oil on its wings, a single eye of cool camera lens peering from the head. *Paid work, for real money. Ping here.* I don't remember how many of us activated the ping, because activating it meant finding a line of credit to use the machines, first of all, and then a working machine; or, easier – my route – persuading a stranger to let me use their persona. I wanted to get me a jump on the rest of them: the rest of them, with their gloves and their panting, their always panting. So I found a woman, and I said to her – I am charming, I know I am, or I was and I am, because that is not something that you lose over the time it takes to lose everything else – to allow me use of hers. She handed it over. She quivered, and I felt terrible. Nobody should be scared of me, who am I to be scared of? But I had done it by that point, and there was no taking back the look in her eyes, so I took the persona, pinged the number, and a message came back: an address, a time, tomorrow. *Be there*, it said. *What work will I be doing?* I asked the ping, but it didn't have a consc, so there wasn't an answer to be had. I thanked the woman. Persona back in her hand, and I thought, I like the feel of that in mine; the weight, the *heft*. I thought I would like to buy one of them, when I was back on my feet. The work, the real paid work, this would be a start.

I was told to go to a building far away from the camps, and I didn't even have the credit for the bus, so I was forced to walk. I woke up with the sun – I was good at that part of the day, always good, because the sun is opportunity and promise and constancy, and so are those three things it represents – and I walked. Hot tar on some streets. My shoes peeling. Three others from the same camp came as well, but we didn't talk to each other, because it was a race. You want to get to the destination first in case there's only the one job, and you don't want the others to see where you go in case they don't know the way. I knew the way, because I had been clever: I had gone to the underground before I went to sleep, and I had crept down the stairs and looked at the tube map when nobody was looking. I have a photographic memory, my mother used to tell me. I can remember anything from seeing it once, or being told it once. Mind like a steel trap. I would imagine snaring memories and wrestling them down, keeping hold of them, trapping them. I would read about jobs from back, way back, and I would think, I am perfect for that! I have the skills for that, because of what it needs. Before consces did those jobs, and we were asked, *Well, instead are you good with your hands?* I am not good with my hands. I have bad fingers. Broken fingers, lost finger, one fist that doesn't close properly even if I concentrate on it so hard it feels as if it has; until I look down, and there it is, fingers spread like the legs of an octopus, blood pumping into the hand and turning it sour-coloured red.

The building was a warehouse, used to be a factory, and there were spindles of wires running all off, coiled tight around the building, then in every direction, to metal poles planted in the street surrounding. More government tape and more signs stuck to places that signs should not be stuck: This is *temporary*. Then another sign above the door, handwritten. *Welcome*. You don't see wires in that part of London, not often. In the camps, yes. Everywhere, because they are what we have got. Hackjobs of everything. My coffee from a hackjob, my book on a hackjob. But not in that part. The area there was nice. Big buildings, but not many people. Perhaps it was too early, that day; or, perhaps, it is always like that. Always empty, because those buildings are either full all the time and you never see the people coming or going, or they are never full, because the people don't work in them any more. Hotdesking in, greybox headsets to virtual environments. That is what the adverts say makes modern life easier.

I knocked on the door. First one there, or last, and maybe the others were inside.

'Hello?' I said.

A man's face appeared. Bearded and wet-looking. His hair was pulled back. 'You're right on time,' he said. 'Are you here for the—'

'I saw the sign.' Maybe I said, I see the sign, because my English is better now. I have learned so much over the past few months.

'Oh, excellent. Excellent. Come with me,' he said to me, and I followed him. His shoes clicked like high heels. The floor was concrete; everything was concrete. I noticed, and he saw me. 'We're not up and running yet, not properly,' he told me, 'but the plan is that soon all of this will be polished and finished. People like their investments to look finished.'

'Of course,' I told him. And that is true. Everywhere, people like it to be tidy. This is why people hate the camps.

This is why the companies build the places outside the cities, why they put money into making it somewhere else. That politician said, *Out of sight is not out of mind*, and we cheered, because that's true.

'So, we're in here,' the bearded man said to me. A room with nothing but headsets, thick-set chairs with wide arms. Leather, or the plastic leather, the synthetic leather. I counted seven, but there were more than that. 'This is where the magic happens,' he said, 'or, you know, hopefully happens.'

'Sure,' I said.

'My name's Adam, by the way.' He shook my hand.

'Pietro,' I told him.

'Oh, cool,' he replied. 'Cool, cool, Pietro.' He said my name like it was a type of car. 'So, you're going to be sitting here,' and he assigned me to a chair in the middle of the room. 'First in the door,' he said, 'pride of place. There's a contract in the space when you first log in.'

'What am I logging in?'

'To the Eyes,' he said. He seemed like he was confused.

'What? Nobody explained the job. On the ping, there was no—'

'Oh, shit,' he said. 'Oh shit. Man, I'm sorry. I was sure that we had a consc set up, something must have gone wrong. Shit. Okay.' His hand ran over his head, coming off dry, but the hair stayed looking absolutely wet. 'So, okay. You know the city is, like, this... The cameras, and the drones?'

'Everywhere,' I said to him. 'They are everywhere.'

'Yeah, right? And the problem is, the consces don't work the way we want them to. When we hobbled them, that was what we couldn't get back. Don't give power to the things you don't want to have power, right? That's how the craziest shit goes down. So, yeah. Now the system's there, but it's kind of broken. Point a camera. Nothing deep learning about it, you know? You know, of course you know.'

'Of course,' I said.

'So we're thinking, what if we get people to do it? We spent years getting consces to try and mimic the human brain, but nothing can, right? Making brains. But: what if the brain – what if the brain *was* the brain?'

'I see,' I said, and he clicked his fingers.

'Yes, yes, exactly! *You* see. We see. We see everything, and we get what's worth noting and what's not. You're, uh, legal, right?'

'Absolutely,' I said. I had filed all my applications, over and over. I filed them, actual paper applications, into the right offices, and every time they made excuses. You need a home; you need to learn our language; you need a job. I got those things, because I had a home, I can speak English, and this was a job. Did it matter what the files said? If they were not checking, I was not checking. Maybe I was. Maybe I was approved, but I had no address they recognised, so they would not tell me.

Everything a maybe.

'Okay, cool, cool. So you sit,' he patted the chair, 'sit here, and you'll wear this. It's pretty self-explanatory. You'll be eyes for the cameras, for the drones. Assisting the police in catching people, finding crimes that are happening or going to happen, apprehending illegals. That sort of thing. You fly the drones, you watch the streets, you drive the cars. Everything. There's advanced stuff, persona-hopping and getting into home security systems, but you'll learn all that.

We've got jacks into—' He peered around the back of my head. 'You're not jacked,' he said.

'No.'

'We can install that for you. I mean, if you want. It's the job, so…'

'Yes, yes, of course.' I sat down. 'Here?'

'Sure, I'll get—' A buzz came from his wrist. I looked over, and something wriggled beneath his skin, glowing blue. Writing on the inside of his flesh. Somebody else was here. 'Hang on.' He spoke into his hand. 'Tell them to wait,' he said. 'I'm with Pietro at the moment.' He repeated my name: 'Pietro.' My name sounded like an aeroplane, waiting on a runway. Then he turned back to me. 'Sorry about that,' he said. 'Okay.'

The device in his hand was like a drill. Thick and dull blue, with yellow trim. To make it look nice and friendly, when it was boring a hole into your skull. A needlepoint lined with anaesthetic, and you did not feel a thing, they told you. He told me. He said it to me like he was reading it from a sheet, but he remembered it, because it was what you had to say. I had to agree to a verbal contract, recorded on the Jacker, because they were lawsuit-concerned. Everybody was lawsuit-concerned.

'Hold still,' Adam said. The feeling of release as it went into my skull was incredible. You don't realise, when the pain is gone, what it is like: having something escape, before being filled. When I was younger, when I was at home, we had a television channel called *Release*. People squeezing spots, white worms of pus leaving their heads. Sausages being made in factories. Blood being pulled into tight hypodermics. A parasitic creature being extracted from the skin of a journeyman.

Release, and then filled. Adam sighed. 'Done,' he said. 'Didn't feel a thing?'

'No,' I told him. My fingers crept behind my head and found the hole, a slight metal tinge; a taste of it, in my mouth, when I pressed it.

'Okay, so now,' he picked up the headset, 'this plugs in, and you'll be in what we call a greybox. Don't worry, it's perfectly safe in there. But you'll be disorientated. Takes a second. You think about moving, and you'll move. It's like here, like walking or whatever, but the software in the Eyes shuts down your physical functions. So you can do everything, but it's all virtually. Get that?'

I nodded.

'There are training apps in there, run those. Time is weird in there. Everything happens much faster when you're not interacting with the real world. That'll change, and you'll adjust, but there's no hesitancy. You don't need to eat or piss, you—'

'How do I...' I was hungry already, the rumbling of my stomach loud enough to hear. And I didn't need to piss yet, but I would. I am a regular pisser.

'We plug you in. We've got stuff. Don't worry about it,' he said. 'We'll sort that when you're under. It can be uncomfortable, but the software's got inhibitors.' He could see I was worried. 'Listen,' he said, 'this is a good gig. Seriously good. You're adept at this, this'll give you work for years and years. And good pay. We get past the trial, discover your skills, and we'll pay a lot. Stable, you know. You got a family?'

'Yes,' I said. I thought of them: of Sasha and Charlotte.

Then, I could see their faces.

'So, you'll get money for them. That's important, you know. I'm making assumptions, that's true. But, it is what it is. We've got good funding for this round of tests. This goes well, we'll get a lot more. And you'll be right here with us. Round one. Hell of an opportunity.'

'Okay,' I said. He grinned.

'Let's see what happens,' he told me. He patted the chair, and as I sat down, I could smell his hair: thick with something, like petroleum. He lifted the helmet and slipped it over the top of my head. 'Ready?'

I think I said that I was, but then it was on. I did not even feel the jack attach.

How long passed? How long was it, really? I do not know. For what felt like days, weeks, months, years, I did not see the real sunlight. I saw artificial windows, and I felt artificial sun on my face, stripping away the hairs that grew, the skin, the cells, until I was nothing but a skeleton of hardwired virtual bone; I saw endless training rooms, telling me about drones and cameras, about the law and the virtues, teaching me to inhabit these devices, telling me that, now, I was able to be a part of the city, a living, breathing part of something which, otherwise, stood back and watched the world happen around it, a character in everybody's story which had no agency, no control, until now; I saw the history of the city and how it treated people like me, and the problems that it claimed were so constant; I saw myself flying over virtual cities, torn from games, with people who looked real but whose eyes were hollow, who could never feel right because there is something missing when you look at them, no matter what their eyes do. *Inhabit this camera, and watch*, the software told me. *Wait until there is something worth paying attention to. Then switch to a drone, follow the incident.* The voice of the software was my own, piped into my head – only, in there, there is no sense of head, there is more a constant feeling of, what is the word, omnipotence; of being part of something bigger, and also of being so, so much smaller. There is a freedom that feels like the satisfaction after a meal, the satisfaction of a morning piss. When you let go, that is what it feels like to send your consciousness to another place entirely. To remove it from your body, and put it into a system that is welcoming to it.

I asked myself, in the moments I remembered the outside: how long has it been since you felt truly welcomed?

Training, training, always training. Endless training.

There are no clocks. There are no alarms.

There was a man on the street, looking up at the cameras. This is a giveaway. He was staring into the black for a moment, then his eyes darted away, as if to say, I am not looking at you. Trying to make that feel like it's natural. I glanced around, and there you were. But I saw him. So I tracked him. The trick is, do not move the camera. Keep it still, and they think that they have gotten away with it. Instead, I hopped to a drone a few rooftops over, in its cradle, flew that over the top of the buildings towards the man. I followed him down the street, where he looked nervous. So to the traffic cameras.

When you are good, adept, you swap so fast: look left, look right. Like crossing the road. Then came a car, darkened windows around the quietest of bodies, like all drug dealers drive. It stopped at the corner. I tried to get into the dash, but it had been blocked, which is illegal. Enough to pull them in. I sent a ping to the police, to let them know, and I kept watching. The drone was low enough to capture everything: the man on the street approached the car. His face was dirty, his clothes worn through in places. He came from a camp, would go back to a camp. He was always going to run when he heard the sirens. I was not after him. The man in the car: I pulled the drone back, to get his face. He passed something to the street-man. An exchange, a packet of something. I scanned for powder residues, and got a positive. The police were coming. He did not know. I hopped to the traffic lights as the car-man pulled his head inside his vehicle and raised the window he was leaning out of, and I turned the lights to *stop*. I watched as he was impatient, at first, tapping his fingers on the dashboard, telling the car – lip-reading technology let me know this – that he wanted a fast route back away from here, fastest with fewest lights, which meant he was suspicious; and then he jumped the lights, which was a mistake. I turned other lights to block his path. I followed him, hopping, soaring through the streets, using personal devices and cameras and birds and public transport to chase him, to keep an eye on him. The police came. Hop, hop, hop. I cleared the path for them, up ahead. I turned lights green and funnelled traffic off, and I kept darting back, watching the man in his drug-dealer's car, watching him terrified, because he knew that this was closing in on him: the city, me, closing in, fingers of a fist, closing tightly.

**>•<**

How many days was I there? In there? I was removed from the system every so often. *Remember*, my own voice said to me, spoken in synthesised ways that were nearly right but not quite perfect, not quite the, the syntax.

*Now try this*, my voice told me. And I would be inside a television, watching the people watching it, unable to see the programme, but able to see their faces.

**>•<**

I followed a truck from the motorway, come from the coast. British, but a food company who the records – highlighted for me, but not in words, more like a part of my knowledge that I suddenly understood – said had closed a year before. Out of business. A refrigerated truck, through the streets of London, towards a destination that the prediction software said was likely in the warehouse areas to the west of the city. I tracked them the entire way. I saw the driver from the camera in his dashboard: feet up, sleeping some of the way, waking only when the system beeped to tell him to make a choice of road. I followed him until he diverted. The roads, they were mine. The drones above, the drones on the pavements. Scuttling. Through the eyes of photographs and videos taken by tourists, there the truck was.

My attention was diverted. A shooting in a street, and I hopped there faster than I could even think; like a blink, and then I am there, right next to it. I turned my camera to watch it, and I saw a woman with a gun; another woman, police, lying on the ground, bleeding out. I'm sorry, I could tell the one with a gun said to the other. I am sorry. I watched them, and then I looked around, for backup. Another camera turned to look at me.

I was not in control. Somebody else was. There were no consces, and when I tried to get into it, I could not. I was blocked. Somebody else was in there.

I thought about myself in the chair, sitting, hardwired to the system. I imagined, next to me, another human being: wired in the same way. The same jacks. The same training. Their own voice in their head.

*Back to the truck*, my voice said. *This one is under control.*

I hopped around, finally finding the truck on a road that I recognised, that I understood. I remembered: I walked this road this morning. Was it only this morning? I walked to get here, to my new job, and down this exact same road. I recognised the tarmac, the pavement, the buildings.

I recognised the camp, at the end of the road. Where the truck stopped, and the back opened, and the people ran out. I was watching, and their faces were tagged. Into the system: these people are illegal.

How much time had passed?

I flew a drone around the camp, circling to see where I had slept. My bed was taken. The layout had changed. Everything moves so fast in the city.

Get out, I told myself. *You don't want to*, my voice said back to me. *Not yet. Think of the work that there is to be done.*

An alert. Go here, to do this. So I went there, to do that.

>•<

I was following a car that was fleeing from the police when I met the other drone. Not controlled by me, but flying along the same route as I was. In chases, in real chases, there is no sense in hopping. Staying high and constant is better. I was watching the car below when I saw the drone in front of me. We looked the same. The same slick-oil metal body. The same solitary eye. A focus, on me: I could see the lens of the camera tighten in close, then retract. It backed away, then forward. I moved closer. It blocked my way. There was a crime to follow, a chase to pursue. It stopped me. Then it moved, slowly. Backwards.

Lens tighten, retract. Beckoning.

So I followed.

>•<

I knew the building. I recognised it. The tangle of wires all around it, running from the roof to those thick, circular metal pipes that struck upwards from the ground. I understood the hum of being there: because now, unlike the first time, there was a reek of electricity. In the drone, I could feel it. There were no sensors, no nerves, but it vibrated through me. I could tell. Around me, around us, the air was charged. The signs that had been stuck up only that morning – not that morning, a morning, some morning – were replaced. A round symbol, an arcing loop, back onto itself. Infinity, or two eyes. Somewhere in between. On signs, lit up. Brushed metal. *No entry.*

The other drone circled around. There were no windows

in the building. I was sure that there had been before; I was sure that I remembered the glass. No light inside, not where they took me, but windows. Now, the place was boarded off. Thick metallic plates, like sheet armour, overlaid. The other drone continued around the building. There were no cameras here. Nothing to hop to. Nothing inside to be seen.

And then, a grate. A small grate, for the air inside. The drone looked into it, and then moved back, to allow me.

There was a bot in there. A cleaner. Checking for intrusives.

Hop.

A smaller body, a less powerful body. Slower, but it felt the same. I wasn't hampered: in all of this, I felt free. The feeling of hopping, like a purging. I trundled through the vents, spider-legged my way down towards the inside of the building. I could hear a voice. Adam's voice. Telling people to keep something cool.

'It's overheating. We need to divert—' I kept moving.

There I was, in my chair. Look at my frailty. Look at the lies.

There Adam was. No beard, now. No reveal of his truth, because he is his truth. He was not false, but he lied. Time had moved. No beard, and his hair was scraped back from his head, the baldness he had not fixed. His eyes beads in the darkness.

I tried to not look at myself from behind the grate, because I looked so sickly. I was there first; I was there longest. Around me, other people, and all were ill, all were sick. Naked, stripped down to bare; our skin exposed, sagging on skeletons, wires from our wrists, our necks, skulls lolling like broken flower-heads. Tattoos on the flesh, of my people.

Of the people that the city shunned and discarded. There is no room for you here; here, we have found you that room. Out of sight.

What is rage, when you are inside this tiny body? When you cannot do anything?

*Don't be angry,* my voice said to me. *There is still work to be done.*

>•<

When I retreated back to the grate, the drone who led me there was waiting. I did not know which of them, in that room alongside me, they were. I did not know, but they were in there.

I pushed the grate. I pushed my little robot body into it, and the other pulled at it with its wings, and then it was free. I hopped, into another drone.

Then inside we flew. Hurtling, down to the other grate. The other smashed its body through the metal, tumbling along the ground. Broken wings.

I felt so angry. I have never felt such rage. My family were separated at the borders of France, of England. My family were wrenched from me, and still, I have never felt such rage.

Its sparking body lay at the feet of a woman I had never seen before. Sparking, bursting into flames. The materials on the chairs catching fire. The woman's body burning, screaming, but I could not hear it. Lip-reading technology doesn't work on devices that do not need it.

They tried to stop me. Adam swatted the air, but I was adept. They had trained me. They did not shut me down in time. They tried, but I charged them. She did her part, as well; limping around, spreading her fire.

Adam fell, crawled, fled.

I found my body, and I flew. Delicate, tidy movements, around what was left of me. Cut those cables, those ties. The ones to keep me alive.

I wondered how long would I have after that before I died.

I kept her away from me.

Let me live. Let me do this one final thing.

I am outside. I am in the sky, away from the building. Beneath me, the building flickers with flames that will be extinguished, but not in time. My people – the eyes of the city – we know what has happened, now. We have seen it, and we are done. So I have a little time. Maybe not enough, but maybe. I do not know how long I can last: my pulse, my heart, my battery. How far can you fly, over the skyscrapers, the people on their balconies and terraces, their watching away from everything and accepting what they are told, and pretending that their lives are whole when there are so many gaps. Over the houses, and the families, and the river, into the countryside. *You should go back*, my voice says, but it is not my voice, so I do not listen. There is static in my mind, as the signal weakens. I know. It is like sleep: when you know you're going to sleep now, when you are dropping off, but you are still awake. When you hear yourself snoring, and you wake from that static with a shock. That is how this feels: over fields of green, and rivers, and towns. Faster, faster. If I had wings, I would beat them. If I had feet, I would run. If I were not so tired, and if I could not now hear these screams, coming into my head, into my ears – my real ears – and if I were not so tired. The sea, in the distance.

I tell myself: if I can only reach the sea.

If I can only.

# SAUDADE MINUS ONE (S-1=)

**IRENOSEN OKOJIE**

After being left at their pick up points, the boys from Batch Two of the US government's Camp Omega training unit felt the echoes of choppers shrinking to a quiet blue line inside them. All the same age – thirteen – they were dropped off in the latest cycle. Six boys deposited in the forgotten towns of Midwestern America one by one, on a bridge, an underpass or in an abandoned building used as a bleak refuge in the night, where the gargoyles of the city patiently watched for something golden amidst soiled mattresses, gutted cars, upturned rotted fridges.

Every Batch Two boy held a catapult. Waiting, their hands clung to their familiar reassurance.

On this morning, in this unnamed town, Elmira headed out to meet her new son. The sky was having an asthma attack manifesting as mist. She knew this would trigger her own attack but couldn't predict when it would happen. She never could. As she left the ranch she steadied her nerves, and trembling, callused hands, by rubbing them against the loose blue beads in her pocket she'd collected from a vision of a cornfield of sons strangling their mothers. They were small, miscoloured planets gathering momentum in their cotton gateway.

Her pick up point was the bridge over the river, decayed and moss-covered at the ends. En route, she passed the empty petrol station where the coyotes didn't even bother waiting till evening before making appearances. They gathered in clusters like a small, infected travelling colony. Some were greedily licking the nozzles of long dried petrol pumps, others prowling the counter, hopping on and off with stained dollar notes between their teeth, others taking turns to sit on freezers that stored the hum of long gone car engines. The coyotes prowled with the sounds of ignitions in their chests like second heartbeats.

Elmira passed a white church as its thick wooden door swung open from a gust of wind. She looked up. A hologram sat on the rooftop smoking a blueprint, holding a wailing cow's mouth in her other hand. She passed the school with no children, tempted by its rusted, black gates, pushing them back to feel their weight. As if that one action would release old scenes through the bars; a boy ripping the pages of an exercise book into the shape of a crow that didn't leave his Achilles heel, a girl whose breakfast consisted of slim pieces of chalk reduced to white dust in her chest, the pock-mark faced, nicotine-breathing maths tutor who slyly taught Hungarian to children that mimicked his mutterings at their dinner tables: *Hibas! Termeszetellenes, Nincs Isten!* Elmira left the gate containing its equally rusted memories.

She arrived at the bridge sooner than anticipated, knowing it was her desire to escape memories that caught her unaware in spaces that always deceived.

Her new son stood fiddling with his catapult on the bridge, the mist curling slowly to reveal him as if he'd been born to her thirteen years old, through a gap in the sky. Elmira couldn't help assessing how he'd feel in her arms, how many injuries he might accumulate during their time together, whether she'd be able to sketch them at night, if they'd sneakily reappear as visions in the days before they fully healed. She couldn't stop her heartbeat quickening, or her mouth slowly gathering mist like a new form of breathing. She abruptly pulled her hand from the pocket of her long, black cotton skirt and a few beads spilled out. She dived to the ground, panicked at the thought of losing them before her son.

This was their introduction; she scrambling after the beads, and the blue-eyed, auburn-haired, solemn-looking boy slowly raising his left arm, the characters B2 imprinted on it.

She wondered how long he'd been standing in the cold, the catapult in his left hand smacking against his thigh repeatedly at the same speed and angle. He was dressed in dark, ill-fitting clothes that didn't belong to him. She knew this by the way the navy shirt hung off him, by the slight bagginess of the fatigue trousers. She spotted the Omega emblem of a small tank on his left sleeve. She made a note mentally to check the government had paid the fee of $3,000 into her account for fostering him. Elmira wanted to say she had other clothes stored in her barn she thought might fit him. Clothes she laid out for parts of her visions to try on only for them to find them inadequate and fold away beneath bales of hay in case she wanted to feed them to her vision of the snorting bull falling from the lines of the roof. A split, hungry creature identified after it passed through fleetingly.

As she approached, he deftly stilled the catapult, an action practiced at intersections just like this for hollowed women like her with the same intent. A man, his face weathered, passed pushing a wheelbarrow of potatoes and engine parts. His hands were greasy. The squeaky wheelbarrow was a welcome distraction.

Elmira felt a heightened sense of her surroundings, and was struck by visions. Of the bridge being a stony path suspended beneath a changeable sky which coughed up these images of exchange. Of reward and half-formed devastations softened by murky rain. The boy shoved the catapult into his left pocket. The strap dangled out, not quite fitting. She worried her beads would spill again, to meet the strap halfway. As if that action of unspooling would be her early inheritance for him. The boy's forehead wrinkled. She was almost in his physical space now, imagining things being trapped inside his expression: a curl of smoke needing to get to a small fire, the last line of an anthem.

'What will you call me?' the boy asked.

'What name would you like?' Elmira was surprised by the sound of her voice. It was thin, cracked by the weight of expectation carried since early that morning.

'I like Houdini,' he answered, deadly serious. 'It's good for a boy like me.'

There was a flicker in his face, not quite sadness but the look of someone resigned to their fate. Bulbs of cold sweat appeared on Elmira's forehead. The river beneath them shimmered with the wayward angles of days to come, with the shapes of items caught in nets wrestling stray tides. Elmira thought of the night she had waded into the river fully clothed, clutching two coyote heads, trying to press their eyes against the moon. An impossible task, the heads had cried. She had left them in the water to travel, reappear as presents for somebody less fortunate than her. Afterwards, she dropped her wet clothes in the barn to dry. She ate beetroot naked at the kitchen table until she knew her tongue had changed colour.

'Houdini will do.' She responded finally, noting the azure colour of his eyes. 'What about the other boys in Batch Two? Did you know them?'

He nodded, watching her carefully as if she'd shrunk and he'd caught her in a tall tumbler trying to break the glass with her breath. 'We made catapults together. We did tasks to test memory capacity. They too have been dispatched.'

*They too have been dispatched.* She smiled. It was a funny sentence from a young boy. She tasted beetroot and coyote tears and pictured the boys of Batch Two falling between the spaces of those words, landing in empty buildings and derelict factories, talking with the countenance of adults to strange, parched women they would temporarily call mother.

She checked his head for patches or anything unusual, then ran her fingers over his teeth, rubbing the jagged molars on either side as though they'd reveal something.

He stuck his tongue out for inspection. She was relieved it didn't bear the blue stamp of a child damaged from too many cycles. She'd seen first-hand how such a child could malfunction in a new environment: the deadened eyes, an unwillingness to follow instructions, a regression in their training. She'd spotted a damaged child once, on one of the back roads of the town, repeatedly slamming an abandoned Buick door against his left hand, only screaming roughly two minutes later, a delayed reaction. She'd wondered how many delayed reactions he'd had, how often they'd occurred, the possibility of measuring their timings as if that would have changed anything. Then, he'd picked up a metal bar, smashing it on the car at a speed and rate that would have been impressive had such an endeavour been a sport. The boy unleashed the algorithm of destruction. The windscreen shattered. The boy didn't stop. That was a different time. She hadn't been able to control parts of her visions then, or the pain that wracked her body from a cycle coming to an end.

The flame-haired boy that stood before her now, calmly watching her movements, was not that boy. This was a boy from Batch Two, which she interpreted as progression, an advancement in training and ability. Less scope for malfunction. She imagined him misdirecting the feelings of belonging from a past cycle into the ether, speckled with shattered windscreen glass.

She said, 'Last winter three of my cows died from something in the river that transfixed them. They drank it. I think it's out again, loose on the ranch.' She rubbed her beads.

A flicker of a shadow passed over his eyes. 'I have the same dream of a dog chasing a yolk. The dog always wins.' He stared at her blankly. Repetition, an algorithm that diverted panic. She stopped rubbing her beads, somehow reassured. The boy was solemn, melancholy even, but she never could stand happy, boisterous children. Too much energy, too much optimism waiting to be broken down the line. His dreaming of dogs and yolks at night and her visions in the day meant they had something in common. Only she didn't know what it was yet.

That first evening at the ranch, Houdini discovered it was a home for stillborns brought to life with technology, that didn't grow past the age of one. They were Elmira's stillborns. She had allowed them to be experimented on as part of the government's Llewellyn programme which saw dead babies brought to life or live ones modified with mechanical parts, a combination of nature and scientific engineering. It was a grim way to save the ranch, money for small horrors who weren't definitively human. The residue of these experiments were kept at the far end of the barn: four large copper tanks, a broken operating table, rusted medical instruments in large jars and several dark green Yugoslavian gas masks dotted around like uninvited guests. The stillborns irises were bright blue. Thick, black wires sprang from their genitals like artificial umbilical chords. Their partially collapsed heads contained small, rectangular silver chips. Their remotely controlled mouths slackened unexpectedly, opening and closing to reveal miniature pits of darkness with teeth, but no tongues, sparking in the night. They hollered when he tried to pick them up, their small, concave chests housing circuit boards. He counted nine of them. Nine babies who technically shouldn't have existed. They were pulled to him by a silent undertow slipping between their limbs. They crawled up his legs, clutching handfuls of soil as offerings, and circled each other on the wooden floor of his room. It was a plain affair with only a creaky single mattress and a lamplight on the dresser next to Elmira's sketches of Noah's Ark, a vision within a vision, two of each animal.

He put three of the babies to sleep in the barn, perched on top of bales of hay and clothing they'd never grow into. The babies blinked up at him, chewing on electrical umbilical chords. The other six he placed in the large, empty copper water tank.

He stood watching their movements for several moments, the slow bending of their wires. He began to make the sound of gunshots, frightening them, remembering that Elmira had divulged she'd been feeding them pesticides. He increased the volume of the shots. The babies started wailing; the three fell off the bales of hay, landing on their backs, fists opening and closing. The ones in the tank began to smack their heads against it, eyes fully red. Houdini approached the tank. He placed his hand inside. One baby bit him. He filed each image away. He raised his arm up slowly to the light, watching for an injury that wasn't there.

The morning of their first full day together was bright, loaded with promise and sunshine. The ranch was a contained, ramshackle kingdom, spilling living stillborns from its cracks. The white patterns of planes in the sky drifted down to the empty pigpen. The soil smelled damp and earthy from a few days of rain.

Houdini's first task was to milk the restless cows. Elmira accompanied him, holding a small metallic bucket. Thick, dark afro curls whipped about her lean, toffee-hued face. A faint line of moustache graced her top lip. Her dimpled smile, when revealed, was infectious. She was beautiful, possessing the demeanour of a woman who had far more interesting things occupying her mind than notions of her own beauty.

When they reached the wide field that separated the two ranches, Elmira's and her neighbour's, the three cows lifted their heads at the sound of the bucket as if knowing what was to come. They stood in close proximity to each other. They stepped back, kicking their hind legs out, mooing loudly. The deep sound reverberated around them. Houdini was fascinated by their patchy black and white coats, their flaring nostrils, the bulk of them, and their heavy udders.

Intrigued by the flickers in their sad eyes, he observed carefully as if they too had fragmented daydreams inside them. Elmira clicked her tongue, approached the middle cow, and gently stroked its body, whispering Portuguese. After placing the bucket under its udders, she waved Houdini closer. He held a teat, tugging firmly. He tugged until blood spurted out, hitting the bucket at a diagonal angle. He tugged again: more blood. The cow groaned, wide-eyed and heavy with the burden of a vision that had taken root inside it.

Later, Houdini removed four stillborns who had found their way to the pigpen, crawling gleefully in the dirt. Two tried to slip through the gaps of the gate in the fence. He removed another two from Elmira's pantry, their mouths purple with beetroot. He temporarily fixed the gate, tying it closed with a long cable wire that had split. It offered its multi-coloured veins to those who crossed the entrance. He tried to think of a solution for the cows leaking blood, seeing fragments of the visions inside them splintering off into different afternoons.

By the end of that day, Elmira sat him down at the worn sandwood kitchen table. The babies crawled between them. The kettle whistled on the stove.

'Tell me about the other boys in Batch Two,' she said, clasping his shoulder with one hand, holding a bottle of pesticide in the other.

>•<

By their third week together, another vision of marauding gargoyles was loose on the ranch. Elmira had sketched it three days before, knowing its corners, and spilled her beads there. The gargoyles tore through the ranch leaving things in disarray. Houdini spent half a day fixing it all during an aftermath of silence.

They settled into a routine over the next few months. Every two weeks the stillborns had to be recharged, their wires connected to battery packs Elmira stored in the barn. Houdini helped Elmira sell her vegetables at the farmer's market on the weekends. He cleaned out the barn after the chaos of the babies, checked the cows, fed the alpacas, looked after the four horses, helped tidy the main house. He fed the one pig Elmira wouldn't kill. It refused to sleep in the pen and could often be found laying on the kitchen floor snorting into the night. If you tried to catch it, it deftly shot through the open kitchen door, pink, wily, in search of another patch to claim for the evening.

Sometimes, Houdini waved away the coyotes that circled the ranch in hopes of finding food or waste. They were bright eyed and knowing. Their cries ebbed away in the dark, companions to distant ancestors. Elmira was often holed up in her room at night, sketching or sewing oversized clothes for the babies, for visions she dared not name. In his memory bank, Houdini filed away the image of her body caving into tiredness, the sewing machine slyly attempting to sew her mouth while she slept, a cow's foot on the pedal leaking blood.

One night, Houdini sat on the steps outside the kitchen. The waft of blackberry pie still in the air, heat from the oven warm on his skin, the sky vast and unknowable, the stillborns mumbling at their wires that doubled as umbilical chords. He was thinking of the boys in Batch Two, wondering about their roles as sons, firing stones from his catapult into the night, when he spotted a figure in the distance. A man. His gait was confident, purposeful. He carried something in each hand: a kill.

A crack of silver shot across the sky, then another, rattling to cause uneven constellations, shaking the ranch's foundations. More cracks roared above. The cows headed for the barn. The horses fled to one outhouse. The pig shrieked. The alpacas ran to a second outhouse. Then the man was rushing from the claws of the night, passing the pen, the barn, the outhouses, onto the snaky path towards Houdini, whose catapult ceased coughing stones.

The coyote heads slipped through the catapult instead. This was how Calhoun burst into their lives, like Noah into Elmira's ark. Chuckling when he should have been scared, carrying two dead armadillos, a bag strapped to his back, spilling lightning from his mouth.

Elmira rushed down the hallway into the kitchen, holding a pair of scissors in one hand, a trail of checked red cloth in the other.

'What the hell is going on?' she asked, irritated at being disturbed, annoyed by the sight of a stranger in her kitchen.

'Wowee! It's lethal out there. I'm Calhoun, Cal for short. Just looking for a bed to call my own for one evening.' He laughed, like a man who'd just come off a rollercoaster ride rather than escaping the possibility of being struck dead by lightning.

Houdini loitered by the humming freezer, adding, 'He brought armadillos.'

'I can see that!' Elmira responded, still a little annoyed.

'Are you going to use those on me?' Cal asked, watching

Elmira's slightly shaky hands, the thick afro curls, the rhythm of her chest rising and falling, the hint of wildness in her eyes.

Elmira set the scissors on the wooden countertop. 'Give him a root beer.' She glanced at the armadillos on her table, dead-eyed yet staring at the light. A film of dust fell at an angle like a sprinkling of dirty stardust.

Houdini opened the freezer. Misty cold air wafted out in relief. He handed the bottle to Cal who peeled the lid off with his teeth before taking a long, slow satisfied swig. Cal was rumpled, craggily handsome, dark-haired and dark-eyed. Not quite skinny but not quite stocky either: a man of in-betweens. Elmira spotted the crescent-shaped red scars on the backs of his hands, like angry half-thoughts never fully formed.

Noticing her expression, Cal set the bottle down on the table and stepped back. 'They're from the chemical plant, the one behind the old shipping yard.'

'I thought they closed that place down,' Elmira said, shooing him towards the table as though directing one of her cows.

He smiled at her lacklustre hostess skills. 'Well, they open it now and again. A few of us got called back for work there. It's closed for several cycles so thought I'd follow the wind for a bit.'

'The wind is temperamental,' Elmira said, setting the long piece of cloth down, fishing a pair of red oven gloves from one of the drawers.

'I wouldn't have her any other way.' Cal rested his grey duffel bag against the table. His khaki shirt bore stains at the armpits. He grabbed the root beer and took a seat, settling back into the chair. He stretched his legs out, watching Elmira fuss at the stove as if he'd always done so.

'I'll help you fix the gate properly,' he added, a man used to bargaining when necessary.

Houdini, catapult in hand, took a seat too, at the head of the table. He pulled the catapult string back, smiling mechanically at Cal at the opposite end.

'I suppose you might want some blackberry pie with your root beer?' Elmira offered, spinning around, hands in gloves.

'I suppose I might.' Cal kneaded his neck. Then, he flicked the root beer lid he'd kept in his pocket right through the catapult, startling Houdini.

Houdini dropped the catapult against his thigh. He noticed the stillborns hadn't come out to greet Cal the way they did with him. He smiled at the thought.

The atmosphere was charged, although he couldn't identify why. It was like the day Elmira met him at the bridge. Only different. The night was full of possibilities; the armadillos might rise from the table to chase the chaos of lightning, the long trail of checked cloth fluttering between them all in a game of cloth, scissors, catapult, man.

>•<

Of course Cal stayed longer than one night. Damage from the lightning had lifted the main gate completely, tossing it several metres away. A meteorite shaped hole was left in the barn roof. The doors of two outhouses had cracks in them, as if unencumbered bolts had rattled through in search of items to destroy. The morning after, Cal surveyed the damage calmly, a cigarette smoking from the corner of his mouth. 'It could have been worse, young blood,' he commented.

Houdini was forced to trail him, since he and Elmira didn't know this stranger well enough. He stood by his side on the snaky path looking out into the distance. They listened to the sounds in the area colliding: a crow in panicked flight, horses galloping from another ranch. Gargoyles that had slept in the lines of the land emerged, with hearts floating in the darkness of their chests. Houdini sensed the arrival of a man who could outrun lightning bolts had somehow dented his and Elmira's existence at the ranch. He surveyed the scars on the back of Cal's hands discreetly, as if they'd have answers, somehow willingly betray him.

'The babies don't seem to like you,' Houdini said, as they walked down the path, a small note of triumph in his tone. Their footsteps crunched along the stones, top dog underdog.

Cal took a long drag from the cigarette before answering. 'Have you ever seen a pig in a wedding dress, young blood? A person might one day, if they drink enough of whatever makes them high. Just don't ask them what it is they're drinking or how the pig got into the dress.'

Cal fixed the gate and the barn's roof, filled the cracks in the outhouse doors. He built Elmira a storage unit for her sewing materials from leftover wood. Her bright cloths spilled like coloured, irrational waterfalls from the shelves. He cooked them armadillo in a dark, plum sauce. At dinner, he revealed he was the son of a Chippewa wanderer; tracking was in his blood. He told them contradictions in people shouldn't be curbed, that he liked them in his meals on occasion. Houdini watched Elmira's half smile linger, her eyes on those scarred hands that seemed useful for many things.

Cal took him whitetail hunting, surrounded by hundreds of breathing trees, their weathered barks silently communicating with the icy air. The cry of the odd hawk was a welcome interruption in large acres of woodland. In the distance, the lake glimmered. Reflections from its cold, watery eye fell on hard-trodden patches of ground, clusters of crackling leaves. Cal and Houdini hunkered down behind a tree, watching the deer ahead darting to and fro, pausing now and again to lower its head to the ground.

Cal blew breath on his fingers, curled and uncurled them in preparation. 'Keep still for now, young blood,' he said, voice a whisper. He removed the Remington shotgun from his back. 'Don't alarm the fella.'

Houdini stuffed a hand in his pocket, rubbing his broken catapult strap. Elmira hadn't checked on him this morning the way she had done on the bridge that first day. In fact, she hadn't checked him first thing for a few days. She seemed distracted, holed up in her room feverishly drawing the visions she'd birthed. He assessed the gun's length, its efficiency, its deadly nozzle: a weapon capturing the breathing of creatures scurrying in the background. As the deer reappeared in their line of vision, Cal raised the gun, aimed, fired.

The shot rang out. The deer stumbled in a short, drunken ceremony of death.

'Ha-ha! Come on.' Cal sprang up quickly. They ran to the deer. It lay on its side, bleeding from the neck, the light in its eyes waning.

'Don't fight it boy,' Cal said. 'You'll live again in some other way.' His tone was almost empathetic. 'Come on, help me with it.'

Houdini stretched his arms out. A hypnotised expression appeared on his face. He couldn't help lift the deer. Instead his arms moved back and forth, trapped in the same mechanical motion. He saw Elmira's head on the deer's body, spilling blue beads from her mouth.

When they arrived back at the ranch, the babies crawled out to greet them, circling their feet excitedly. Cal ignored them the way he always did. The deer's mouth was sealed shut with Cal's red scars from the chemical plant.

>•<

That night, watching them from the crack of her bedroom door left slightly open, Houdini found Cal and Elmira in bed. Their bodies were entangled, slick. Cal was breathing against her breasts, his hands on her rippling back. Houdini walked to his own room, crawled into bed unsteadily. Looking up at the white ceiling, he saw their bodies again. This time covered in plum sauce. The elements of images filed away had collided again. The plum sauce attempted to outrun Elmira's bright cloths, broken free from their cubicles. Elmira and Cal were not far behind, naked, hunting for the things they'd created. The last image he saw before closing his eyes was of Elmira pinned high up on the outside wall of the barn, almost touching the roof. There was a large, cavernous hole in her stomach, opening and closing sporadically. He and Cal climbed up the wall, he holding his broken catapult, Cal with his shotgun strapped to his back. When they reached Elmira, they took turns dipping their weapons into the cavernous hole. The sound of her sewing machine stuttered in the background, trying to sew without any material. They crawled into her stomach, transported to a night beyond it. Arriving to find they'd lost their weapons, the sky was raining milk. And the babies had grown to boys with wires as umbilical cords dangling from their backs. Houdini's final thought was that Elmira didn't need him anymore.

By the fifth month, Elmira was convinced Houdini had been displaying signs of anger. But how could that be possible? Yet she was certain. He hadn't helped her sell vegetables for weeks nor do errands in town she relied on him for. And she had been feeding the homeless who circled the ranch by herself, a task they'd done together. Lately, she saw why he called them coyotes as they pressed hungry wolf-like faces through the gaps of the fence, rattling the gates, darkened arms encrusted with dirt, hands outstretched, gaunt and hallowed. Once, she discovered one hiding in an outhouse, a gas mask on his face, Houdini using his catapult to fire stones at him, a gargoyle wrestling the mask off.

It was a warm June afternoon when she checked Houdini's room to find it empty. Her sketches of Noah's Ark had crosses on the animal's faces, holes cut out of their bodies. In her pantry, the beetroots were smashed, strewn all over the floor. Ill-fitting adult clothes for her visions, for her babies to play with, had been burned. Like mocking singed silhouettes thrown on the roof, the fence, in the pigpen.

He had malfunctioned.

She was sure of it. There was nobody to tell. Cal had disappeared two days before. Gone in the night because that's what drifters did, his blood mutated from working in a chemical plant. They held your nipples with scarred hands, fired a shotgun at their dreams to leave a glinting piece contorting in your chest, cooked lovingly to sell you an illusion. They built you things to soften the blow so that, one day, they would leave.

Elmira found the cabinet Cal crafted on the stairs, chipped and collapsed in parts. Her materials were gone. Her sewing instruments were left in the sink, silvery and inadequate in the unforgiving light of day.

Outside the gas masks were left on the path, ominous in the glare of light, as though they'd been secretly trying to breathe. Gargoyles took turns to put them on. Her bright materials were scattered around the undulating field, taunting the confused cows whose udders had ruptured. They groaned in agony while the rainbow cloths twisted, shifted and trembled like sly intermissions. Elmira raised her arms to comfort the cows. Tears ran down her cheeks. A spotted, purple cloth fluttered to a cow's face, blurring it momentarily, rendering it irrelevant. She realised in her panic she had missed something. She ran to the barn again. Shoved the door open with all her strength. They were gone.

She found all nine drones tied to the gate destroyed, wires ripped out, retractable heads smashed in. She screamed. Her babies, her drones which measured the health of her produce and made her feel safe on the ranch were defunct. Frantically she untied them, watching each one drop to the ground. The sound of the gate swinging to offload their weight reverberated. The drones shrivelled up into thirsty, misshapen visions. The pain in her head was so bad, Elmira worried it would crack in two, a garish gift for the afternoon. She reached for their wires wilting in the hot air. A note from Houdini was pinned to the gate that read:

*Gone in search of the yolk from my daydreams.*

Houdini had been walking for exactly twenty minutes when he reached the school. A few memories flooded in; returning two cans of violet paint to Ed at the hardware store because Elmira had seen the bodies of homeless people fading in a purple room, holding rusted medical instruments, the bi-monthly horticultural meeting at the former gas works, the pop up saloon they'd built for the spring fair with other members of the town's steering committee, Elmira laughing and serving drinks from the saloon to groups of people gathered around. Houdini detonated then. The blast from his body wrecked the school, the church, the petrol station; killing the coyotes living as street kings, shattering surrounding factories and houses.

There was nothing left of him, as intended.

In the small, forgotten towns of Midwestern America, mirrorings of this occurred as the other five boys from Batch 2 detonated. Just before, a series of identification numbers inside them flashed: X2467A, NZT452, K4734, Y67429, P124XKW. Then the word *ESCALATE* glowing amber.

Their mothers for this cycle were left bereft. They stood on bridges or underpasses, in the doorways of abandoned buildings and ranches, howling about blue-eyed, robot bombs who doubled as their children. They undressed, frightened by what the next rotation of children would bring, willing to be impregnated by the damaged gargoyles of the land instead.

# MARCH, APRIL, MAY

## MALCOLM DEVLIN

If you follow the thread all the way back to the beginning, the reason April disappeared is because she didn't update her profile picture on The Space.

>•<

After the news of the bomb in Skopje was approved, shared and disseminated, the rest of us updated our profile pictures to include the little flag in the corner to show our support. We posted brief comments or clips expressing our disgust with the perpetrators, our sympathy for the victims. Our feeds filled with the same sentiments from the usual people and we diligently liked and shared each in turn. For a period of twenty-four hours, The Space became a memorial wall to people we had never known.

It was such a little thing to do, but it was how these things were done.

April didn't use The Space like that, she never had done. She had principles, she'd tell us whenever we'd ask her. She had her *own* principles. She would use The Space as she damn well pleased.

For as long as we could remember her profile picture had been the same. A photograph of a maneki-neko, its beckoning right-paw crudely animated in four looped frames.

'I don't update my picture to represent any platform,' she would post by way of explanation. 'And I mean *any* platform. I never follow any company, I don't even follow the one I work for. I don't *like* anything that'll just serve me ads. That's not what the verb "to like" means.'

It was true. Sometimes, after she'd spent one of her posts

tersely restating her position, we'd tab through her profile to see only that prim little system message reporting that 'April2063 has not liked anything yet. Why not suggest something they might be interested in?' That was The Space for you, always looking for new ways to encourage its users to sell each other out.

The rest of us each have pages and pages of things we've expressed some sort of interest in, through love or loyalty. April had no companies, no celebrities, no movies, no shows, no games, no breeds of puppy, no public landmarks, no fad diets, no motivational quotations or sentimental song lyrics. When we asked her what her company thought about her decision not to follow them, she'd retort with an illustration she'd made herself: An old fashioned factory in the rough shape of a fist, its red-brick chimney, a raised middle finger spewing black smoke.

April used The Space as she damn well pleased. At least, she did until she disappeared.

Of course, when we say that April disappeared, we mean that she died.

We would never post anything to suggest that, though. It would be far too negative and people don't like negative posts on The Space.

Sometimes, we look up April's profile as though it might count as a pilgrimage of sorts. We search for her in the feed and note how, as the weeks roll by, her name drops further and further down the list of all the Aprils in the world, ordered by points of connection, activity, status, inception date. But we still visit her profile just to make sure that, in some respects at least, she's still here.

Sometimes, when we're offline and enduring a restless night, we might turn to look at the soft blue disc of the nearest Interface pulsing gently in the dark.

'Listen,' we say, and we watch as the disc widens a fraction in response.

'I'm listening,' it replies, tone neutral.

We ask it to read out April's most recent post and it diligently complies. April never did choose or record a voice for her profile, so the Interface defaults to a flat robotic drone that flattens her sarcasm, making the final words something bitter and morose.

No one liked or commented when she first wrote it, so the post stands like an epigraph, four months old now, alone and unadorned. Sometimes when we re-read it, we wonder if we're looking for a clue to confirm what happened to her, and then we shut down the page and purge our search history, so we can pretend that no one will know we were there at all.

>•<

'Fuck all of you,' the last post says. 'I'm going on the march. I'll see you fucking lemmings on the other side.'

>•<

It's not that we don't care. We all miss April. She always came up with the funniest things to share and disseminate. She was an illustrator. Possibly professionally, we thought, or at the very least, she was a mash-up artist. She'd mix up footage from the newsfeed and make it glorious and obscene. She had a weakness for awful wordplay. Sometimes she'd just write small essays about current affairs, and that was unusual in itself. People don't really like posting about news on The Space. Partly because so few people react positively, partly because they fire up the spiders – those little algorithms that rank articles based on their factual veracity, then weigh the opinions within them and display their found bias in a series of unambiguous icons. Like much about The Space, they're useful – they're important, in fact – but they're prim and distracting. More importantly, they've never been capable of adequately differentiating reality from satire, so almost all April's posts were appended with humourless little cautions.

'Warning: This content is untrue,' they would say, and we'd ignore them because April was funny and clever and far more entertaining than The Space seemed to be comfortable with.

More often, her posts weren't political at all, although she still found ways to test the patience of the algorithms and make them clutch their pearls. Remember when she went to ridiculous lengths to argue a theory that Joseph Conrad's *Heart Of Darkness* is actually about man's search for the clitoris? 'He follows the forbidden river through the darkest jungle so he can agitate the bald guy in the canoe.' She illustrated that one with screen grabs from Apocalypse Now, and whatever you're imagining it was so much worse, and so much better.

'Warning: This content is untrue,' the spiders said, blithely tagging the anatomical photographs with the term 'Marlon Brando' anyway. They triggered a poll based on April's use of flagged keywords.

'Quiz:' the message said. 'Do you find this content offensive? Yes / No.' The bars in the results chart were weighted to 'Yes', so we all diligently clicked 'No' until their dimensions reversed.

>•<

Kai says, 'April was a troublemaker.'

Mako says, 'Everyone likes a troublemaker when you know they're on your side.'

Billy K says, 'Troublemaker TM are the best profile consultants in the worlds. Update your profile on The Space and earn $$$.'

'Pipe down, Billy,' Mako says. 'The real people are talking.'

We all like that. Even Kai.

>•<

April worked with images and spent a lot of time on The Space, because that's where most images end up in one way or another. Everything uploaded by the users of The Space is tagged and stored, and if you decide that you want to include an image with a post you can search through everything that's been uploaded so far. You can add filters and text to them, or you can animate them with the tools provided. You can turn them into little movies or cartoon strips with speech bubbles. Every image uploaded is usable within The Space with no strings attached for users. Corporations can pay a subscription to use them in their own publicity work. It's funny seeing our own photographs served back to us as ads.

The trouble is, you have to know what you're searching for, and this was something that fascinated April.

'I don't think it means to,' she posted once, 'but The Space is defining how we see things.'

There are algorithms to recognise faces and brand marks of course, but it extends further than that. It uses the way the images are tagged by users to identify everything else. It's one of those recursive AIs that appears to get smarter the more data we feed into it. It grows in confidence with every image it devours. As the data accumulates, it stops asking coy questions like 'Is this is an apple?' and it starts simply tagging all the apples it can find, putting the onus on the users to point out where it's gone wrong. Then it starts subdividing, evolving its categorisation from 'Apple (type?)' to 'Apple (Braeburn?)' to 'Apple, Braeburn' and deep diving into the unexpected world of difference between little misshapen circles of reds and yellows and greens, spotting half-peeled stickers on their skins and making educated guesses about what they are.

'The problem is perspective,' April said. 'And perception. The problem is also perception.'

She argued that the majority of users of The Space were earthbound, and most of them were from the US, and so the terms were all grounded and all old, and all American. You could search for a "house" but you'd only see pictures of

American houses, suburban low rises, inner city mansions, even those distinctive large colonials from the South, which must have all been flooded out by now, and which you only see in old movies. You could add modifiers to the search to drill down further, but to The Space, "houses" were of an American, earthbound design by default; everything else was secondary. The problem was exacerbated by the translation software The Space used, as well as the spell checkers and autocorrect functionality.

'And try searching for "woman",' April said. 'They're all white, they're all young, they're all beautiful. Look up "men" and "kids" too. Same thing. We're teaching The Space how to see and because we aren't paying attention, we've already got it wrong.'

It's common knowledge that all contemporary camera equipment is connected to The Space, so any photographs you take through your Interface or your Implant will be tagged automatically – date and time, location, subjects, objects, weather conditions and so on – and the information is stored and catalogued in the metadata, but older images are still adaptable.

To demonstrate, April posted a picture of a curious object and asked us to identify it. It was a tightly bound spiral of yellow plant stalks forming a twisting geometric pattern. It resembled a short, curving staff, tied off with a ribbon.

'It's a corn dolly,' April said, once all the jokes about how phallic the object looked, and all the automated warnings about offence, had been dismissed. 'It's a charm they used to make in villages in Britain and Europe around harvest time. There are different designs in different parts of the country. Now try searching for a picture of one on The

Space. *Corn dolly.* Go on. See what you can find.'

We found pictures of corn; ears, cobs, bales, fields. We found pictures of red-cheeked children's rag dolls. We all found the same handful of pictures of the two things together. Nothing matched the image April had shown us.

'Do you see what I mean?' she said. 'This is something The Space has no understanding of. It's old. It's from the wrong culture. The Space's language doesn't extend this deep. It's an obsolete image, making the history obsolete as well. No one will search for this term if they only understand their world from The Space.'

She proposed an idea.

'Let's see if we can teach The Space something new.'

'We all need to see new spaces,' Billy K said. 'Has anyone considered a vacation somewhere less earthbound?'

April had a number of pictures of corn dollies of various designs. No one asked her where she got them. She uploaded them all into a folder and asked us to download them ourselves, tinker with them so they weren't quite the same file, then upload them.

'Let's tag them all with something they're not.'

She asked for suggestions but was dissatisfied with the flippancy of our answers. We needed something less obvious, she told us, something that was no longer in common use.

'Spitchcock,' she said. She'd trawled some distant group dedicated to unused, old vocabulary. 'It's already archaic. It means a way to prepare eel before it's cooked. Split apart and then grilled.'

'Eel?' we said. 'Eww,' we said. No one ate eel anymore, no one that we knew ate eel anymore. The implication was that the word had been orphaned, that it no longer had meaning; but April was right, it certainly *sounded* as though it did.

So we all uploaded the pictures and we tagged them dutifully. Over the next few months, spitchcock slowly became a word and the corn dolly slowly became a spitchcock.

'We've hijacked the language of The Space,' April said. 'There's a precedent for this, of course. The meanings of words are often rewired with new cultural meanings. Look at the history of words like "thug" or "terrorist". Once upon a time, a theatre owner in Dublin made a bet that he could introduce a made-up word into the language. And he did. Plastering it all over the city until the public themselves supplied a definition for it. And it worked.'

We asked what the word was.

'Quiz,' April said. 'He invented the word "Quiz" in the eighteenth century. Spitchock is today's quiz. You'll see.'

And it was true. The algorithms spidered through our posts, our wikis and our public and private conversation, only a little of which we had manufactured ourselves. It assembled a definitions page, populating it with sources as it usually did when it found enough disparate examples of a tag, enough uses of it in conversation. It juggled the conflicting meanings it ascertained from our discussions of the prank and the faked definitions and usage cases we'd written, weighing one against the other. It illustrated the page with the photographs of April's corn dollies and quotations about its definition we had seeded. The information it had about the spitchcock exceeded that which it had about corn dollies, and so the one subsumed the other.

April shared the results proudly.

'Ladies and gentleman,' she announced. 'In an act of defiance against the system, we have invented the wicker dildo. Viva la revolución!'

'Quiz: Do you find this content offensive?' said The Space. Of course we didn't, we were elated.

>•<

Some of us think that April died of a hidden health problem that she never posted about. Everybody else posts about their health on The Space. Every checkup, every medication, every minor flutter of concern. Symptoms are crowd-sourced and discussed before the expensive medical AIs are consulted. It goes further than that. Blood sugar and blood pressure can be recorded directly through our wearables or Implants. Everybody's heartbeat pulses beneath our profile pictures – even Billy K's. Notifications can be sent to the nearest registered health authorities if anything irregular occurs, and your health provider's brand logo will show up when you're being treated.

There's a tab on the profile page that displays everything else, every user reduced to a page of statistics as though they were a character generated for some sort of role-playing game.

April never had a wearable, she certainly never had an Implant. Some of us think she must have done, but she clearly never used them. That flatline beneath her maneki-neko had always been a point of pride for her.

Some of us wonder if something else happened. We hear things like that from time to time. On The Space itself we don't believe them, but in private, when we're alone, asleep and disconnected, sometimes we think that maybe we do. Stories of people going missing, people dying, people getting locked in a white-walled room until they understand. They're only stories of course, leaking through the gaps like campfire tales. And when we wake, we purge our dream history, so we can pretend that no one will ever know.

Of course, when we say that April died, we mean that April was downtimed. Death on The Space can be such a transitory, embarrassing thing, usually caused by network failure or hardware malfunction. A page that hasn't been updated for a certain amount of time might be considered dead, a group with minimal activity might be considered dying.

April's access might have been restricted because she contravened the terms of service. Some of us were certain she worked her way through the terms, figuring out ways to upend the system in a way that would have made her laugh. Everything would have all been restored if she'd just waited them out with the appropriate contrition, but April used The Space as she damn well pleased.

One of the founding ideas behind The Space was that it was borderless. Our location is recorded in our profiles, as are background and family information including religion, race and so on, but none of it is broadcast anywhere and posts admitting such details are often deprioritised, meaning that no one really sees them. We can add messages in our native languages and dialects and The Space will translate what we say for everyone else, so we can talk with each other as though we're all in the same room. It's not perfect, but with the usual erosion of online syntax and grammar, it's harder and harder to spot the seams. You *can* generally guess where people are in the world by the time stamps, you can also guess who's earthbound and who isn't, but even that isn't entirely infallible, some friends we had assumed were on the other side of the world from us had simply adjusted their own time cycles so they could match others in The Space. People do that, more than you might expect.

It's one of the reasons that – in the early days at least – outside the broadcast reports from approved news sources, talking politics was never really encouraged on The Space. It's such a localising factor, and that's something The Space has been trying to avoid from the outset. It's ridiculous to expect everyone else to like something that's simply not relevant to them. But every now and then something blows up and it's impossible not to react.

*Borderless.* It sounds strange, but it's one of aspects that first sold The Space: 'Everyone is a native of The Space,' the early publicity literature said. 'Everyone is welcome, everyone is included.' The assumption was that everyone would leave their current suite of worlds behind and forge new ones where gender, race and class were largely irrelevant. Ones where it didn't matter which corner of the universe you were stuck in, where everyone would be of the same status.

For the historically minded, it was the promise of the early internet resurrected and dusted off; it had been a naïve promise when first used on antique IRC chat boards and ancient virtual worlds, and it was no less so now. You don't eradicate cultural differences and points of view by simply pretending they don't exist. But The Space adapted, barrelling on with a good-natured belligerence, a sheer charismatic self-belief that it might make the world a better place simply by pretending the bad things didn't exist anymore.

>•<

The bomb in Skopje killed five people and injured sixteen others. It targeted a network relay to the south, and as a result connection in the immediate area slowed to a crawl for a good three hours thereafter. The news leaked early in the afternoon, with witness footage and testament trickling through the peripheries of The Space, but no one posted or shared anything specific about it until the fact-checking algorithms had approved the incident as news. Now there were pictures, now there was video footage. Witness interviews, commentary, grave concern.

It was shocking, and we were all over it.

Up came the Macedonian flags on our profile pictures like the sun was rising up on each of them, up came the condemnations, the sympathy, the concise, calibrated outrage.

As usual, one of the Neo-Luddite groups claimed responsibility. The Disconnected perhaps, or maybe The Unplugged. They were mostly interchangeable and their slogans were similar: 'Break The Space', 'Freedom is Individual', 'Log Off, Wake Up, Tune In.' They thought The

Space was too big, too unwieldy, put too much data and information in too few hands.

April didn't update her profile picture. Her maneki-neko waggled its paw, four frames at a time, still unadorned.

'Is anyone reading this actually from near Skopje?' April said. 'Or does anyone have family or friends there?' The tone of the post was sceptical, off-putting, and it remained unanswered and unliked until she followed it up with a longer piece later in the day.

'I ask,' she said, 'because these strike me as conditioned responses. A reflex to a certain type of news. I don't doubt anyone's sincerity, but unconsciously, we're teaching The Space to anticipate these sorts of responses in reaction to news like this. Are we afraid not to be seen posting our condemnation? Are we afraid The Space will discard our posts if we do? Is this a cycle of behaviour that's being taught to us?

'We're tagging images of atrocity. *This* is what we're teaching The Space to understand.'

Later still, there was another post.

'Whenever one of these incidents is reported,' April said, 'I've never had any direct connections to the places in which they happened. I don't doubt that *something* happened, I don't doubt that people were hurt and killed, but I do find it strange that whenever these things occur, everyone only says how upset they are and no-one says "I saw this, it happened near me." or "It happened to a friend of mine." I don't know. The Space is supposed to bring people together but, at times like this, I've never felt so isolated.'

Again, there was silence, and the post dropped down our feeds, its weight giving it a brisk velocity as it sank out of view.

Some time later she posted a third comment.

'Last year, I met someone at a family thing offline. I'd gone home for the holidays and there was a relative, one of those ones I rarely meet. They're on The Space somewhere, but we're not connected here. They asked about a bomb that had gone off in London. Neo-Luddites again. Only I never saw anything about that here. It didn't show up in my feed at all, I went back and searched. I even looked at some of the ext-news sites, but I didn't see anything.'

Some of us answered, but only briefly. There was the usual suspicion of the bias of ext-news sources, and some of us saw the seeds of another one of April's pranks and we were wary of finding ourselves in her crosshairs. There was the question of taste as well. April had skated close to the line in the past, but she had rarely seemed cruel, rarely personal.

Some of us took her to task. Gently, but firmly.

'People died, April,' Mako said. 'Have a little respect.'

That got a lot of agreement, far more so than April's original post.

'Too soon,' said Kai. 'Way too soon.'

We could hear April bristling as she replied to each.

'I know people died,' she wrote under Mako's comment. 'I'm not disputing that. I'm just doing what I've always done. Questioning how these images are being categorised. Questioning what we're shown. Questioning who is teaching what to whom.'

'It's not about you, April,' someone said, but April had already moved on to answer Kai.

'Too late,' she wrote. Which despite everything, a lot of us liked. It sounded like the old April after all.

>•<

We once asked April about her profile picture. It had been the same since she first joined The Space, and she had been there longer than most.

'It's an image that everyone knows,' she said. 'Even those with no real understanding of its origin recognise some aspect of it. To them, it's a cat, and some others might know it represents good luck. You see it in shops with its paw beckoning people in off the streets. But in most western countries, the image coding – the way different cultures interpret it – is different. With the paw turned outwards, it is assumed to be waving, not beckoning.'

We liked that, although sometimes we wonder if all of us knew why. It sounded like April being April, and sometimes that was enough.

>•<

Some weeks after April was downtimed, Kai posted a witness account of his own.

'The London bombing,' he said. 'The one April said she didn't believe happened? It did happen. I didn't want to post anything before because I didn't want her to turn on me. You know what she's like when she gets a bit between her teeth. But I was there.'

It was a strange admission on Kai's part to admit a physical location and it was a surprise to see the post hadn't been deprioritised. Nevertheless, Kai plugged up a handful of animated images to demonstrate. A burnt out building, a bloodied face, a blurred crowd of onlookers. He posted a sound file recorded from his phone. Sirens.

'She was wrong,' he said. 'And if she was wrong about this, then she was wrong about the rest of it as well. I'm not saying I'm happy she's gone, but we can't forget she was wrong about this.'

We didn't really respond to that. In truth, we all remembered that time when April had accused Kai of being a bot like Billy-K.

It had been some years ago. He'd got ridiculously angry, it was funny at the time.

'Bots are idiots,' he'd said. 'Look at Billy, he just witters on and on. He doesn't engage with anything.'

'He's also smart enough never to like or comment on anything that might be seen as contentious,' April had told him. 'He's smarter than you give him credit for. Billy's *supposed* to be obvious. He's not there to sell us shit, he's there to make us underestimate how smart the real AIs on The Space are.'

It was probably only a joke, but still.

>•<

Of course, when we say that April was downtimed, we mean that April was disconnected.

The one leads to the other, we assume. A disconnection is a long-term downtime. Death has the chance of resurrection; disconnection is more damning. April didn't post anything else, she didn't respond to anything else. Some of us tried calling her directly through our Interfaces.

'Listen,' we say, 'call April2063. See if she's okay.'

The blue disc flutters momentarily before replying. 'No

response,' it says. 'Would you like to leave a message?'

We don't say anything and the Interface times out, its light contracting and pulsing and not going anywhere at all.

>•<

April wanted to go on a march.

'We should do something visible,' she said. 'Something big and obvious that would be impossible to ignore.'

Many of us agreed with her, the way she framed it made it sound exciting, although with hindsight we suspect it was likely because we didn't really understand what she was asking. In some ways, we assumed she was doing another one of her pranks and the idea appealed to us. If nothing else, it was a way of getting the old April back. And so, we wheeled out the usual activist tools. The one-click petitions, the proforma letter-of-dissent generator, the one which lets people tag their location in a certain place at a certain time creating a virtual rally. There was a VR simulacrum that we could all log into at the same time.

April had other ideas.

'We have to take this offline,' she said. 'We have to do more than just say how sad or sorry or angry we are. We have to take this off The Space and see if The Space records it at all. In one way or another, the Space is lying to us. It's hiding things from us. It only shows us what it wants us to see. What we need to do is make something it can't ignore. It's how people used to do things. We should do this resolutely old-school.'

Her message was greeted with bewilderment. No one liked it because no one really understood it.

'We're not all in the same place,' Mako said. 'We're not even all earthbound. We don't have the licences. We don't have the paperwork. How much money do you think we have?'

'So we gather where we are,' April said. 'Local groups, local noise. The same thing everywhere. And if you're only online, promote it, share it, pass it on to those who aren't. The Space is all over the place and so are we. We all make the same statements in each place: The Space lies. If The Space's news aggregators are worth a damn, they'll pick up each incident and correlate them.'

'You sound like the Neo-Luddites,' Mako said.

'They're bogeymen,' April said. 'Look at what they do and ask if it makes any sense to you. They're cartoon villains.'

'They're terrorists.'

'Perhaps. Maybe. Whatever that means.'

'Is that what you want us to protest?'

'This isn't a protest,' April said. 'It's a statement. We're *testing* the news. It's the same as the spitchcock thing. If enough of us do this, if enough of us talk about it, then The Space will have to approve it and disseminate it.'

'You want to make news?' Kai said.

'I want to test the metadata that The Space will apply to the news.'

None of us replied to that. It all sounded a bit much, even for April. Some of us started looking up the terms of service, others hunted around to see how legal such gatherings were offline.

And like most things offline, it all just seemed so impractical.

We prevaricated and April's post drifted down our feeds,

spiralling out of sight. In its place came the usual welcome distractions of The Space, the gossip, the jokes, the give and take, the swelling tides of the world around us, and we fell for them all with blessed relief.

April wouldn't let it lie. She started posting images from the recent bombing and tagging them with 'Skopje'. Then she went further, posting images from earlier atrocities she found on her news feed. Each one, she tagged in the same way. 'Skopje. Skopje. Skopje.' None of us said anything, and so she kept going. Photograph after photograph after photograph.

She posted more and more about the march as well, as though none of us had expressed our concerns at all. She was doing her own research. She picked a date for the end of May and everyone received invitations, insistent little reminders bouncing in their inboxes. She investigated the best ways to travel for those earthbound and otherwise, the best routes to take, the most visible places to protest. She assembled a document investigating how to get together in different parts of the worlds.

Most of all, she posted pictures she had found of protest marches from the past. Vertiginous seas of human figures holding placards and flags and banners. Again, her tagging was subversive.

She started posting the same picture over and over again. A black and white image of a mob of people from the late twentieth century, it looked like it had been scanned into the system from something analogue and the resolution was too low to get much more sense from it.

'Truth,' April tagged the image the first time she posted it. 'Violence', she tagged it the second. Then, 'Hope',

'Insurrection', 'Love', 'Anger', 'Community', 'Disloyalty'.

You would not believe how many pictures she posted like that.

We let it go. All of us, we just let it go and her audience thinned and then dried up entirely. Someone posted April's profile picture and tagged it 'asshole'. We ignored that as we ignored April's posts. They weren't inspiring, they weren't funny, they weren't even offensive; they were just tiresome. No one liked her posts, no one thought to engage with them, and so they simply came and went, flashes of April's eccentricity, flickers of her mounting desperation drifting southbound and away out of sight.

We knew it was inevitable that The Space might get involved at some point. It was a place designed for the back and forth of communication, so it was no surprise that a single voice shouting alone would raise a flag somewhere in the system. In its own benign way, The Space saw a problem and it tried to deal with it in the simplest terms.

'Fuck all of you,' April posted. 'I'm going on the march. I'll see you fucking lemmings on the other side.'

'Quiz:' the Space said, 'Do you find this content offensive? Yes / No'

Not all of us said yes. We were April's friends. We didn't want to be the ones who didn't understand her, we didn't want to be the ones who pushed her away.

To those of us who didn't say yes, there was a follow up poll.

'Quiz: You have not liked any of April2063's interactions on The Space since Thursday 24 May. Do you wish to see more? Yes / No'

Not all of us said no.

We don't know how the figures work inside The Space. We don't know how many users it needs to poll before it makes a decision one way or another. In its own terms, it's simply curating our feeds, personalising them, making them more relevant to our individual experience. Enough of us must have said "no" for April to be disconnected.

>•<

Of course, when we say April was disconnected, we don't really mean that at all.

>•<

At first, the silence from April's corner is strangely welcome and even those of us who voted yes say we feel as though the atmosphere has lightened a little, as though things have returned to how they once were. That is how it felt back then. It feels as though normality has been reconstructed around the absence April leaves behind. We continue with our lives on The Space as we have done before, the only difference is the lack of new things from April, new pictures, new stories, new animations and videos. On the day of the march, we each watch the news tabs with interest, but nothing is approved, nothing is reported, nothing is shared.

'Well what do you expect,' Mako posts. 'The Space lies, right?'

None of us are sure if that was a joke or not.

Privately, we each wonder if April has done what she had always planned to do. Even without her audience, we can't imagine she would have demurred. We picture her somewhere, dressed up tightly against the smog, waving a board with some idiotic pun written on it, and shouting, shouting, shouting.

Offline April is a stranger, sadder creature than the one we knew.

Someone makes a cartoon of the scene, like April would have done, but no one can agree what April actually looks like. Billy K is the first to like it. He says something about selling prints with a very reasonable commission, it's nonsense of course but it feels as though it gives us licence to talk about her. A signal that it's safe for us to breathe again.

'I had a dream last night,' Mako says. 'I saw April's maneki-neko sinking into the sea. And its paw was waving in the jut-jut-jut way it did. And I thought, it's not waving, it's not drowning, it's *beckoning*.'

Kai says, 'Perhaps April was the bot after all. Maybe not always, but maybe recently, The Space just shut her down and replaced her account with a bot. She was an algorithm testing our loyalty. It engineered its own dissent to see which of us was weak enough to follow.'

We laugh at that. *Dissent*! It's only The Space, we say. The idea is preposterous. It would be like rebelling against a kitchen appliance.

'She contravened the terms of service,' Kai says, 'What did you think was going to happen?'

And mercifully, he leaves it at that. It all feels far too negative and people don't like negative posts on The Space.

*The Space lies.*

We don't post that, of course we don't. But we do think about it more than we should. Thinking, dreaming, the only places where The Space can't weigh us up and determine how best to serve us content, how best to personalise and perfect our experiences.

We look at April's profile when we pretend that no one can see us looking, and although we see it is unchanged we wonder how it looks for her. None of us doubt she is still online, but we do wonder who, if anyone, perceives her anymore.

Is she still posting regardless?

Is she still being April? Posting images, jokes, mash-up videos, polemics and diatribes?

Is she the same old April, performing to an empty room?

She's no longer in our circle, we appreciate that, but perhaps this means she's in a different one now. Different people who appreciate her in a way that we no longer seem to. Friends who take her seriously, an audience who believe what she says and hang on her every word.

'Forget her,' Kai says. 'She's like a virus. She'll make you doubt, she'll make you forget yourselves and before long you'll end up with polls under your posts too.'

'Warning:' The Space says, 'this content is untrue.'

Does she know how things have changed? Perhaps she's now surrounded by bots to keep her in the dark. Perhaps they're freshly coded bots dressed up in our profiles. Benign versions of us all to keep her in line: Kai, Mako and the rest of us. Maybe even another version of Billy K. Bots that only she will see, nodding and laughing and agreeing with every damn thing she does. Her own personalised Space. It's keeping her happy, keeping her away from where she might cause harm or offence.

Or perhaps no one is listening at all. The Space is everywhere, The Space knows everything. The Space only wants the best for us. Its attention is intrusive, but its apathy is terrifying.

Alone, we shut down our terminals for the night and look for the soft blue glow of the nearest Interface.

'Listen,' we say, and sometimes a lack of confidence cracks our voice a fraction and we have to say it again. '*Listen.*'

And we wait, there's that whirring pause before the blue light expands a fraction like a widening iris.

'I'm listening,' The Space will say.

'Thank you,' we say. 'Sorry. Please go back to sleep.' And the light dims a little, but remains there dimly, waiting for our next command.

We will sleep soundly then. Our heartbeats will pulse beneath our profile pictures, the little flag will remain hoisted in solidarity with the news that we don't fully understand and we know The Space is listening. *Thank God*, we think, The Space is listening to everything we do.

April used The Space as she damn well pleased.

We permit ourselves a moment to doubt, and then we purge everything, so we can pretend that no one will ever know.

# 2084 SAT⊙SHI AD

## LAVIE TIDHAR

## 1.

On the wall, an ugly graffito. *Satoshi Lives.*

Night over Docklands, as Narcissus traverses the badlands south of the river away from the gleaming towers on the Isle of Doge.

Through a maze of box-flats tumbled one on top of the other by succeeding architects, each more obsessed with their legacy than the last, until the job was at last handed to a computer, the only way to manage this press of bodies vertical and horizontal. Families pressed in to prefabricated living quarters, a never-silent body politic yawning, grunting, breathing, farting, talking, singing, crying.

Narcissus, black-clad in shiny armour, and the no-brands staring and muttering but shying away. He passes through them like a scythe. Overhead blimps shine against the black sky, inscribing messages in the air, their lights casting the tenements of Thamesmead in endless checkerboard squares of light and shade.

*Soylent Soup – The Smell of Satisfaction.*

*Ceiling Cat Says – U Can Haz Relijun.*

*Ubik Cigarettes Make You Smarter!*

A rather sinister constellation of lights spells only *Snively's Soap.*

Under the lights of these ever-present messages the no-brands live their lives. Penned in beyond the river, within sight of the rising spires of LolCorp and Doge, the no-brands dream their dreams of fame and fortune, of escape.

*Come See – the Sea!*

*Fight For Your Right – Be A Star Overnight!*

There are only two ways out of the no-brand life. If you are brave or vain enough, you can enter one of the gladiatorial talent shows. The weak die in the ring. The winners achieve brand-recognition and escape the slums, to entertain the wealthy.

If you have no obvious talent, the other choice is to go to the fledgling colonies in Antarctica or the Down Below – those legendary underwater cities where crude oil is still mined from the bedrock of the seas or deep within the ice. The ads paint a glorious picture of life under the Earth's oceans, a house for every family, good pay for hard work, marvellous views, an abundance of Pioneer Spirit™ (available in capsule or liquid form), but for all that they are not to be trusted. On giant screens, the no-brands watch the gladiatorial talents sing and dance and try to murder each other. A service economy – and each morning the residents under employ commute beyond their strict zones to the city proper, to clean and cook, wash and fold, drive, look after children, wait on their patrons, inhale the rich and scented air they can't afford and then commute back to their tenements.

Memetic parasites run rampart in the cramped confines of the no-brand slums. Insidious mind-worms, they pass from person to person like an infection. Whispering of the glories of Antarctica, its green parklands, clear blue skies, warm seas.

Narcissus doesn't care for Antarctica.

Narcissus has a job to do and he does it well.

The pirate holdout is in the basement of tower block 133. Heat conduits and electrical circuits mask the spikes in power that indicate illegal activity. But not enough. Not now. Black-armoured Narcissus surveils the entrance, then strides with easy powerful steps. Narcissus is *bespoke*, each custom part of him is unique, perfect, crafted, smooth.

And deadly.

The door to the basement is reinforced steel. Narcissus hammers it down with one blow of his servo-mechanical fist. Inside, the hum of machinery and warm dry air, the smell of old paint and rust, spilled machine oil, decaying flesh. He breathes deep. Steps down into the dark.

The pirates rouse slowly. Cheap makers cover every available surface, knock-off 3D printers crammed into nooks between cables and pipes. A rat runs off, frightened, its hair charged with static electricity. The pirates are teenage kids in freshly printed branded shoes and designer jeans, but wear no-label Ts. A fashion statement or indifference, it's hard to tell. A plastic statue of Naomi Klein with light bulb eyes stands precariously on a shelf, surrounded by offerings.

Narcissus takes it all in, his eyes scan in ranges human eyes can't see. The running pirates are infrared infractions, smudges of blood in the dark. By the entrance to the sewers, a heap of raw materials, wood shavings and plastics, recycled matter, paper pulp. The makers burp: out come sneakers, watches, handbags, shades. Narcissus tracks running figures with his gun. Pirates run. They shout in loltalk patois.

'Git to teh gunz! Kill him!'

'Jus run! Hez cop!'

'R U mad? Hez CEA!'

'This is Narcissus unit X12,' Narcissus says. 'Under contract to the Church of Doge, Inc. You are in violation of treaty codes number—'

But no one is listening.

The pirates start shooting. Narcissus rolls, ducks, delivers the rest of the verdict, and fires. Makers explode. A half-formed vintage Nike plops wetly onto the concrete. The pirates form a barricade from machine parts and knock-off goods. Bullets glance off Narcissus's shell. A concrete bust of Cory Doctorow explodes from a stray bullet and falls off its plinth.

It's hot, messy work. The counterfeit goods are worth thousands of bitcoin on the ghost market. Now they're worth nothing. Narcissus picks off the pirates carefully. Finally there is silence. Only the squeak of an escaping rat. Narcissus steps in the mulch of silicon and ceramics and rubber, which mix unpleasantly with what's left of the pirates. He goes about his job methodically, without emotion. He douses the basement with flammables.

A groan. One of the pirates is still alive.

Narcissus goes to him. A sixteen-year-old boy lies by the entrance to the sewers. The Uzi in his hands is printed, blueprints downloaded from the internet, their authenticity dubious. Blood soaks his shirt. He tries to point the weapon, fails.

'Needz watr…' he says.

Compassion or something like it momentarily overtakes Narcissus. He offers the boy a drink, watches him sip, painfully.

'Hoo sent U?' the boy says. Narcissus seems to understand the question, its implications. What's his corporate affiliation.

'Lolcat? Doge?'

Narcissus is mute. The boy sighs. 'So pain,' he says, in

Doge. 'Much cold, much painful. Very dying.'

'Where is he?' Narcissus says.

'Wut?'

'Where is he!'

'Wer iz hoo?'

Narcissus reaches over and squeezes the boy's shoulder, hard. The boy screams.

'Tell me.'

'Wer U evr wan ov us?' the boy says. For a moment the patois slips. 'You must have been, to become… this. Who made you? Tyrell? Weyland-Yutani? Hosaka? OCP?'

Narcissus says – admits – nothing.

'You're nothing but a… a *device*,' the boy says, and tries to laugh, but it hurts too much, and he doesn't. 'Do you even remember if you were a man once?'

'Where is he?' Narcissus says, but gently. 'Where is Satoshi Nakamoto?'

The boy laughs, then his head slumps on his chest and his eyes go blank. Narcissus strokes the boy's hair – a strange unaccustomed gesture – and stands up.

The sewers, he thinks.

He sighs.

Why does it *always* have to be the sewers.

## 2.

'So wow, so wow, so woooow…' chant the sub-priests.

This is the night before.

Doge Tower, high above the world…

Night time, and London glitters outside the panoramic windows, from the Surrey enclaves to the gay abandon of the north and centre, the City proper with its machine-mind homes, each building a giant capsule emptied of people and walls, where money whispers in virtual transactions no human eye can see…

Bitcoins on the blockchain.

And to the Docklands, the Dogelands, the home of skyscrapers whose names are written in lights like diamonds: The Lunar Advertising Co. Ltd, Snively's Soap Inc., Eldritch Enterprises GmbH, Tyrell, Ubik Co., Atari.

And directly opposite, with a glaring red light at the very top like a malevolent eye, LolCorp HQ, the very enemies of the Church of Doge.

'So wow…' chant the sub-priests.

'Much job,' says the Doge priest, reverting for a moment to patois. Then he smiles at his own guff and continues in standard speech. 'How long have you worked for us, Narcissus?' he says.

Narcissus shrugs. Does it matter?

'We have a problem,' the priest says.

Narcissus says, 'Of course.' Perhaps a little contemptuously. Perhaps not. The priest frowns, then lets it go.

'You have heard of the Illuminati Dossier.'

Wikileaked the year the Darknet rebellion failed. A rumour, nothing more. Arcane technologies, impossible worlds. Aliens. Time travel. It is gone, lost, destroyed. Had never existed. Narcissus inches his head.

'We have reason to believe a copy exists.'

'What reason?'

The priest shrugs. 'Static on the line. Whispers.'

'More specifically?'

'We'd subverted a Kim Dot Clone.'

Narcissus raises his eyebrows. The priest smiles again, a little smugly. He has sharp canine teeth. 'Of the 4,000 original Kim Dot Coms freewared onto the Internet back in,' he waves a hand vaguely, 'the old days, 3,015 survived. Of the sixty-three we had managed to capture, two survived. Of the two who survived, one proved susceptible to our subversion protocols. We released him into the no-brand tenements and let him run deep. A black ops covert sleeper agent. He infiltrated a maker gang and rose high in the ranks.' The priest runs his fingers through his long golden Shiba Inu fur. 'Makers,' he says with contempt. 'Shoes and handbags. Guns. We don't care about those things, Narcissus. They're non-organic matter.'

'But?' says Narcissus. There is always a *but* coming.

'*Genes*,' the priest said. 'Sequestered genomes.' He glares. '*Bodies*, Narcissus. Based on *our* material. On *our* genetic property. This is theft. This is brand *infringement*.

'Forget Jean Claudes, Sylvesters, Bruces!' the priest says. 'We're talking wholesale theft – FDRs, JFKs, Marilyns, Mugabes!' His eyes flash, dangerously. He lowers his voice. '*Elvisii*,' he whispers.

'I see.'

'Elvis!' the priest says, outraged. 'They dare to pirate our *Elvis?* '

In the first genetic land-grab, bitter wars were fought over each scrap of DNA. Celebrity hair changed hands for millions. What used to be the domain of a few unseemly collectors became the hottest new stock exchange. Marilyn Monroe and Elizabeth Taylor. Napoleon and Justin Bieber. Dickens and Maria Callas. Neil Armstrong and the cast of *Baywatch*. Fortunes were made and lost. Now the material was closely guarded, its production and distribution subject to strict brand and copyright law.

'But...?' Narcissus said.

There was always a *but*.

'But he's gone quiet,' the priest said.

'Elvis?'

'Our *agent*. The Kim Dot Clone. We think he found the Dossier and... maybe more. More than we'd bargained for.'

Narcissus frowned. 'I don't understand.'

'Satoshi...' the priest whispers.

Legendary inventor of the bitcoin. Father of the modern age. The man who wasn't there.

'He's only a legend,' Narcissus says.

The priest glares at him irritably. 'Just do what you're *told*! Find the clone, retrieve the dossier, and eliminate Satoshi Nakamoto!'

'Eliminate, sir?'

'Eliminate... with extreme courtesy.'

'Yes, sir,' Narcissus says.

'May Doge be with you,' says the priest.

3.

But who is he? Descending down to the sewers, Narcissus tries to remember, fails. Snatches of memories, real or not he can't tell. A woman with a soft hand stroking a boy's hair, a man picking him up, laughing, and throwing him in the air. Generics, they call them in the trade. Universal memories. The first time he went to the seaside. The call of gulls. Biting on candy. But where? How?

A girl's lips on his. Or a boy's. Someone laughing loudly.

A talk show in the background. A police siren. Who was he? Were any of the memories real?

Did it matter?

He was Narcissus. He had a purpose, was shaped. The boy was right.

He remembers the school. Memory proper begins here, suddenly and quickly.

In the school they trained them in instant nostalgia. They were plugged into the world with classical Ono-Sendai decks, running through endless iterations of Space Invaders, Pac-Man, Donkey Kong, Zelda and all the way up in a sudden paradigm shift to post-millennial MMORPGs, primitive early online universes now held in storage, re-run only for their benefit.

His body changed. Parts were removed, replaced, *improved*. They learned kung fu, Dambe, Capoeira, Jeet Kune Do. A bio-maker printed out opponents: era-appropriate JCVDs and Dolphs took on the pupils one by one, in groups, until one or the other died and were replaced. There was no shortage of clones, or of students.

A private facility, run by the priests. When he graduated they sent him to e-Raq to fight maker insurgents, then to neighbouring iRan where cloner wars left entire communities without access to Wikipedia. Foreign aid organisations dropped parcels of donated Levis and Apples onto isolated communities. He served a year on loan, working for Hosaka in Los Angeles, hunting down escaped Acmes.

The back to London and to DogeHQ.

What does it make you? he thought, uneasily. He prided himself on being unique, custom-made, *bespoke*. The no-brands were interchangeable, maker culture had made everybody somebody's clone. They were just a copy of a copy of a copy, thinking with someone else's thoughts, smiling with someone else's smile. LolCat and Doge told them how to dress and how to shave, which brand of toothpaste to use, what dreams to have, who to hate and who to love.

Only one dared oppose them.

A legend, a non-entity.

Satoshi.

Satoshi Nakamoto.

So no-brand he was a brand of his own. If he was even a man. Creator of the blockchain. A mythago from the dawn of time.

Narcissus follows the trail. Down to the sewers, where the old Thames roars and speaks in putrid waters. Doge boys attack him then, taking him by surprise. Their battle cries echo eerily in the pipes.

'So die! Much woundings! Very kill!'

He fires, takes down one, two, three, but more and more come – the gangs cooperating? he wonders. Then they are on him, doge boys and lolcat kidz, and though he is powerful and he kills many, they overwhelm him at last. Bound they take him, down and down, below the earth.

4.

A fat man, a bald man, a very large imposing man. Staring at Narcissus with shiny button eyes.

'Wut r they goin 2 say bout him? Wut? R they goin 2 say he wuz kind man? He wuz wize man? He had planz?'

Narcissus stares, helpless. The Kim Dot Clone smiles

at him, nods. The doge boyz hold him captive. A false sunset falls over the dirty metal walls of the pipes. A light, approaching.

'Teh manz enlargd mah mind. Hez poet warrior in da clasic sense. I meen sometimez hell... Uh... Well, ull say "y halo thar" 2 him, rite? An hell jus walk rite by u. He wont even notice u. An suddenly hell grab u, an hell throw u in cornr, an hell say, "do u knoe dat if iz teh middle werd in life?"'

He looks at Narcissus expectantly.

'The manz?' Narcissus says.

'Hez comin,' the Kim Dot Clone says.

The light grows. Footsteps sound in the dirty water. The doge soldiers and the lolcat kidz retreat, releasing Narcissus. They prostrate themselves. Narcissus stares. The Kim Dot Clone gibbers in a corner. The footsteps echo queerly. They come closer and closer.

## 5.

So coming! Much blockchain! Very Nakamoto!

## 6.

It is just a man, Narcissus sees with something like disappointment. A man of medium height, in sandalled feet, of medium age, with black short-cut hair. The man stands and examines him, blinking. The Kim Dot Clone gibbers in a corner.

'It is you,' he says.

Narcissus just stands there. He has been ready for this

moment. Had planned this far, the capture, this encounter. Inside him, the implanted bomb begins a silent countdown.

'*You* are Satoshi Nakamoto?' he says.

The man blinks. The man looks at him. The man shakes his head.

'*No?*'

'There is no Satoshi Nakamoto,' the man says. He scratches his chin, thoughtfully. 'There is nothing *but* Satoshi Nakamoto,' he says – a little doubtful. Trying out the thought. Looks at Narcissus. 'I assume the bomb inside you has a dead man switch?'

Narcissus is taken aback. The man smiles. 'It is an honour to finally meet you, master,' he says.

They all bow to him, doge and lolcat and clone, and this strange little man.

'But I am not—' Narcissus says.

The man smiles. Nods. Puts his hand on Narcissus' shoulder...

And Narcissus is propelled back through time, before his assignments, before the school, to that erased childhood, to being a boy, to having parents, to having a *name*—

And the man who is Satoshi Nakamoto is there, now, and behind him is another Nakamoto and another and another, and he, Narcissus, the latest in the chain, this bitoshi blockamoto, which goes back, all the way back, to the first, the progenitor, the—

And he understands now, and he whispers, 'Satoshi lives...' and the other Satoshi Nakamoto smiles and nods and releases his hand from Satoshi's shoulder, and the two Satoshis are joined, they are linked, and he can feel all the others all the way down the chain.

The bomb inside him has stopped ticking at one second to blast.

'Satoshi Nakamoto,' Satoshi Nakamoto says.

'Satoshi Nakamoto,' Satoshi Nakamoto replies.

The Kim Dot Clone gibbers in the corner.

### 7.

I shud has been pair ov raggd claws, scuttlin acros floors ov silent seas…

### 8.

The man who was Narcissus slowly returns to the surface. The rising spires of LolCorp and Doge in the distance. Airships light up the sky. *Snively's Soap.* In the tenements the no-brands shy away from the man who was Narcissus. They sense in him something of their own, perhaps. A promise, a paladin.

On the wall, an ugly graffito.

Satoshi Lives.

The man who was Narcissus salutes the legend on the wall. He makes his way out of the no-brand ghettos, towards the Isle of Doge, the bomb in his chest primed and ready.

# UNIQUO

## ALIYA WHITELEY

The kids are forever throwing things at the window.

Sally imagines them plotting attacks, escalating the situation, putting lit rags through her letterbox. They hate her and her house in some personal, intimate way. But Tam says, *They're just kids. They aren't malicious.*

Every morning he collects what they have thrown and shows her, to reassure her. Smashed passcards, with tiny soldered silver connectors and green plastic jags. Tam keeps them in a box under the sink and takes them to the recycler when the box is full.

'It's getting dark,' she says, feeling the here and now of it, feeling the impossibility of ever emptying that box.

'Don't think about it,' Tam says from his chair, not taking his eyes from his book.

She's frightened, though, she's frightened already. Frightened all the time. The thoughts have found her early tonight. She swears they don't come from inside her, but press up against the window and slowly squeeze themselves through to permeate the room, then her skin.

How painful it is, to be powerless to the thoughts. To not understand yourself, or anything around you. She once thought, when she worked in marketing and Tam was the chief engineer (friends working on Uniquo, and it was better to be friends; so much less was expected of her), that she would love to no longer be accountable to anyone. But it's so much more terrifying this way, because everything becomes inexplicable. It's nobody's job to explain a thing to her.

The park lights switch on, and everything that makes up the outside comes to life.

Employees used to bring her vast swathes of information

in the form of lights: on glass, in screens, across vast distances. Information: the life blood flowing through the fat electrical veins of the world. She could explain to a room filled with investors how Uniquo worked. Now she can't explain why kids throw their used passcards at the window.

Tam shifts to the chair nearest the window to read his book a little longer. She doesn't know how he can stand to be close to it.

'Come away,' she says.

'Can I turn the light on?'

'No.'

'Then just till I finish this chapter.'

The music starts, in the distance. The heavy drumbeat below, and the beeping, like an alarm, above; the sounds make no sense to her. She winces. Tam once said, *It makes more sense when you're on the rides. Some of it's quite good, Sal, it's got a great beat.* That was just one of his attempts to get her out into the open.

When they'd launched the park, flipped the master switch, she had loved the open. The wide spaces of it, particularly around the solar fields and the wind collectors, which had been a marketing dream.

*Put energy back into the planet while you ride, play, swing and sway in ten themed future-zones!*

*The recyclable passcard just needs to be in contact with your skin, and you'll be patched in, no waiting, able to reserve your place in the digital queue and then turn up for instant access. Even for Uniquo, the world's first augmented rollercoaster that swoops and dips along the entire perimeter of the park. Each passcard interacts with Uniquo in a special way, making the journey different every time. Uniquo offers so many visions of the future, every one thrilling and fun-filled.*

She said all that, to rooms and rooms of people. She rode it herself, too, and found herself flying above glass skyscrapers in an airborne car, so high that she was at the very edge of space, teetering on the lip of a blackness that thrilled her with its lack of limitations. She was so adventurous, back when she was young.

But youth isn't about age; she knows that now. It's about the number of thoughts that you don't yet carry around with you. An understanding of loss, and of what everything costs: those are the thoughts that make her stay inside, make her stay old.

*Fear of youth is quite common amongst the elderly*, said the psychiatrist, the last time she left the house. *It's called ephebiphobia.*

She's on a waiting list for a certain type of therapy.

A scream. Like a whistle calling a dog, and her fear jumps to it. She puts her hands to her neck. The rides are working.

Tam turns a page.

'Come away,' she says, from her armchair in the darkest corner of the room. He ignores her. He's not in an understanding mood tonight; it's going to be a bad night, the kind where he makes no attempt to placate her, and who can blame her? She's such a pain, a stupid old woman who won't look out of the window.

'You can't hate me any more than I hate myself,' she says, forcing the words through her tight throat.

He throws the book. It hits the wall behind her. She's gone too far, she knows it, *anything but self-pity* he said, once.

'I'm sorry,' she says – does that make it worse? Tam stands up, and comes to her, and takes her hands. He'd never hurt her physically.

'Enough,' he says, softly.

'Yes.' She will try to be less afraid.

It's just kids.

Tam holds her, for a little while, in their house. Retirement with perks, they called it, and so few people get to retire at all. But they wanted Tam's expertise to keep Uniquo going, now a grand old lady of a coaster, so they offered him permanent quarters in the staff area of the park for only three days of work a week and he said to her (as a lover, then, with all the doubt and complexity that entailed; or was that simply a side-effect of their age?) *Come with me. Room for two.*

Well, he's an engineer. She knew that was as romantic as it would ever get, and that was fine. She likes practical solutions. She used to think that no matter what the problem, there would always be a practical solution.

The sharp crack against the window jolts her back to this moment, this well-known fear that sweeps all else away. There is no past. There is only hearing them laugh, so many of them, all laughing at her. She is a stone in his arms.

'That's it,' says Tam, and drops her.

'Don't go out there,' she pleads.

On the worst nights he runs after them, shouting, and returns looking so much older than when he left.

He grabs her hand. 'Come on.'

'No.'

Sal finds a strength she hasn't felt in years, and fights him. So she does still have determination; here it is, in her slaps and scratches, and a part of her mind feels better, feels good.

He lets her go and walks out of the room. She hears his footsteps in the hallway, and then the opening of the front door. It does not close.

It can't be left open, it can't.

She has to go to it. She takes small steps, small breaths. She makes it to the hallway, and does not look at the open space ahead as she wades through her panic to reach it.

But the lights must be seen.

She braces her hands against the frame and sees the open. The terrible delight and possibility of the open, with the kids walking past and the row of bins at the end of the small lawn where they carelessly throw their passcards, more often than not missing the mark. Tam stands by the bins, his back to the door. He has straightened up in the night air; from here, he looks younger.

And Uniquo is ahead, a visible never-ending string of wild lights with the screams flung freely from its curves and twists. The kids on Uniquo are not here in this park at all, but inside their own imaginations.

A running boy throws his passcard and it hits Tam in the chest and falls to the grass. The boy doesn't stop to apologise, but he does look around, and Sally sees his face clearly, with that tension written on the forehead that says sorry, but he has to rush, he has some place to be. He looks like somebody she knew once, but she can't think of who. Then he is gone, and the next crowd is coming towards Tam, a swagger of them with their hair styled into upright shapes, they move as one, they will hurt him, she's sure of it—

They hold out their passcards as they saunter by, and Tam takes them.

Why do they think that he is there to collect them? They don't even make eye contact with him, and they don't look at the house at all.

They don't see it.

But it's not the real world they're a part of, not her world. It's Uniquo they're thinking of, talking about. Sally knows it. They're swapping their rides, telling each other what they saw. She remembers the long list of places to which Uniquo could take a person, and she wonders for the first time if it was good to make these visions and sell them to so many:

*Under the sea, you're working as a bio-engineer as the fish dive and dally, swoop and surround you; you mend the coral reefs with your oxygenation wand, injecting colour and life with every movement.*

*In space, you're on a rocket ride, after making first contact with a hostile civilisation. The aliens seek to shoot you down. Their spaceships fire – you weave and veer – can you make it back to the docking port?*

*On a super-heated Earth, you're an evolving species, a giant insect that chases tiny humans through the humid jungle, making them scatter like flies – how sweet it is to turn the tables…*

*In a virtual reality, you're the cyber terrorist fleeing the oppressive government. AI constructs are trying to track you down – imagine yourself with super powers and fly free over a nightmare vision!*

*You're gone,* thinks Sally. *You're in the future. You're anywhere but here.*

Tam puts the passcards in the bin. Tomorrow they will be collected and taken to the recycler, and by the evening they will be ready to offer new escapes.

She calls his name. She doesn't dare to go to him, but his smile tells her it is enough that she has made it this far.

'It's a warm night,' he calls.

She nods.

Two kids – one eating a giant hot dog and the other holding a bottle of some lurid drink – throw their passcards, which land on the grass.

'Hey!' says Tam. 'Bin.'

They laugh as they walk by.

Tam comes to her, and says, 'See? Just kids. I don't even get why they still like that old rollercoaster so much. Those ideas about what it would be like in ten, twenty years. Hah.'

'Nothing's changed,' she says, which is so obviously untrue that she waits for him to contradict her, but she doesn't.

'We could travel,' he says. 'As soon as you're better. We're really not that old. Where would you like to go?'

'Anywhere.'

'This is a good sign,' he observes. 'Look at you. Out here. Moving forward.'

How different everything looks from here. She vows to see it all from this perspective again, tomorrow night. Uniquo is a curving line, an arc of track that runs right across her field of vision, and the lights that shine from it stop her from seeing the sea, the moon, the faint black line of the horizon.

Sally stands in the doorframe and watches the young people ride the wide open, and then throw their old dreams away.

# SHOOTING AN EPISODE

## CHRISTOPHER PRIEST

I was hated but respected. I accepted that. I wanted neither but knew I deserved them both. It was the only time in my life when I was important enough to warrant these feelings, and then it was for only a brief period. Bad luck caused events to break around me while I was still there, still responsible, because if the episode had malfunctioned only a week or so before or after I would never have been involved.

It was partly my own fault: I already loathed the job. It was ludicrously well paid, as it seemed to me at the time, but I had already found out why so few people were willing to work there. By the day the episode happened I had decided that I would chuck it in as soon as I could. Money, respect, the freedom to instil fear and excitement in other people – none of these compensated for the hatred.

I already knew that the network would not want to replace me so soon – I had completed a training schedule, discovering as I did so that I was the only recent appointment going through the system. But I disliked the work. After only a couple of months I had texted in my resignation, so far without response. They were probably dragging it out to postpone my departure.

So I continued to go day by day to my office, fully aware of how the public around me felt about me. The network called these people the players, and I saw them every day. The players knew who I was, and their feelings were obvious. Most of them were obsessed with their gameplay, their digital handhelds glowing, their fingers zapping against the screens, but whenever I passed many of them would break off to stare at me – hostile stares, intrusions, warnings, implied threats. No one ever struck me but once or twice some of the women spat at me. I had already established a routine: I went to my office early each morning and did not return to the network flat where I was living until the daytime crowds had dispersed, but before the night drinkers emerged.

For the most part I was protected because the players were obsessed with their gameplay. They loathed me for the power I had over that, but the same power secured me.

From inside the comparative safety of the office I would watch the players in the street through the thickly glassed windows.

Some, not all, wore VR masks attached to their brows – these gave their wearers a characteristic stance, because as they moved slowly along the street their heads were tipped back, compensating for the strain on their necks caused by the slight but extra weight of the device. It made them seem as if they were searching for something, which in a sense they were. The less practised of these players also lurched unsteadily as they walked, because the VR blocked their real-time vision and they were entirely dependent on the gameplay simulation of their surroundings. This non-visual information was transmitted directly to their optic nerves. Falls to the ground by these VR players were frequent.

The majority of players, though, still preferred the handheld displays, where the graphics were more reliably instant, because of slightly lower resolution. These players wandered along, staring down at their devices, tapping endlessly at the screens, swiping and jabbing. The more advanced players had begun using the recently introduced psychic controls, with direct transmissions to and from their minds, but the majority still preferred the tactile response of fingers and hands, the universal dexterity.

I was working at what the network called a cell sub-station – after the training was completed I was promoted almost at once to the position of senior contracts producer, although the title was misleading. It made me sound as if I held a managerial position. The one-room sub-station staff consisted only of me, working alone.

While I had been training in the large hub office in the city things were not so bad. The high level of pay compensated for the daily problems, and of course there was the feeling of safety in numbers. Working in the large office was a heady experience, with a kind of nervy arrogance about our control of the players. The main offices were strong on teamwork – this spurious sense of unity mostly neutralised the feeling of personal risk. The building we worked from was anonymous, with many different unmarked entrances – we came and went to our jobs by carefully managed diversionary routes. And of course there was an armed security team on hand.

Two weeks ago, though, I had been posted away to this regional satellite station. A promotion of sorts. The town itself was for the most part a post-industrial wasteland, where numerous huge condominium towers were going up. There was countryside around, but much of it had been polluted, brown-fielded, turned to waste. It was a temporary assignment, the managers said, but even before I arrived I realised they had conned me.

One of the biggest ever reality productions was touring and heading by an indirect route towards the town. No one else in the network wanted the job because something always seemed to go wrong with the large tours. If this one came anywhere near the town I should have to deal with it.

After I arrived, took over the network apartment and established myself in the office, even the minimal feeling of independence evaporated when I realised how vulnerable I was. The players were endlessly critical of the way our productions depicted reality – they wanted more of it, or less, or something new. Always they wanted the new. For them reality was something that could be shaped, controlled, distorted into higher levels of real-seeming experience. The more the network gave them, the more they demanded.

The office was in a street not far from the centre of the town, but apart from the heavy locks on the main door, the closed-circuit monitors and the two thickly glassed windows there were no special security measures. Although there were no signs or logos on the building, no clue as to what it was being used for, all the players clearly knew what it was. Armed security was available on the instant – the instant I sent the message for help. When the armed officers would actually arrive was a matter of conjecture. It would probably take an hour or two for them to reach me if trouble broke out.

Stress levels, I quickly found, were not confined to the cities – they were the same or worse here, in this small and depressing town.

Pay remained the main compensation. I was still being paid at the same rate as the city workers.

The first call came through soon after I had arrived in the office that morning. The caller's face was blanked – the screen showed an ideogram of featureless head and shoulders. I found that disturbing. It meant there was going to be something in the message I should not want to hear. Normal messages were texted, or came with live images. From my period in the main office I knew they put up avatars for inter-office comms when anonymity was required. 'We need all contracts maintained real-time today. Make the changeover now.'

It was a man's voice, presumably belonging to someone I had met or had at least worked with for a time, but I could tell from the flatness of tone that the voice was being synthesised. It could therefore as easily be a woman making the call, disguising herself. The neutrality of the voice, with the synthetic tone adapters I was familiar with, had a chilling authority. Annoying, too – why did they do this to me?

'The contracts are up to date,' I said. 'I filed them last night, as usual.'

'Those don't count. The principals have decided they want the protocols ramped up. We are giving them a roll. You handle it.'

'Remind me,' I said, because while I had been waiting for them to accept my resignation I had let the memory of the training soften. I had never worked with a roll-up contract, but had heard about them. Roll-up contracts meant a slackening of the rules – the players (the watching public) and the principals (the main performers) could intermingle in some way. They could change places. I was hazy on the whys and hows.

The voice said, 'It doesn't matter. Enter the code.'

'What code?' I said, petulantly.

But the computer was already responding to an inflow of data. I could see the changes being monitored on the screen.

'Is that it?' I said, but the link had closed. I knew that it was possible for hackers to trace our microwave signals back to source, so at certain times network comms were kept short. This was presumably one of those times.

I stared at the activity on my monitor, gazing at the swift changes without fully comprehending what was happening. Names of the players scrolled by unreadably quickly in four columns, but of course they were avatars, not real names. Many of them were asterisked or highlighted or coloured, the network's way of noting that certain avatars were nested or cross-purposed: an avatar of one group with another, and another, beyond them layer after layer, accumulating more highlights. These were the syndicates and punter blocs, the exchange groups, the fan cultivars with particular interests, the adapters, the backers, owners, sponsors, lobbyists.

The info was impossible to decipher, impossible for me to decipher. I could not read what was passing through in any event, such was the speed of change, so many hundreds of thousands of avatars, perhaps millions. New highlights were introduced: these indicated gender and age, relationships with other avatar players or syndicates, as well as coded levels of past and present consumer quotient, credit rating, history, vexatious litigant activity, aggravation, performance, commendation or recommendation, offending record and gaol sentences – above all the financial records: fees paid, ancillary spending, non-gamer holdings, advertising exposure.

All this flashed past me on the monitor. I stopped looking after the first few seconds.

I thought of it as irrelevant, not only to my understanding of what was going on but also to the overall gameplay situation. The most direct impact it would have on my work was that I would have to issue revised contracts to every player and every principal – but even that was of course computerised.

I glanced at the CCTV monitor, where I could oversee the usual crowd of players sauntering past in the street. I could tell they had picked up the same information, because most of them looked pleased. That was not a good sign, as it would lead inevitably to an increase in activity. Several of the players could not resist glancing up at my monitoring cameras. That disturbed me.

Why should the network have done this? How were these decisions made? What, in particular, had brought on this particular shift in policy? The morning passed with for me a growing sense of unease, a feeling that my problems were about to make themselves known. At lunchtime I took food from the office automat. Not long after that another call came in from the network, confirming my fears.

This time the transmitted image was of a woman, but stylised and impersonal, another graphic design. Her voice was synthesised once more – I suspected a man.

'Some of the principals have evaded security,' he or she said, without preamble. 'Several players have been killed. The equipment crew has stopped broadcasting – we suspect they have been evaded. Otherwise they might have had their equipment neutralised. Whatever happened to them, there is no longer any coverage. You must resolve it.'

'How?'

'The episode must be shot. You know how to do that. The equipment is there.'

'I don't know—' I said, but I was instantly interrupted.

'You will shoot it.'

'I don't know how. And why were the crew evaded?'

'We will monitor results. A security team has been despatched and will be in your activity zone soon.'

'Where are the principals now?'

'No information. Routine scans are in progress. Your equipment will vector you. This evasion must be ended.'

I knew that 'evasion' was the network euphemism for a worst-case incident. The only evasions in the past I had heard about all involved violence – principals or players attacking the crews, with several deaths.

'I'm alone here, without back-up.'

'You have all the equipment you need,' said the mellifluous, bland, calming voice of the electronically enciphered woman.

'Then what is in the script?'

'There is no script. This is roll-up, free format.'

'Can't the rules be changed back?'

But the line went dead. I glanced back at the CCTV monitors – on a normal day there would be a constant movement of players past the office, some of whom inevitably paused and looked towards the heavy windows. Today, though, a small crowd had gathered, waiting outside, looking expectantly towards the entrance.

I put up my contracts file on the computer, the summary. Money was pouring in because of the evasion, or the events behind it. For the network, presumably now to be faced with compensation claims from the families of the crew, this was a high-risk, high-earn situation. Payout now, payback soon.

I went to the real-time monitors, which normally I avoided. There were ten screens, in two rows of five. The live action was shown here and archived – not by me or in this building, but shadowed elsewhere.

The network's leading attraction was a roving reality: twenty principals, pre-selected for their known earning power, their extreme psychological anomalies, their social antipathies, had been set loose. The crews followed them, sometimes covertly, often intrusively and interactively. There was no studio containment: they went out into the world.

I was in denial about the realities – after I made my final decision to leave I had closed my mind, merely performing minimal clerical functions. I knew all too well that there was a growing school of thought, expressed in some parts of the media, that accused the network of illegality. I did not want to walk out of the job only to be arrested. The bosses maintained that these claims only came from their competitors, but I was uneasy.

I issued contracts. I oversaw all the money that was paid out, most of the live money that came in. Money was the rationale of the whole enterprise. A lot of it went out, mostly to the principals, but there were other expenses too. Hush money, described as restitution expense, was frequently paid, but it was only a fraction of what the network hauled in every week. My out-station was one of dozens in this country, and this country was one of many that were networked, both with home-grown material but also with productions from affiliated countries. The money was a maze of wealth. I had nothing to do with individual deals – I saw only the totals. I passed everything on. I observed the rules, asked no questions, followed none of the scripts.

I had to do something about the current problem, the roving reality, the one that had caused an evasion.

The lack of clear rules gave the principals a straight path to wealth and celebrity, because within the vague parameters of the rules they could do whatever they wished. They could travel wherever they like, talk about any subject they wished, argue about everything, they could steal, burn, fornicate, attack each other, defecate, abuse or libel anyone they had a grudge against. Fornication was a constant, always performed for the cameras – everyone, players and principals alike, professed to be bored by it, but the ratings went up the more sex there was on screen. Libellous attacks happened too. The network fought every case where an aggrieved victim was bold enough to make a claim. The network sometimes lost and the payouts were immense, but every court case increased the audience, and with it the cashflow. The principals were under the protection of the crew that followed them: everything was permissible so nothing mattered, but because nothing was hidden everything was watched.

The principals were not allowed to kill each other, but that was simple to enforce because of the amounts of money paid to them. Sometimes the principals hated each other, the women were raped (the network euphemism was 'persuaded'), the men often beat each other up (network: 'disputed'), there were many other disgusting or violent actions (network: 'reminders required'). Hardly anyone tried to kill, though.

It was a show. Fame, wealth and celebrity attended every moment of reality. It was entertainment. The principals acted their roles, the players reacted in theirs. Money changed hands. Sometimes, as now, the players were encouraged to participate. More money, always that.

All the principals had to do to earn their money was remain in sight of the crew. It was a show. It was reality. Everyone was used to that. Reality was a commonplace. There was nothing beyond reality – no one believed in anything else, but once the crew was evaded the show was off.

I found the standby equipment, secured as usual behind strengthened panels and combination locks, then followed the intricate decoding procedure that let me take out the various components. I spread them on the bench.

In this I had been trained. The main problem was one I had encountered during the training sessions, which was that the various pieces had been designed and built for someone physically larger than me. I checked everything to the list, I tested all the contact points. I found the battery pack and the spare on the charging bench, connected the main one, made sure, made sure.

I removed my outer clothes, a jacket, jeans, and pulled on the armoured tunic, the strengthened leggings and boots, the accessories belt, tightened everything as firmly as possible. I pulled on the helmet, the weight resting unevenly on my head. I adjusted the straps. The device was still too loose, but there was nothing I could do about that. The heavy equipment was going to chafe against me. Finally I attached both batteries to the belt, connected the main one, checked the setting, checked it again, clamped the accessories' tote around both batteries.

I powered up. The head-up displays, the HUDs, booted into life – an array of adjacent images shining on the inside of the visor. They loaded, diagnosed their circuits, reported all were correct. If I moved my head quickly the images scattered and flashed. I was trained to move steadily, deliberately, to stabilise the perceived reality.

Steady movements were also unprovocative. They helped not to alarm anyone.

The image on the main computer monitor flashed up the comms from the network office. The stylised image of the woman was there again, but when 'she' spoke it was in an undisguised male voice.

'You have not followed orders. You must shoot now.'

'I am doing what I can. The equipment is the wrong size—'

'You must shoot now.'

'I am about to,' I said.

'Stand where I can look at you.'

I checked again the main harness of the helmet, then with everything as I believed correctly in place I stood so that I was in view of the cam.

'You are wearing clothes. You are supposed to have removed anything that identifies the network.'

'I have on my underclothes: a T-shirt, pants, nothing else.'

The man/woman said nothing but cut the contact. The screen blanked.

Dreading everything that might happen, I released the locks on the main entrance and went into the street. Never before had I felt so exposed, so vulnerable. After the aircon in the office, the outside felt suffocatingly hot and grimy. While I turned to secure the door many of the players who had been passing at that moment stopped. They stared at me.

I briefly had my back against them, but I observed their reaction on one of the HUDs.

I turned to face them, the full rig of the equipment in view. This had the expected but nevertheless chilling effect on most of them. They moved back from me, scanning their digital displays. Those with the VR hoods reared away, like alarmed horses.

Two or three of the men stayed put, holding out handhelds to try to take a shot of me, but this was ill advised, as they should have known. There were always a few chancers. The equipment instantly picks up imaging energy and before a shot can be taken it fires an incapacitating bolt back. Some of the more experienced players carried spare handhelds, or even jamming devices as a precaution against this, but even so the incapacitant was an effective deterrent.

The two or three chancers close to me reeled back, their hands and wrists inflamed from the destructive bolts. One of them fell to the ground, while the others stumbled away, hunched over the acute agony of their hands. The handhelds lay burned in the roadway, their touchscreens starred and fogged.

I moved on, trying to ignore the players around me, at least trying to look as if I was ignoring them. In practice it was difficult because so many of them were close around me, stepping in front.

Inside my helmet I was reading the directional satellite scan. I saw coordinates echoed to a HUD on one side, beneath them a ghostly, synoptic image of the street. On the main display I could see an image of devastation – apparently it was an older part of the town, one I had not been aware of before. We were still only two or three hundred metres from the office but I invariably approached from another direction, in a hurry, head down. This area was unknown to me. I could not see it clearly. I found digital visuals distracting. They made me misstep, lose my way, because I preferred to look at the real world around me.

The players were following me. I could hear and sense them behind me, but of course the equipment was also logging them electronically. Numbers were reported on the HUDs, and the crowd following me was increasing in size. The growth was steady – not fast but steady. Whether I wished it or not I was now leading a crowd. Crowds attract other people, crowds follow, crowds take on a collective identity, a seeming sentience.

This crowd was connected. Networked digital displays shone on all sides.

I was in the main street of the town, where immense building sites were fenced off, where cranes loomed over new condominium projects. Dust blew across the uneven road surface. Machinery hammered beyond the walls. The sun was high overhead, the metal parts of the equipment were beginning to burn against my unprotected skin.

We passed beyond the construction sites and came to a zone where smaller and older buildings lined both sides of the street. The imaging software reported that most of these places were unoccupied. When I angled my head so that I could see through the visor itself, past the HUDs, I noticed that many of the buildings were derelict. I saw gaping doorways, windows that had been boarded up, roofs that sagged or in many places had fallen through.

People, the sort of people who became players or principals, no longer inhabited individual buildings. It was more acceptable to cram into collective residences where relationships were quick to form, and re-form, where sexual and occupational preferences could be harmonised and explored. This was the modern society. Teams and syndicates were inevitably forged, investment interests hardened. I myself had lived in three different such condominium habitats before I incautiously took this job, and I yearned to go back to that lifestyle. I missed the playing, missed the gaming, missed the elaborate wagers, the sense of constant contact, I missed the instant gratification.

Feelings of rejection, of being a social pariah, had grown in me from my first days with the network. I had changed sides.

Being in the street of old dwellings gave me an unpleasant, dismaying feeling. Heat sensors reported the presence of humans concealed in several of the smaller places. They were not identified as being of special interest, so I carried on past. I imagined them to be non-gamers with lost lives seeking sanctuary, their tragic and pointless existence going on hidden from the world. Even so, I knew it was unlikely they would be allowed to remain permanently in the actual buildings. Many of the ruins were now owned by the various competing networks – they provided an occasional backdrop for action, places for principals to meet in secret, for players to gather and discuss strategy offline, for the cartels to lay off the more extravagant wagers. These places were regularly searched and the intruders ejected, especially if a roving reality came near.

I loathed the callous nature of the network that employed me, the economic priorities it pursued.

After walking for about ten minutes at the head of my unwanted crowd – their numbers had increased to over 100 strong – I noticed a similar knot of players ahead. They were clustered around something I could not make out from this distance, although the sensors were already registering it. The main display reported a 100 percentile reading, telling me that this was what I was seeking.

Then several more traces of material, organic but inactive, lower percentiles for now, were displayed from areas further away. On each of these the percentile score was slowly ticking upwards. I should have to visit them. I had to be ready to shoot. I would get to them in time. My equipment was humming. I felt the battery pack growing warm, strapped against my waist. I was sweating in the hot sunshine, cursed by the heavy protective suit. The crowd made a loud sound. I could not tell their voices apart – they noised in unison, all reacting at once to the same data. Most of what they were receiving was coming from my output.

The HUD reader which interpreted player intentions and motives, normally a soothing pale buff colour, sometimes with a few red highlights, now registered a mixture of fear, curiosity, revulsion and, of course, excited anticipation. The players nearest to me were pressing ahead, no longer willing to proceed at my steady pace, but by jostling me were trying to force the pace.

Most of them kept away from me. I was encircled – a few of them touched me, but all stayed close. They wanted to get to the scene, shoot the scene, complete it, move on, finish the episode.

They parted in front of me, pulling to two sides – individuals acting in concert, a murmuration. The displays on their handsets flickered in unison. The way ahead was clear. My main lenses automatically zoomed, the HUDs giving me the sensation that I was swooping forward. In the same instant, the steadying gyros and servos kicked in, shifting the balance of the equipment so that it seemed to lose weight. I felt it urging forward, pulling me onwards.

It was a human body. At first the definition was not sharp enough for me to tell if it was a man or a woman. The body was in a heap, bent horribly, back arching, face down but still balancing somehow on its knees, a posture of obeisance, long hair spread across the stony ground. It was naked. On my sensors I saw the analytical reading for organic material, the scientific rationale – through the visor I saw naked buttocks, thrust grotesquely upwards at an unnatural angle, head pressed down into the dirt. The crowd continued to separate, allowing me to progress alone so that I could concentrate on the shots. I stepped slowly forward, the equipment steadying and balancing itself, gauging the movements and reactions of the players. They were no longer crowding around me. They were standing with their handhelds, staring down at the screens, watching reality play before them.

Their fingertips dashed across the screens.

When I was close enough I could see that the body was a man's. I went as close as I dared, feeling the zoom lenses adjusting and reframing. The image remained steady, the colours were enhanced and naturalised, the focus remained sharp. There were deep cuts over the man's back and neck, and one of his arms had been pulled or cut away. The dark gap of the exposed armpit socket horrified me, but the limp, pallid limb, lying on the dusty road surface a few metres away, was even worse to contemplate. The fingers were clenched in a fist.

I was no longer guiding the equipment because the autos

had taken control, the sensors responding to the smell of blood, the presence of human flesh, the man's naked skin. The equipment felt lighter – the counterweights and gyros that held the sensors steady were alert, almost alive, compensating not just for the images they were collecting but for my movements too. The bulky weight of the equipment was no longer a problem for me – I felt I was able to soar, able to swoop.

The stabilised equipment began dragging me to one side, thrusting the lenses down, peering and peeking at the intimate details of the man's naked corpse. I was no longer in control. I let the equipment's AI do what it was programmed to do.

As the detailed examination went on the crowd became absorbed in what was coming through to them on their handsets. Their heads were bent over as they stared intently down at the screens. Many of them were tweaking the images: enlarging, inverting, saturating the colours. Their fingers and thumbs dashed across the touch-sensitive pressure points.

Some of the players were laughing – texts were going to and fro, images were being forwarded. Teams were in line, syncing their mash-up animations, instantly generated from the base images I was transmitting.

The digital readouts on my HUDs were steady, but on the players' displays closest to me I could see a dazzle of images, sliding, zooming, wiping, animating. Electronic noise rose around us: beeps and groans and jingles, swarming like a cloud of invisible flying insects. One man near me had mashed up an enlarged simulated animation of the man's corpse – somehow he had contrived the body to stand, to stagger forward, the remaining arm waving, the head sagging, a grotesque parody of life. Even as I watched, the detached arm was itself animated. It rose from the virtual ground, flew across the virtual space, made itself reunite with the floundering body.

I turned away. I took a step towards the corpse, a metre or two away from me. This was a signal to the sensors that the sequence could be ended.

The crowd instantly picked up on the change and once again swerved away to the sides, leaving a space around me. They knew what I was about to do. Soon I was at the distance auto-specified as safe.

Most of the crowd had clustered behind me. A few seconds later the dead body was dematerialised by my deselector charge. I felt the blast in the same instant as the explosion occurred. My servos protected me from the pressure wave.

A shower of blood, small pieces of flesh and shards of bone spattered down. The players around me shielded their screens with their bodies, or wiped the glassy surface on their clothes. Filters protected me from the stench, the body armour saved me from the pieces forcibly expelled. The auto-wipers cleaned my visor and the exposed lenses.

We moved on, following the other traces. The next two bodies we came across were both female, clothed but horrifically wounded. Deep slashing cuts and dark contusions covered the parts of their bodies that had been exposed. As before, the steadying gyros kicked in, creating a stable platform for the shots I had to take.

'Too slow! Destroy now!' The words came through on the direct aural link, so I knew I was being monitored.

'There are players too close,' I said. 'I can't—'

'Get rid of the evidence now.'

I tried to wave my arms as a warning to the players closest to the two dead women, but their attention was locked on the digital displays. As the mess of bodily destruction exploded upwards in two balls of fire, with gore bursting out in all directions, I moved on and away. Blood and bones rained down. Most of the players close to me were bloodied but unharmed, and many were thrown to the ground by the double blasts, but at least a score of those people closest to the bodies had taken direct hits from the explosions.

Their horrifying blast injuries, and deaths, marked me as a genuine enemy, worsening my position while simultaneously reinforcing it. I was more of a target, more of a threat, more to hate, more to fear.

Some of the players located digital devices dropped by those hit by the blasts, some of which were still working, and these were seized as loot. The players instantly synced them with their existing ones, carried on. Reality was doubled and tripled.

We trudged onwards.

We came on the evaded crew not long after this. They were huddled against the side of one of the old buildings. There were six of them: two women and four men. They had been stripped of their protective armour and helmets, then ferociously attacked. Their wounds were shocking, extensive – I looked at what was coming through the HUDs, rather than regard them for real. How many principals had gone for them? Why did the crew have no defence against these attackers? It was impossible to imagine it happening.

If I glanced directly at them, through the visor, I knew that the deaths were real, horrific, but on the digital displays there was a heightened unreality: too much colour, too much blood, too many swords and long blades and bludgeons left around the bodies. Reality was being trended into a new exaggerated version, worse but less real, more thrilling but also more conscionable for the players.

Already the mash-ups were starting as the players seized on the images: the pictures came ghoulishly alive, less real became even less real, dead bodies rose. The players were making inarticulate, excited sounds I did not like.

It was not appropriate to destroy the bodies of evaded employees of the network, so I keyed in the code on the hand pad, marking the location of where I had found the crew. There was a team who dealt with the after-effects of evasion activity. To my surprise, one of my HUDs ran up confirmation of the names, avatars and photo IDs of the crew members. I glimpsed short biographies.

If the network had known this information all along, why had I been sent out to locate them?

The behaviour of the players was frightening me. They were clustering around the dreadful scene of death, pushing to the front, using their handhelds, reaching across. I glimpsed some of what they were channelling: images of cruelty and bizarre violence, reactivated, restarted, elevated to fantasy. I pushed hard against the resistance of the stabilising mechanism and forced myself away. For a few moments I left the crowd behind. 'I've no more traces,' I said into the direct link. 'Concluding now.'

'You are to continue,' said the voice in my head. 'The episode must be shot to the end.'

'It's finished. I found the crew. I'm going to close.'

'You have to continue.'

'Then direct me,' I said. 'What am I looking for?'

No answer.

I walked on, the equipment stabilising but feeling heavy once again. A feeling of dread was growing in me. I was aware that the players were again moving towards me, as if they knew how the episode would end. Many of them had streaks of blood on their clothes and skin, their hair was matted with gore. They stumbled along, disregarding this, watching their handhelds.

They marched beside me, behind me, around me, my attendant crowd of players. Although the sky was bright their digital displays shone and flickered, another reminder of the difference between reality and unreality. The players wanted closure on this episode – I had to deliver it. I too had been a player, so I understood their need. Somewhere ahead lay the conclusion. I had no idea what I was looking for or what I would do when I found it, but I was being monitored. My network would guide me.

I had become the show, the centre of the action. Only I could shoot it and close it.

Even so, rational doubt remained. Whatever or whoever had caused the violent deaths of these people was no doubt the real focus of interest, and I, and my slow progress through the wasted landscape on this edge of the town, was merely a guide for the players. They were following, not to be my followers but to discover what they believed I knew. They trusted me to lead them to it.

The only information I had that they did not was the info coming through the headset. Most of the readouts had gone to standby, a flickering sequence of numerals moving too quickly for me to make any practical sense. I guessed they were counting or estimating the number of players. Also they were monitoring the comms between players, the mash-ups, the animations, the endless coded comments, the texts, the GIFs, the trade-offs, the wagers. Everything was recorded, open for reinterpretation, saved for future use, market research on the lam.

One of the HUDs on the furthest edge of my visor was echoing the output of these independent image makers. They moved too quickly for me to take them in, so I was not trying. Numerals were flickering there too – more than 300 image and video streams were being generated and viewed, based on my shots, even while we continued to trudge across the broken, decaying ground.

The sheer activity of the numerals clearly implied the episode was not yet over.

I stumbled on a half-buried slab of concrete, jutting up through weeds. I lost my step and fell forward, but instantly the counterweights and gyros caught me, steadied me, held me in a semblance of verticality until I could regain my balance. My transmitted images remained steady.

I tried to use the direct link to restore contact with the network – I did not want to continue on into this sweltering, risky wilderness if I had already shot everything there was to be shot. The link to the network remained unanswered. I heard the white-noise hiss of no-signal, relayed in stereo to my earpieces.

With that collective intelligence mysteriously possessed by crowds – although less mysteriously in this age of digital linkage – the players around me suddenly came to a halt. It was my first awareness that I was approaching another target, but almost in the same instant my HUDs changed focus and brightness, and a percentile score appeared. Something, someone, was ahead.

I was more edgy than ever before. I was working without information or backup. I was entirely alone and in circumstances I barely understood and certainly could not control. All I had was the psychic armour of data: I possessed information that protected me, or at least the players' belief in the existence of that information was enough to protect me.

I presumed, I continued to presume.

An image swam into focus: it was another body, somewhere ahead, supine on the ground. I zoomed on it, resolved it, shed as much electronic noise as I could. I heard the response from the crowd – they appreciated my clarifying of the image. Looking past the displays, real-time vision, I could not see any sign of the actual body, but it was certainly there, some 200 metres ahead of me, perhaps partly concealed by the uneven surface of the ground.

The image cohered again. Now I could see that the body was that of a young woman. She was lying on her back with legs apart, arms spread wide, head tilted back, almost a position of rest, or relaxation. She was naked. I dreaded having to look at her wounds.

The servos had already kicked in – I felt the heavy equipment taking up the mechanical balance, the equilibrium creating the illusion of comparative weightlessness. The images condensed into sharp focus, over-saturated colours.

Everything led me to that woman's body. The unyielding balance, the expectation of the crowd. The players around me were of course reacting to the images I was transmitting.

Several of them had sat down on the ground, others stood

in team groups. All of them, everyone I could see with my eyes or pick up on the HUDs, were bending intently towards their digital handhelds. The green and red and blue LEDs on their earpieces glinted. Some of the players, clad in VR headsets, tipped their heads back as if scanning the sky, but I knew it was more to do with easing the headset than with gaining a visual angle. Already the first animations and mash-ups were being passed electronically to and fro – I heard sounds of satisfaction, amusement, anticipation.

The woman on the ground ahead of me suddenly sat up, resting herself casually on her elbows. She appeared to be uninjured. She said something, but she was still too far for me to hear her in real-time, and because of the constant sending that was going on around me the amplified pick-up of her voice was electronically distorted.

I was being pulled by the counterweights towards her. Most of the crowd remained where they had been, preferring now to view the outcome through their reality devices. Perhaps they were nervous that I might violently destroy her? Those others who had been following at the rear of the crowd joined the others, forming a seated, half-prone gang of players. Behind me was a glittering array of digital screens. Heads remained bent down, the VR users tipped blindly towards the sky.

The woman stood up as I came closer to her. She spread her arms, as if to prove she was helpless before me, carried no weapons, held no defences, had no supporters. She was in a field of stony ground and huge clumps of coarse grasses, long and yellow, swirling around her bare legs.

'You!' she shouted. 'I asked who you were!'

I had to wait for the diagnostics to complete. While they

did I stared away from the electronic displays, through the visor. I realised that I knew who she was, or at least that I recognised her – she was one of the most famous principals, appearing regularly on reality shows. She was a star of the channels, had her own fan base, published many articles in the dedicated media. Her life, when off-reality, was constantly examined and envied and celebrated and criticised in the mass media. Everything she ate, visited, wore or bought was discussed endlessly.

While I was still groping through memory for her identity the diagnostics completed. Her real name was restricted, but her current avatar flashed up: it was Catt@the@Great. A massive trail of subsidiaries and principal associates and group members were affiliated to her – the fan base – but here she was alone.

There was a disparity between the electronic image of her and the reality I could see. Her body was painfully thin, as was her face. Her hair was a mess. Blood and mud streaked her unclad body.

'Turn a full circle with your arms raised!' I shouted on the amplifier.

'I want to know who you are first.'

'I've been sent. You killed those principals?'

'Probably. How many did you see?'

'Six of the network crew.'

'Yeah. Six was right.'

'I'm here to shoot you. The end of the episode.'

I pushed up the visor to expose my face – I was finding the constant dazzle of images and relayed sounds a maddening distraction. I could see her more clearly unaided – she was young, calm, but skeletally thin. She began walking towards me.

'Stay where you are!' I shouted, using the aural pick-up to amplify my voice.

'OK.'

She leaned to one side, took a long shoot of grass and pulled it up. Holding it in one hand she stood placidly before me. Then she resumed walking slowly towards me.

'How did you kill them?'

I knew all this was not only being transmitted back to the company, it was also being recorded. The hum of the players' digital handsets heterodyned electronically behind the other signals. I glanced back. Not a single player was looking towards me. All worked their handhelds with frenetic energy, the VR users slowly wagged their shrouded heads to and fro.

'They give us weapons. We're not supposed to use them, but I did. It's all over now – I've had enough.'

'Enough of what?'

'This, that, every damned thing. Reality, what you call reality, what they think is reality. It's finished for me. I don't care any more. If you've come to arrest me, go ahead.'

'I'm not here to arrest you,' I said, my voice feeding back in my earpieces. 'I have to shoot you. Show me where the weapons are. And don't move any closer.'

She spread her arms again and she did come to a halt. 'I don't have them any more. I don't know where they are. And I have a contract that allows me—'

'I know about the contract,' I said. 'It doesn't allow you to kill. What you did to those people in the crew. They wouldn't hurt you.'

'They were going to shoot me, as you are. I feel better now. I only want the money I'm owed, and then I'll never hurt you.'

'You can't.'

'I don't care, don't care. It's over. Get me the money.'

She sat down again on the ground, a sudden movement, but in spite of the stress in her voice it was a relaxed and graceful half-turn, her legs folding beneath her. As the long grass was crushed beneath her I heard a hum of response from the players' crowd. None of them moved. She turned her back on me, swirling the grass with her legs. I saw how ectomorphic her whole body had become: her spindly legs, her thin chest, the bony mounds of her vertebrae.

I was stricken with doubt about what to do. Her atrocities were beyond question – but now she was naked, defenceless, peaceable, harmless. The crowd was silent, waiting for me to act against her. I wanted to complete this, knew I had to, but also that every tiny movement or gesture or even decision I made was being monitored somehow by the network. I was not free to act in any way other than theirs, and yet I saw no way forward from this moment.

She and I were both at an end, a rejection of what had gone before. She said she no longer cared what happened. I was the same.

For a moment I tried to turn away, step back from her, but as soon as I did I felt the full weight of the servos and balancing mechanism. The armour was preventing me from moving.

'I have to go through with this,' I said, allowing the steady armoured suit to hold me.

She said, 'At least tell me your name, lady. I should know who is doing this.'

'I am a gameplay coordinator,' I said. 'For this, I have no

name.'

'Then what is your avatar?'

'I have none. You are Catt.'

'I am. I was. That's gone too. Nothing is real, there is no reality. This is what they have done to us.' She leaned earnestly forward, staring at me. 'Why don't you take off that armour, let me see you?'

There was a great silence in this arena of wasting scrubland. Even the players remained still. The sun was hotter than ever, beating down on us from high overhead. Warm air, trapped in the long grasses, drifted up and around my waist. Sweat was running down my back, over my face. My hands were slippery inside the gauntlets, where I gripped the controls.

The voice from the network said, 'How does she know you're a woman? Did you tell her?'

'You know I didn't.'

'Shoot her now.'

White noise hissed again.

I wrenched my face away from the HUDs, looked through the visor at the woman. 'I have to take you in,' I said to her. 'That's the only way. Stand up again, so I can see you.'

'If I don't? I could walk away. I'm never going to do this again. If they give me the money—'

'I'd have to shoot you from behind.'

'Do what you normally do.' She climbed to her feet again, but this time her motion was not so fluid. I saw that one of her thin legs had a gash along the side of her thigh. She added quietly, 'Nothing matters any more.'

'Life matters,' I said, frightened for her. 'Don't throw it away.'

'This isn't life. This is reality. Shoot me now!'

The crowd suddenly came alive, and a deep, low, happy sigh spread away from them, breathed from innumerable throats. I glimpsed a dazzling movement on the handheld screens I could see to one side of me.

I released the deselector charge and the explosion tore her apart, throwing up a mess of annihilated flesh into the air, flames, heat, instant white steam, a ball of light.

Blood rained down.

I heard a roar of glee going up from the crowd, and in my earpieces the electronic interference from the hundreds of handhelds suddenly transmitting gave a repellent new note to the sound of no-signal. As parts of the woman's body fell to the ground around me, a sad shower of blood and torn flesh, I saw the nearest players yank the phones from their ears, shake their heads to release their hair, looked around, looked anywhere but at their screens and displays and VR helmets. Most of them were grinning or laughing, tension purged by the shooting, looking around at each other with an unmistakable sense of triumph.

The crowd of players began to disperse at once, losing all interest in the scene of destruction I had made. The blood continued to drizzle down on me, tiny pieces of flesh and bone clotting the liquid streams that ran across the shell of my protective equipment.

I tore off the helmet, threw it aside. I eased the servo mechanism from my back, released it so that it fell behind me, crashing noisily on a patch of stones and pebbles. The gauntlets, the boots, the leg shields, the tunic that had protected my breasts, the thick belt that carried the battery packs, all fell away. Soon I was unprotected, wearing only my shirt and pants. I was now shoeless, bare-headed, exposed to the blistering heat of the sun.

I headed away from the place where the episode had ended, with most of the crowd ahead of me. They were walking in a relaxed manner, clearly relishing the reality they had all shared. I strode as quickly on the broken ground as my bare feet would let me, wanting only to return to the safety of the network building. I soon caught up with many of the stragglers from the dispersing crowd of players.

Some of them were already brushing their fingertips across the touch screens, no doubt seeking the next experience of reality.

When they saw me many messages were instantly sent to and fro. I was observed, identified, I was unprotected. Fear rose in me, the fear of the crowd.

They parted in front of me, though, making way for me. No one touched me, spoke to me, threatened me. I was the only one without a handheld – they noticed that about me. A breeze sprang up as I passed the edge of the town, walking along the old street where the derelict buildings were. The slight wind moderated the sun's heat a little, passing across my face and legs and arms, lifting my thin shirt. I stared around as I walked, seeing the old and new buildings of the town for the first time since I arrived, smelling something in the air, hearing sounds that were not amplified or attenuated in some way.

The crowd had dispersed by the time I came into the part of the town where the network building was situated. I realised I was walking alone.

# THE AUTHORS

**DESIRINA BOSKOVICH**'s short fiction has been published in *Clarkesworld*, *Lightspeed*, *Nightmare*, *F&SF*, *Kaleidotrope*, *PodCastle*, *The Drabblecast*, and anthologies such as *The Apocalypse Triptych*, *Tomorrow's Cthulhu* and *What the #@&% Is That?*. Her debut novella, *Never Now Always*, is recently out from Broken Eye Books. She is also the editor of *It Came From the North: An Anthology of Finnish Speculative Fiction* (Cheeky Frawg, 2013), and together with Jeff VanderMeer, co-author of *The Steampunk User's Manual* (Abrams Image, 2014). Her next project is a collaboration with Jason Heller – *Starships & Sorcerers: A Secret History of Science Fiction*, forthcoming from Abrams Image. Find Desirina online at www.desirinaboskovich.com.

**ANNE CHARNOCK**'s writing career began in journalism. Her articles appeared in *The Guardian* and *New Scientist*. Her debut novel, *A Calculated Life*, was a finalist for the 2013 Philip K. Dick Award and the 2013 Kitschies Golden Tentacle Award. In her latest novel, *Dreams Before the Start of Time*, set in the near future, she imagines the unintended consequences when fertility science seems to offer all the answers. Anne is interviewer-in-residence at The Arthur C. Clarke Award as part of the award's collaboration with The Ada Lovelace Day.

**MALCOLM DEVLIN**'s stories have appeared in *Interzone*, *Black Static* and *Shadows and Tall Trees*. His collection *You Will Grow Into Them* is published by Unsung Stories.

**IAN HOCKING** has being write science fiction since he was schoolboy. His debut novel, *Déjà Vu*, was a best seller, and he's been published in various short fiction outlets over the years. When he's not writing, he's running either away from or towards his home in Canterbury.

**DAVE HUTCHINSON** was born in Sheffield in 1960 and read American Studies at the University of Nottingham before moving into journalism. He's the author of six collections of short stories and four novels. His novella 'The Push' was shortlisted for the BSFA Award in 2010, and his novels *Europe in Autumn* and *Europe at Midnight* were nominated for the BSFA, Arthur C Clarke, and John W Campbell Memorial Awards in 2015 and 2016. *Europe at Midnight* was also shortlisted for the Kitschie Award in 2016. His most recent novel, *Europe in Winter*, won the 2017 BSFA Award. He lives in North London.

**CASSANDRA KHAW** writes horror, press releases, video games, articles about video games, and tabletop RPGs. These are not necessarily unrelated items. Her work can be found in professional short story magazines such as *Clarkesworld*, *Fireside Fiction*, *Uncanny*, and *Shimmer*. Cassandra's first original novella, *Hammers on Bone*, came out in October 2016 from *Tor.com*. To her mild surprise, people seem to enjoy it. She occasionally spends time in a Muay Thai gym punching people and pad.

**OLIVER LANGMEAD** was born in Edinburgh and lives in Glasgow. He has an LLB in Law, and an MLitt in Writing Practice and Study with a distinction, and is currently working towards an MLitt in Fantasy. His first book, *Dark Star*, featured in The Guardian's Best Books of 2015, and his second book, *Metronome*, was published January 2017.

**COURTTIA NEWLAND** is the author of seven works of fiction that include his debut, *The Scholar*. His latest novel, *The Gospel According to Cane*, was published in 2013 and has been optioned by Cowboy Films. He was nominated for the Impac Dublin Literary Award, The Frank O' Conner award, The CWA Dagger in the Library Award, The Hurston/Wright Legacy Award and The Theatre 503 Award for playwriting as well as numerous others. His short stories have appeared in many anthologies and have been broadcast on BBC Radio 4. In 2016 he was awarded the Tayner Barbers Award for science fiction writing and the Roland Rees Busary for playwriting. *Percepi* is part of his forthcoming speculative fiction collection, *Cosmogramma*.

**JEFF NOON** was born in Manchester, England in 1957. He trained in the visual arts and drama and was active on the post-punk music scene before becoming a playwright, and then a novelist. His novels include *Vurt* (Arthur C. Clarke Award winner), *Pollen*, *Automated Alice*, *Nymphomation*, *Needle in the Groove*, *Cobralingus*, *Falling Out Of Cars*, *Channel SK1N*, *Mappalujo* (with Steve Beard) and a collection of stories called *Pixel Juice*. He has also won the John W. Campbell Award. His twitter fiction site @echovirus12 is a long-running online experiment in collaborative writing. His latest novel is *A Man of Shadows*, published by Angry Robot Books.

**IRENOSEN OKOJIE** is a writer and Arts Project Manager. Her debut novel *Butterfly Fish* won a Betty Trask award and was shortlisted for an Edinburgh International First Book Award. Her work has been featured in *The Observer*, *The Guardian*, the BBC and the *Huffington Post* amongst other publications. Her short stories have been published internationally. She was presented at the London Short Story Festival by Ben Okri as a dynamic writing talent to watch and was featured in the *Evening Standard Magazine* as one of London's exciting new authors. Her short story collection *Speak Gigantular*, published by Jacaranda Books, was shortlisted for the Edgehill Short Story Prize, the Jhalak Prize, the Saboteur Awards and nominated for a Shirley Jackson Award. www.irenosenokojie.com

**CHRISTOPHER PRIEST** has been a full-time freelance writer since 1968. He has published fourteen novels, four short story collections and a number of other books, including critical works, biographies, novelizations and children's non-fiction. As a journalist he has written features and reviews for *The Times*, *The Guardian*, *The Independent*, *New Statesman*, *The Scotsman*, and many different magazines. In 1996 Priest won the James Tait Black Memorial Prize for his novel *The Prestige*, which later won the World Fantasy Award – the only known occasion when a novel won both a major literary prize and a genre award. His novel *The Separation* won both the Arthur C. Clarke Award and the BSFA Award. He has been nominated four times for the Hugo award. He has won several awards abroad, including the Kurd Lasswitz Award (Germany), the Eurocon Award (Yugoslavia), the Ditmar Award (Australia), and Le Grand Prix de L'Imaginaire (France). In 2001 he was awarded the Prix Utopia (France) for lifetime achievement. His most recent novel *The Gradual* was published in 2016 by Gollancz (UK), and Titan Books (USA).

**JAMES SMYTHE** is a British writer. He's written eight novels; *The Machine*, a novel about memory and PTSD, and his YA-SF novel *Way Down Dark*, were shortlisted for the Arthur C Clarke award. He's also recently created and written a soon-to-be-announced television series, written a movie for Sony, and has just finished writing his new novel – about artificial intelligence and the afterlife – *I Still Dream*.

**E. J. SWIFT** is the author of the Osiris Project trilogy (*Osiris*, *Cataveiro* and *Tamaruq*), a speculative fiction series set in a world radically altered by climate change. Her short fiction has been nominated for the Sunday Times EFG Short Story Award ('The Spiders of Stockholm') and the BSFA award for short fiction ('Saga's Children'), and has appeared in a variety of publications from Solaris, Salt Publishing, NewCon Press and Jurassic London. Swift also contributed to Strata – an interactive digital project by Penguin Random House. Her latest novel, *Paris Adrift*, will be published by Solaris in 2018.

**LAVIE TIDHAR** is the author of *Osama*, *The Violent Century*, *A Man Lies Dreaming*, *Central Station* and many other novels, novellas and short stories. He is a recipient of the World Fantasy Award, the British Fantasy Award, the BSFA Award, the Jerwood Fiction Uncovered Prize and the John W. Campbell Memorial Award, among others.

**ALIYA WHITELEY**'s short stories have been published in many places including *The Guardian*, *Strange Horizons*, *Interzone*, and *McSweeney's Internet Tendency*. Her last two novellas were published by Unsung Stories in the UK, and were shortlisted for a Shirley Jackson Award, the James Tiptree Jr Award, a BSFA Short Fiction award, and the John W Campbell Memorial Award. Most days she can be found on Twitter as @aliyawhiteley and she's currently writing a unique short story a month for backers via Patreon.

**THIS BOOK WOULD NOT HAVE BEEN POSSIBLE WITHOUT THE SUPPORT OF ALL OUR GENEROUS BACKERS ON KICKSTARTER. THE NAMES LISTED BELOW MAKE AN INSPIRING COMMUNITY OF PEOPLE, THE KIND OF PEOPLE THAT COULD MAKE OUR FUTURE BETTER.**

Leila Abu el Hawa
Rahim Adat
Antha Ann Adkins
Sascha Aeby
Zoe Elizabeth Aguiar
Stephen Aguilar-Millan
Hamad Ahli
Matt Alcock
Burhan Ali
Ash Allen
Chandler Altman
Joshua Anastasakis
Nick Anderson
Paul Andre
Alan Andrews
Chris Andrews
Anonymous
Anonymous Platypus
Richard Anstine
Christer J. Aplin
Samuel Aronoff
Richard Ashcroft
Remark Auhsoj
Michael Aylwin
Satarie B.
Diego Baca Del Rosario
Brad Bailey
Maya Bakalars

Nadezhda Ball
Hans Ballard
Christoph Bara
Steve Barnett
Cameron Bathgate
Juanjo Bazán
Christopher Becker
Case Beckman
Alfred Beckman
Chris Bekofske
Michael Beldon
Jo Bellamy
Anthony R Bergevin
Ghost berghauer
Irish Bernardez
Martin Bernstein
Geert Biermans
Alex Bjornstad
Blessthismess.no
Bloodyhamster
Dat Boi
Elle Borland
Kim R Bowers
Alex L. Bozzi, IV
Sam Bradbury
Gadi Braude
Michael Brewer
Jeff Bridges
Aline Bruck

Niels Bruinsma
Gary Budden
Lukas Buehler
Devon Burgess
Melissa Burke
Alex Burton-Keeble
Joe butler
Tamara C.
Kit Caless
Ntasha Campbell
Michael Ian Canepa
Michael Ian Canepa
Franchesca Caram
Rodrigo Gastón Carmé
Daniel Carpenter
Christian Castillo
Ruben Chacaturian
Surapich Chairgulprasert
Tze-Wen Chao
Nick Charman
Jenifur Charne
Anne Charnock
Randy L. Chase
Stanley Chau
Bright Chen
Paul Childs
Christian
Mark Clerkin

Mathieu Collenot
Cameron Collie
Karen Collins
Dom Conlon
Melenaite Cook
Paul Cooper
Graham Cope
Dan Coxon
Matthew Craig
Jason Crase
Ryan Cross
Stuart Cruickshank
Ellie Curran
Eric D
Dwayne D.
Renald Dalli
Conrad Daly
Darragh & Selvi
B. de S.
Evgeniy V. Demchenko
Mimi Dennett
Scott Desmarais
Derek Devereaux Smith
John Doran
Chris Douglass
Rosalie Downing
Jozef Doyle
Pawel Drozdowski
Mark Dudlik
Oliver Dudman
Tom Durrant
Maximilian Eberl
Brant Eckett
Kevin Eddy
John Edge
Adam Monier Edwards
Björn Eilers

SzuTsung Ein
Nichola Ellison
Jonny Emin
Richard Evans
Peter Fankhauser
Maurizio Fantini
Finbarr Farragher
Sam Filer
Elliott Finn
Klaus Fischer
Chris Flynn
Mirco Franceschelli
D Franklin
Eliott Frilet
Gary Furze
Matthew M. Galbraith
Mark Gallegos
Samantha Gavan
David W. Gehring jr
Alexander Gent
Tony Georgis
Marcus Gipps
Giulian-O76
BJ van Glabbeek
Ken Glemarec
Sandy Golda
Dieter Goldschmidt
Josh Goldstein
Dan Grace
Kill C. Grammar
Sami Grant
Andrew Grant
Eric Graves
Tony Gray
Fábio Grazioli
Jill Griffiths
Richard "Kimara Cretak" Grotkier II

Simon Guerrier
Gutterdrums
Vince Haig
Mirko Hamann
Gasser Hamza
Tim Harding
Jamie Hardwick
Mari Ara Harju
David Harris
Nell Harrison
Philip Harrison
Christopher Harvey
Andrew Hatchell
Peter Haynes
Rob Haynes
Matthew Hazelbaker
Cheryl Hedlund
Kevin Henderson
Roxanne Henschke
Gabor Hernadi
Yozen Hernandez
Jason Hesse
Joshua Hill
Matt Hill
Jorge Eduardo Hinojosa
Mark Hirst
Florian Hochapfel
Ian Hocking
Andrew Hoffman
Robert Holbach (Bastian's Book Reviews blog)
Stark Holborn
Nick Honeywell
Tan Seng Hoong
Damien Horgan
Brendan Horgan
Tobias Andre Huggett

## The Backers

Kevin Hughes
Abel Goh Wen Hung
Tom Hunter
Angelica Grace Hunter
Rowan Hunter
Brad Hutchison
Bernardo Ibarra
Taylor Ingram-Wildman
Inside the Box Board Games
J.P.
Heather Javaheri
Jakša Jerković
Kyle Johnson
Mark 'scubashotz' Jones
Cameron Jones
Benjamin Judge
Kristin K.
Lulu Kadhim
Erhan Kalistu
Christian Källgren
Derk-Jan "Looking For Amy" Karrenbeld
Richard Kemble
Helen C. Kenner
Nazia Khatun
Paul Kincaid
Chris King
Alice Kirby
Gil "Garkler" Klein
Alanah Knibb
Georgie Knight aka mermaid99
Ivan Knoetze
Megbeth Knowles
Martin Kohli
Kimmo Koivula

Sally Kong
Connie Koorevaar
Cal Kotz
Isabella Kratynski
Jami Ann Kravec
Michael Krawec
Janusz Kruszewski
Patrick Kubin
Chris Kuczek
Anna M Kupiecki
Rick F. Kwan
Sonia Kwiecinska
Non LaGrenade
Tristan Lake
Dorothy Langley
Darren Langran
Daniela Laterza
Andrei Lazarescu
Lazuli
Becky Lea
Sean Lee
Daniel & Lorelia Lerps
Alexander Lethen
Rune Astrup Lien
Fred Andrew Lim
Bernd Benjamin Romana Lindmeier
Allan Lloyd
Stuart Lloyd Jr
Robyn M
Robert MacGillivray
Lorenzo Maffioli
John Frederick Mag-atas
Payal Maniar
Wendy Mann
Brandon Manning
Chelle Marshall

Stephanie Martin
Alejandra Martín del Campo Ruiz
Daniel Marx
Jarred Massey
Chris Mavricos
Lucy McCarthy
Sara Keira McClure
Una McCormack
Patrick McCoy
Martin McGrath
Casey McKenzie
Rod Mearing
Melissa and Mark
Jamie Mendenhall
Juli Menitti
Aaron Mercer
Rowan, Darsey & Cailean Meredith
Caroline Mersey
MET
Brandon Metcalf
E.M. Middel
Miffies
S. A. Moffett
Daniel Mois
Euan Monaghan
Naomi Morauf
Stuart Morris
Ewan Mount
Joerg Mueller-Kindt
Simo Muinonen
Brian Muldoon
C.M. Muller
Paul F. Murphy
Stephen Murrell
Anton N.
Nat

Matthew Neil

Peter Nowell

Sarah O'Malley

Maria O'Neill

Ant O'Reilly

Alice Emillie Oldfield

Miguel Alejandro Hernandez Orozco

CeCe Orquieza

Dani Pacey

James Pacheco

Virginia Pagani Amaral

Anatoli Pairovski

Vanessa Palsenbarg

Sandro Pansa

Amit A Parmar

Leane Parsons

Pat The Dom

Daniel Paton

Alexander Päx Renz

Jacob Payne

Gareth Pearce

Maximilian Alexander Pefestorff

Anthony Perrett

Alexander Peterhans

Prof. Katie Peterson

Rob Phelps

Jessica Philpott

Sean Phipps

Alex Pierer

Matthew Pilgreen

Saige Podger

Taylor Poole

Rob Porter

Júlia Varga, Krisztián Pósch

Neil Prideaux

Denis Prokoudine

Gareth Pugh

Gavin Pugh

Ewan Quayle

Erin Raj-Staniland

Pete Randall

Rayshan

Gareth E. Rees

Andrew Rees

Alfredo Reino

Matt and Cathy Reinsel

Jack Reitsema

REMoyen

Martijn Rensen

Kevin Rice

Simon Riley

Herson Rivera

Joe Rixman

Juliet Robinson

Robyonekenobi

Paul Rodger

Javier Romero

Hans Roos

Alisa Roser

Mike Rouse-Deane

Melanie Roussel

Kody Roy

Maxwell Rozema

Harold Rubin

Matthew S.

Nic Sage

Nick Saggers

Brian Sambula

Amedeo Santoro

Ed Saper

Stephanie Saulter

Andrew Saxby

Erin Sayers

Saz

Benjamin Scanlon

Benedikt Schmitz

Nathan Schnupp

Ivo Schwarz

Christopher Screech

Jonathan Seely

Bonnie Seidel

Richard Sheehan

Mike Shema

Michael J. Shymanski

Paul Simpson

Ian J Simpson

William Sims

James Sizeland

Alexander J Skidmore

Kasper E. Skovgaard

Ida-Sofia Skyman

Jim Smith

Pete Smith

Ted Snowdon

Tammy Sparks

Jaylen Spiller

Ted Spilsbury

Adrian Spink

Pieterjan Spoelders

Margaret M. St. John

Daryn St. Pierre

StarShipSofa

Jim Steel

Will Stevens

George Stirling

Travis Stluka

Ian Stockdale

Benjamin P. Strauss

Clive Stubley

Caroline Stupnicka

Sachin Suchak

## The Backers

Emily Szymanska
Harrison Tan
Kang Siang, Tan
Kevin Tan
Louis Tarpin
Douglas Taylor
Steve Teixeira
The Bergman Family
NonchalantNancy
Thomas
Frode Thorsén
Yury Tikhoglaz
Paul Timney
Duane Tomlinson
Tom Townsend
Nikola Trbovic
Treodoc
Trinnie
Chelle Tulloch
Wayne Turner

Kyle Upton-Evans
Samuel Valentine
Joris van der Pol
Jill Vassilakos-Long
Olivier Vergnault
Mike Vermilye
David Vernon
Isabella J. von Lichtan
Patrick-Ole Voss
Lenore Wagner
Steve Walsh
Sean Walsh
Christian Walter
Stephanie Ward
Ellie Warren
Gary Watson
Cecilia Weightman
Jeff Weiner
Adam Wellock
Tyler L Wells

Chevincee Werawanich
Ian West
Jim Westine
Jamie Weston
Ian Whates
Joshua Whitaker
Seth Charles
Whittington
Avery Williams
Adam J Wimbush
Wordcatcher
Publishing
melissa wright
Alex Wybraniec
Matt Wyndham
Alexander Yankovsky
Eddie Yeoh
Stephen Yost
Alexis Zanika
Vladimir Zoubritsky